# REVIEWS FOR THE WORK OF ALYSSA RICHARDS

"I'd happily read anything Alyssa writes next." —Jeannie Zelos Book Reviews

"...undoubtedly Alyssa Richards has just become one of my new favourite authors for this year." —Living in Our Own Story Blog

"This is well written with complex characters who reveal more of themselves as the story progresses. It is a great mystery with paranormal elements that make it enthrallingly different and captivating."--Splashes into Books

"I felt like I was standing right in the middle of a Movie Set of something between Pierce Brosnan's "The Thomas Crown Affair" or Sean Connery's "Entrapment". I was sucked into the story from the beginning and I could not stop reading. It was such an interesting mix between the paranormal – romance and crime elements that kept me reading and wondering what might happen next."--Jeri's Book Attic, THE FINE ART OF DECEPTION SERIES

"An intriguing read that kept my interest until the last page. Very enjoyable and definitely recommended."--Archaeolibrarian, THE FINE ART OF DECEPTION SERIES

"This book was loaded with mystery and suspense. The plot was well executed and kept me on the edge of my seat. The sizzling passionate scenes between Addie and Blake were red hot." --Smut Book Junkie Book Reviews, THE FINE ART OF DECEPTION SERIES

"The plot is unique in a way that you will keep thinking of its awesomeness for a long time after finishing this book. There was so much positives in the book, that kept me awake with my Kindle at night, in spite of my recently sleep deprived life. This book has exceeded my expectations in every way. You should definitely read it, if romance, suspense or paranormal genre suits you."-- Books are Magic, THE FINE ART OF DECEPTION

"I was very drawn to the characters. Richards did an excellent job weaving you into their world whether it was the good guy or the bad guy you just wanted to know what they were thinking, doing and their next move. I definitely recommend."--The Reading Pile, THE FINE ART OF DECEPTION SERIES

THE HAUNTING OF ALCOTT MANOR is a fascinating tale of tragedy, ghosts, and soulmates. Mystery fans will enjoy this heroine's efforts to track down clues -- both tangible and ghostly -- while trying to find the truth about a woman's death. Romance fans will adore this match-up of a strong heroine and an enigmatic yet endearingly charming and earnest hero. —Fresh Fiction Review

This was a great read, great twists and turns. ...and the end...? WOW! What's really getting me right now though? Henry and Gemma at still with me....days after I've finished the book! I cried with them, I loved with them, and they touched me deeply! —Amazon Reviewer, THE HAUNTING OF ALCOTT MANOR

A MURDER AT ALCOTT MANOR is very definitely a thrill-a-minute tale of evil trying to keep a stranglehold on the living. This is a perfect book for readers who enjoy non-stop action and suspense with a dash of sexy. —Fresh Fiction Review

# THE FINE ART OF DECEPTION SERIES
# SOMEWHERE IN TIME

## BOOK 2

### ALYSSA RICHARDS

Library of Congress Control Number 2015917429
Ebook ISBN-13 978-0-9792265-6-4
Paperback ISBN-13 978-0-9991555-3-0
Editing done by Book Alchemy, LLC
Proofreading provided by 221bBakerSt.net
Cover Design by: Danijela Mijailovic

**Sign up for Alyssa's newsletter at to receive special offers and news about her latest releases.**

You can follow her on:
Instagram

Contact Alyssa at:
authoralyssarichards@protonmail.com

# 1

Cloaked in Blake's button-down dress shirt, I crept barefoot through the darkened salon of his New York penthouse apartment. His scent laid heavily on his collar and I brought it to my nose. I breathed it in deeply as if the aura of him could protect me when he was away.

I stopped at the floor-to-ceiling windows where the cold, winter breeze disturbed the long, white curtains. Searching the twinkling cityscape, just as I'd done every night for the last twenty years, I wondered where my father and grandfather might be. Their presence or the trails of their energy couldn't be sensed anywhere and my heart ached from their absence.

They were out there. Somewhere.

Were they were warm and being fed well? Were they in good health? Were they hurting? They appeared well when I'd seen them just a few months ago, but I didn't know how much of that vision I could trust. It had been so unusual.

The surrounding walls of my fortress inched into my view. Along with it crept the concern that being safely tucked away and being a prisoner were too much of the same thing.

Blake stirred in his bedroom.

Blake Greenwood. My protector, my defender, the love of at least two of my lifetimes. In our last life together we were Jack and Sarah, star-crossed lovers from the 1920s. In this life our names were different, but we were the same souls, in love with one another even before we met, happiest when we were together. Nothing and no one could get to me when he was near.

I wasn't sure if it was his intent or some energetic force-field he created, or the effect of his endless love for me. I was pretty sure I could lie naked in the middle of Central Park at midnight and no one would bother me if Blake were nearby.

Strangely, this all-encompassing love didn't bring me peace or confidence. Because when the love of my life finally appeared, the flip side of that reality became crystal clear. I knew that if I ever lost him, that loss would be insur-mountable. And that insight left me on the ridge of a double-sided coin, stuck between fear and gratefulness. I could easily pitch to either side.

Blake snuck behind me, gently drew me to him, and that was all it took. I was surrounded by love. Total protection. If only time could stand still.

"Going somewhere?" Tired-eyed and pillow-haired, Blake's voice was thick with sleep.

"Definitely not." I spun in his embrace and snuggled against him. Typically, the gentle rise and fall of his chest was the steady cadence that comforted me and set my world to right. Though not this time. Not when worries played with one another in my head like caffeinated children on the playground.

Soft and slow, he kissed the top of my head, "Can't sleep?"

"I gave up. I was on my way to the kitchen to see if you had an espresso machine."

Blake leaned back and gave me strong "don't be ridiculous" smirk. "Wouldn't be home without one."

He led me by the hand to the small kitchen where broad, cream-colored cabinets and dark wooden floors greeted me with surprising warmth. Most of the New York penthouses I'd visited were chilly with sophistication and excess, but this room breathed comfort. There was also a shielding sensation I noticed when we first stepped inside the apartment late last night, and I knew I was safe here. At least for the moment. The outside world rang with chaos, but in this home, there was peace.

With only Blake in residence, the kitchen wasn't quite the center of his home as it was with most abodes, the steady pulse of its heart beat beyond the far wall. Whatever room that was, that was where Blake had spent most of his time, dreaming, thinking, living.

"I miss Paris." I sipped the hot espresso and it heated me from the inside out. Memories of endless museums by day, outdoor cafes for lunch, and remarkable dinners laced with jazz that lingered until wee morning hours danced between us. With only a visit, Paris seeped into your soul. "And I miss our quiet life in the country, too."

Blake leaned against the counter and savored his own cup of espresso. "Then we'll go back. Just as soon as Otto's trial is over and he's in prison. Where he belongs. We'll stay as long as you like." He kissed my neck and the corners of my mouth rose. "We just need to get through these next few days, then we're on our way."

My smile slid into a grimace and I tried to hide the fact

that my heart had taken a shot of adrenaline. I didn't want to think about Otto Albrecht's trial. Or testifying in it.

"You'll do fine." Blake rubbed my arms.

"I'm so nervous," I said.

"William just wants you to tell the jury what you saw in the vault—that there were two of every painting, a forgery and an original. Obviously you don't need to mention that you used your gifts to figure out which was which."

"Yeah, I'll leave that out." I paced the small kitchen. I didn't even know why William needed me. My testimony on its own didn't amount to much. He had several of Otto's former clients testifying that they turned their priceless paintings over to his firm to be restored or appraised, and then they got a forgery in return. He also had FBI testimony that they found the originals in his vaults. And he had Blake's testimony of everything he discovered when he was undercover. In order, those were the most important witnesses in his case.

Blake exhaled hard and scratched the fresh, dark stubble along the lower half of his face. He and I knew that since William didn't get Otto on the murder of Frank, one of Otto's former underworld associates, or the Isabella Stewart Gardner art theft he should have been put away on, that he wasn't going to take any chances. He'd have the neighborhood cat testify if he thought it would help put Otto in jail.

The ghost of Otto's murder victim entered the room and the swinging door moved a little. "I'll testify," Frank growled and his icy presence appeared behind me. He shook his head and the brown, side-swept bangs moved a fraction from where they'd hung near his eyes. At this early hour he still reeked of some brown liquor.

Blake and I frowned at him for the uninvited guest he

was, and I quickly crossed the room and stood next to Blake. The chill from Frank's murderous soul unnerved me.

"Too little too late, Frank." Blake pushed off the counter. "Get out."

Frank's cold, dead eyes stayed glued to me while he drifted through the wall and out of the room.

Blake's text alarm rattled on the counter and I jumped. Blake grabbed his phone and stared at the screen. "William. He wants me in earlier to give us more time to go over my testimony."

"Do whatever you have to do to put this man away. I want us to get on with our life together." I glanced at the wall where Frank had disappeared to make sure he was really gone.

"My plan exactly." Blake's bravery filled the room and I breathed in the scent of it. It felt good to be strong in the face of a monster like Otto.

"It's a big day," I said.

"Maybe not the biggest." He reached out and skimmed the back of his fingers against my cheek. "Or the most important. That would be the day I finally found you." He held the side of my face in his hand. I turned and laid a kiss in the center of his palm.

"Granted, it's up there. I'd do anything to keep you and my mother safe," he said. "Family is everything."

"That it is." My thoughts drifted to the missing patriarchs of my family.

"One more?"

"At least."

He took my demitasse cup, placed it under the spout, and pressed the button on the silver machine. It gurgled, steamed, and brewed. He made my espresso on most mornings now. One of our relatively new traditions that gave me comfort.

"There's a marshal posted outside if you need anything while I'm at the courthouse." Blake opened his hand in front of me, a quiet gesture of support. I placed my hand in his and he kissed it gently. "Another one will pick me up to take me to the courthouse, and I'll call as soon as we have a break."

Blake's eyes were steeled with focus and readiness to face today's battle, to put away Otto—his own father—who had hunted him and his mother for most of their lives. Not that Otto knew that Blake was his son. Blake had kept that carefully hidden from just about everyone.

My heart, however, was neither steeled nor steady. It rode the currents of the wind that howled and whipped along the rooftop patio. I hugged Blake, grateful to rely on his strength and firmness, and yet frightened that there might not be enough to protect him.

"You have to have faith that this is going to work out." He kissed the top of my head. "If you spend all your time worrying, there'll be no space left in there for me." His thumb caressed the thin skin that covered my heart.

His soft lips met mine, heart and soul. And true to my early morning wish, time stood still.

"You're okay?" He asked.

I gave him a confident smile and a thumbs up sign.

Our new life was finally about to begin.

## 2

"Just drive around the block and try again." Blake noted the clipped edge on his words. His eyes narrowed when he searched the back and side windows, for threats. He'd waited a near lifetime to put his father in prison for making his and Carolena's life a living hell. After today he, his mother, and Addie would be free to live the lives of their choosing. It couldn't come soon enough. Today, he was not in the mood for risks.

Thomas stopped the black town car one half block from the courthouse. "I don't think I'll get any closer," he said. "I can drive around again if you want."

U.S. Marshal Roxy Dalton held her phone to her ear. Her shoulder-length, blond ringlets were a mismatch to her job. "No, we'll get out here." Her light blue eyes combed the fairly sparse crowd and hunted for anything unusual. "I'll walk you in," she said to Blake.

Blake eyed the gun at her waist when she wrestled her jacket over her shoulders. Then he texted William: on my way in. He stepped out of the car then leaned in to speak to

Thomas. "I'll text you when we're finished. Don't go far. I don't want to leave Addie alone for too long."

"I'll park on the street," Thomas said. "I saw a couple of spots a block or two back."

Blake looked north of the courthouse and saw two parking spaces ahead. He turned to tell Thomas but he had driven off.

"Straight to the front door." Roxy placed a hand on Blake's back.

Blake buttoned his long, black wool coat, then stuck his fists into his pockets and braced against the New York winter. He knew it was as much hate as it was the need to protect his loved ones that had driven him to this moment. He was okay with that price, as long as Otto ended up in jail.

All they had to do now was get inside and let justice take its course.

Blake noticed everyone who passed by, including the two men who quietly exited their car and caught up to him and Roxy. They appeared to be lawyers or businessmen.

Except that the man with blond curls that peeked out from the edges of his black hat changed directions too quickly. He pushed close to Roxy and jabbed a small needle into the back of her neck. He held it there, camouflaged by his hand. To passersby, he resembled someone who had wrapped his arm around an old friend. Barring Roxy's wide-eyed look of horror.

The darker-haired man with a triangle protuberance of beard beneath his bottom lip sidled up to Blake. His perfectly aligned, too-white smile belied the gun he jabbed between Blake's ribs. This wasn't the first time Blake had felt the barrel of a gun in his side and he slowed his gait. Roxy struggled to get to her gun, but the man's grip was tight and she couldn't reach it.

"Right now you can survive the dose I've given you," the blond man said with a grin. "Make my job difficult, I'll give you the rest and you'll be dead in about three minutes."

Roxy closed her eyes.

The dark-haired man guided Blake to the alleyway next to the courthouse. The gun pressed harder into Blake's ribs and panic swept through him, along with thoughts of Addie.

The alley was empty this time of year. In warmer weather courthouse employees traipsed up and down the narrow pathway as a shortcut to lunch spots. In the icy winter of New York no one was making any unnecessary trips on foot. Which meant no one would see what was happening to them.

Blake hoped that Roxy wouldn't pick up on what he was about to do. Or at least that she wouldn't remember. He inherited one good thing from Otto, a gift that had gotten him out of more than a few tight spots. He had the ability to push his intention onto others, to make them feel what he wanted them to. As a result he could often make them do what he wanted them to.

"You want to put that gun down." Blake pushed the dark-haired man energetically when they rounded the trees on the side of the building.

The man lowered the gun a couple of inches.

"What are you doing?" the blond man asked his partner.

The dark-haired man raised the gun again.

"Put the gun down." Blake drove his intent with a force that left the gunman no choice. He lowered the gun in hypnotic motion. Blake grabbed it from him and turned toward the blond man whose jaw had fallen slack.

"Remove the needle from her neck and let her go." He pushed in case the gun wasn't threat enough.

The blond man let go, Roxy's drugged body slumped to

the ground, and her head knocked against the pavement. Her light blond curls spread across the concrete and Blake's focus shot to Addie. If these men were here for him, one or two others would probably be after Addie. He hoped she hadn't left the penthouse.

"Move away from her," Blake said with a wave of the gun.

The blond man took one step away.

The dark-haired man frowned and blinked several times.

Blake maintained his aim with the gun. He fished his phone from his pocket and dialed Addie's number with one touch and held the phone to his head. There was no ringing sound. He glanced at the screen, no signal.

The dark-haired man lunged from the side and Blake felt a jab to his neck.

He held the gun on the two men and tried to make his way into the crowd for help. A warm, relaxed feeling came over him and drained the strength in his limbs. He felt the cold concrete hit his knees and then slap the side of his face.

His last thought was of Addie, the one he was supposed to protect. The white scuff marks on the black lace-up shoe were the last things he saw before his eyelids fell shut.

THE BLOND-HAIRED MAN snatched Blake's cell phone, and crunched it against the pavement with his heel. Both men rolled him under the cypress tree where he would be out of view.

"What the hell just happened?" asked the blond-haired man.

"I don't know. I—I didn't have any choice—" The man

with dark hair shook his head again, tried to clear the remaining effects of the cloud that had taken him over.

"Did you give him all of it? Otto said it was no great loss if they died."

The man with the small beard scanned the area then threw the syringes into the bushes. "He got all of it."

He briefly turned his face to the falling snowflakes, adjusted a dark green scarf to cover his neck, then both men blended into the pedestrian traffic.

## 3

**B**y the time my phone rang into the quiet of Blake's home I had spent most of the day curled up on a sun-warmed, overstuffed and velveted perch overlooking the city from the main salon. Second glass of red wine in my grasp, I listened to other people's lives play out far below, while I floated on a pond of cooled hope.

Blake was at the courthouse to testify. Now I had to sit and wait for him to come back and tell me our next steps. And those were three things I didn't do well—sit, wait, and have someone else tell me what to do. I'd tried reading a book, but I was too distracted to concentrate. TV really wasn't my thing. So, now I sat with a glass of wine and an aged issue of Paris *Vogue* that I'd picked up on our travels.

My stomach tightened when I saw the phone screen: No Caller ID.

Maybe it was Blake calling from an FBI phone. His phone battery might have gone dead. Or maybe, my neurotic side spoke up, it was someone connected to Otto.

I made several faces before I finally decided to answer the call. "Hello?"

"Adeline, this is Ellen."

"Ellen."

"I'm sorry to bother you." Ellen had never spoken kindly to me when we worked together. Except there was the one time when she saved my life. A fact I'd never forget. Though last I heard she still worked for Otto. So I had to question which side of the fence she parked her loyalties.

"I'm fine," I said and hoped I was telling the truth. "I hope you're well?"

"Yes, I was away from the firm for a few months, while— Well, while all of that police mess was carrying on. They wouldn't even let me near the building in the midst of all that. Now I'm back and at the courthouse for the trial. We're on a break. I just stepped outside."

"Is everything okay?" I asked.

"Addie..."

"Yes?"

"Do you and Blake have plans for after the trial?"

"I...um..." I knew I couldn't tell her the truth. Except there was one question I wanted to ask her. Just in case she might be willing to help me again. "We haven't firmed up any plans. Though I do hope to find out what happened to my father and grandfather are. If you know anything, I'd be very grateful."

I felt Ellen's heart soften, then ache. She and my grandfather had been so close.

A pause filled the space between us. Horns from traffic honked in the far distance like the beeps from toy cars.

"I understand," she said without giving me any information. "Addie, whatever your plans for after the trial, you need to get a Plan B," she said quietly. "Just in case things don't work out as you...thought they might."

The air left my lungs like someone just punched me in the stomach. "I'm sorry?"

Ellen was quiet as if to say, "you heard me."

"Make your plans. The sooner the better. Take care of yourself, and Blake." Ellen hung up without saying good-bye and panic drove through my chest like a marching band.

*Plan B?*

A warning. Things were not going to go as planned today.

**4**

---

I padded barefoot across the cold wooden floors of Blake's salon and checked my phone screen every third turn or so. I'd called and texted Blake several times but he hadn't yet answered. I assumed he was in the courtroom, and that his break had been filled with meetings with William.

Ellen's warnings chased around my head and I had a building migraine: Get a plan B, the sooner the better.

This meant only one thing. The trial would not go the way we wanted. How, I didn't know. William was being overly careful, I knew. Each witness had federal marshal protection, just like we did. Though if she were right, and if Otto was soon on the loose, Blake and I couldn't stay in New York.

Otto wanted revenge on Blake for getting him arrested and for the loss of his firm—essentially the loss of his life. And he wanted access to my gifts, so he could finally move the priceless art he'd stolen from The Gardner Museum over twenty years ago.

I could just see Blake storming home at the end of the

day to say that Otto was a free man and we had to leave. Immediately.

I stopped pacing, stared out the window at New York, and a metallic taste floated across my tongue. This was good-bye. We were only going to be safe if we lived some-place where Otto couldn't find us.

Fine. I would do that. We could leave again. I thought of everything I would leave behind and my heart cringed. All the things I'd left at my townhouse when I thought I'd only be gone for a few months. Jewelry rich with memories that my family had given me. Childhood photos. They were the last of few mementos I had of my father and grandfather. Pictures of us together when I was young. Pictures that still trapped my relatives' precious energy. It was the only way I had been able to connect with them since they'd left. One touch to the photo and I was with them again. I would have to have all of those things.

I peeked through the peephole of the front door and caught sight of the leg of the U.S. marshal who sat at his post, waiting for trouble. Unfortunately, as soon as Otto was free, trouble would come knocking and we'd no longer have the marshal's protection. If I wanted to collect the photo-graphic conduits to my father and grandfather, I'd have to do it now. Otto might be in his trial until the end of the week. Or only until the end of the day.

I knocked on the door and cracked it open gently. It was a bad idea to startle the man with a loaded gun.

"Everything okay?" he asked and stood to face me. He was SWAT-worthy with his all-black uniform and clean-cut dark hair. Maybe he was SWAT. Otto's connections were certainly dangerous enough to warrant such protection.

The migraine had produced a blind spot in my vision. So I kept moving my head this way and that to try to see around it. Unfortunately, I was out of my migraine medicine.

"Yes, I'm fine." A pain shot through the left side of my head and I pressed my hand against it. "I need to go by my home and pick up a few things. Is that possible?"

## 5

When we arrived at my townhouse Marshal Mitch Sandersen insisted on clearing my home before he'd let me in. When he was sure that no one was lying in wait, he allowed me to enter.

"No more than thirty minutes, okay?"

"Okay," I agreed.

My home smelled stale from nonuse and too much recycled heat and I wanted desperately to open a window for fresh air. Mitch would consider that a security risk, I was certain. Junk mail and magazines were littered across the island where my sister Alexa had tossed them in my absence. The thermostat was too high, another sign of Alexa's presence.

Since I'd run out of my migraine prescription, the bathroom was my first destination. I fumbled through a small basket of plastic bottles in the cabinet until I found another bottle of my medicine, popped the plastic top, and swallowed two tablets with a sip of tap water. The prescription would take care of the pain, though it would also make me sleepy. For that reason and a few others, I typically tried to stick to natural remedies, but I was beyond that today.

In my clothes closet, I grabbed an empty, oversized shoebox from the top shelf. I filled it with several framed photos of me with my father and grandfather, me with my sister and mother and grandmother. From my dressing table in the bathroom I gathered a few pieces of jewelry.

My fingers traced an antique silver frame, which sat on the wooden countertop of the dressing table. It encircled one of my favorite childhood memories of my father. He held the tow-headed, one-year-old me in his arms, my pink cotton dress sufficiently delicate for his princess. His proud smile was bright enough to light up the room, and I beamed when I placed a tiny hand on either side of his face.

I held my hand over the photo and hesitated, not wanting to feel what would inevitably come when it was over. Reliving what used to be was all I had now. I shut my eyes, then pressed my fingertips onto the cool photograph.

The smell of his cologne reaches me first, and then the sound of his laugh thunders in my ears, takes over my heart, and makes me feel invincible. His love for me and the rest his family makes each of us feel like superheroes.

"Addie, my angel," his voice echoes from beyond. "Promise me you'll never leave me."

I lean in with the limitless love that all baby girls feel for their daddies and hug his neck. As my palms flatten against the gold chain normally hidden by his shirts, his worst fear reveals itself to me: he would be without us one day. I squeeze him a little tighter.

The vision fades and emptiness crept in with the silence. At least the sound of his voice held strong this time. I missed hearing him call me Addie. The past went to its place in my history, and the present became clearer.

I sighed and stared at a small, jeweled container that held my former engagement ring, the one Jeremy had given to me so long ago. I decided to leave that behind. That was a piece of my past I didn't need anymore.

I climbed the stairs to the small bonus room on the second level. When I first moved in to what used to be my grandfather's townhouse, my grandmother allowed my occupancy on one condition: that I not move or get rid of anything. He had a number of expensive books and pieces of artwork. So I agreed and mostly complied. Though I did move some of the knick-knacks to a box and stored it upstairs.

The fat armchair slid along the carpet easily. Behind it was a small square door that lead to the attic space. Once opened, I dragged a cardboard box from the dark. In it was an old black phone, a ring of keys, a radio and cassette player, and a stack of cassettes. There was also a German beer mug full of pens. I selected two pens, one thin black one, and a fatter burgundy one with a tiger insignia on the side. Both had been among his favorites and they held a strong tune of his energy.

When I returned to the library I collected the rest of the family photos. The glass and metal from the frames clinked when I layered them on top of one another. I placed the box on the floor and stared at it.

That was it. That was everything I needed. It was odd and yet sort of freeing to know that you could put all of your most precious possessions into one simple cardboard box.

Glancing up at the mantle clock on the bookshelf, I saw that I still had a few minutes to spare. Nostalgia washed over me when I realized that this would probably be the last time I would be in what used to be my grandfather's townhouse. I might not be back. Or at least not until Otto was dead and forgotten.

I hoped on every prayer that he hadn't told his sons what I could do. Because I didn't need Otto Albrecht's sons chasing me down to help me build their fortune. Wooziness fell over me at the suggestion, though mostly from the medication. Strong stuff. The jet lag and lack of sleep from the night before didn't help.

I put my phone and keys on the side table and they clanked on the glass. Then I laid on the couch, wet washcloth on my forehead, mineral water with a dash of baking soda—magical healer of nausea—within an arm's reach. My nerves were a frayed mess. Sick exhaustion crept over me like a fog, surrounded my brain, and worked hard to pull me under.

I finally let it. Mitch would bang on the door shortly, which would wake me up. Meanwhile a power nap would reinvent me.

The conscious dream of my father and grandfather's visit replayed through my mind—some part of these two men had called upon me the last time I'd been here. I'd heard the pounding on the door and saw their worried faces, heard their voices telling me to wake up, that I was in danger.

When I awoke, the nausea had passed. I felt better. Though a little too rested. It seemed like a lot more than a few minutes had passed, and the air was cooler now, less stuffy. There was even a faint scent of cologne or men's soap. The whiff made my stomach drop, though I couldn't place why.

I shifted to my side, opened my eyes a tiny bit, and knew I was still dreaming because Otto was sitting cross-legged in the vintage french square armchair my father had picked up at the Paris flea market years ago. Maybe I had a fever.

Otto wouldn't be in my home. Otto was at the courthouse.

I slid the now warm washcloth from my forehead to my eyes. Without the ability to see, I always saw more clearly. And that's when I felt his presence. Otto's presence. My eyes shot open inside the washcloth. My heart stomped fast and hard and a pain shot down my left arm. I was going to have a heart attack before he had the chance to kill me. Kidnap me. Or both.

I had to assume that Otto had gotten rid of Mitch, that I didn't have any protection. Thoughts flew through my mind in wild chase of an answer to the question that beat at the inside of my skull: What do I do now?! Otto knew about my gifts. Knew that Blake and I were together. Obviously knew that Blake had worked a sting for the FBI Art Crime Team to catch him on the Gardner theft. This was all bad.

Otto cleared his throat. My cue while the curtain opened on Act II of My Life: The Nightmare Continues.

My hand pressed against the washcloth and I held my breath for a second to steady my heart. I tried to prepare myself for how I expected to feel when I saw his face after so much time. Perhaps terrified, as was my usual reaction to situations like this. So I lowered the cloth from my eyes, girded myself against it, and rose to a sitting position.

Surprisingly, all I felt was fury.

"Why are you in my home?" I squeezed the washcloth tight at my side.

Otto's eyes were immune to his smile. He tilted his head like a cat. Like he was about to bat me across the room like a ball of yarn. "Well, that's no way to greet a life-long friend. I just wanted to check on you. I hope you don't mind that I let myself in. No one answered when I knocked, but Ellen told me she thought you might be back in New York. So I knew you were here." His artificial smile lingered.

"Why aren't you in jail, and how did you get in to my home?" I asked flatly.

Otto's laugh was the amusing one I'd heard him use at receptions, it was the one he used when he wanted to put someone at ease. "And isn't that something? It seems the prosecutor didn't have as much evidence against me as he thought. "

I muzzled my impulse to strangle him in light of the fact that he was more sizable and stronger than I was. Too, he might have someone waiting in the wings. Someone with a gun.

"Otto. As much as I appreciate this...visit, I really don't feel well today. And I'd hate for you to get whatever I have. Why don't we catch up as soon as I've had a few days to get on my feet?"

"Of course. Of course." His light Welsh accent gave a false lilt of kindness and he studied my face with serial killer intensity.

I stood and glanced at the side table where I left my phone and keys, but they were gone. Otto smiled without moving. His desire to possess me slid around me like a boa constrictor. Just as Carolena, Blake's mother, had once described him.

"I hope you'll be well soon? That it's not too serious?" Otto leaned back and I noticed my keys and phone on the table beside him.

"I don't think it's fatal." I took a few steps toward the door. His eyes came alive with challenge.

"Let's hope not. Because I have big plans for you, you see. In fact, I'd like to discuss a special job with you. It's something of a pet project, and I'd like for you to be a part of it. Willingly, of course."

Otto said it like he was gifting me some kind of special award or consideration. Of course what he wanted was for me to come with him by my own choice. Blake had told me that Otto threatened him that he would be without me one day. That I would be Otto's ally. The suggestion was absurd. Yet here he was with his deluded offer for me to work on what I knew was stolen art, like I would proudly accept.

A chill wafted through the room and my psychic sight shot toward its source. Frank smiled his crooked smile at me while he sauntered toward Otto, then leaned on the wall next to him.

Otto simply stared at me.

"It's separate from the firm's business, you understand. The pieces are exceptional. Unlike anything you've worked on to date. You might say it's a once in a lifetime opportunity." Otto's eyes were electric and probing.

"I'm not available for a project right now." It felt good to put the boundary between us, though I knew he'd trample it.

Frank's lifeless eyes stared through me. He shook his head and clicked his tongue three times. "What have you gotten yourself into now, hmm?"

"Well, it's an...authentication project. For a private client. A very prestigious assignment," Otto said. The late afternoon light cast through the windows behind him. It was a heavenly glow that he didn't deserve.

"Henri would be better at authentication than I am. I don't have any real experience at it."

Memories of my childhood visit to the vault came to mind. How my grandfather presented me with forgeries and authentic paintings, and how I could tell the difference by simply placing my five-year-old finger on a raised bit of paint. I also remembered Otto watching us from the shadows. Nausea rolled again and I placed my hand on my stomach.

Otto leaned forward, elbows resting on his knees. "Adeline, I've always prided myself on being able to see a person's true potential, and I think you have a natural gift for authentication that we haven't yet begun to tap. I think once we bring out your natural talents you'll discover just how much you enjoy using them. You're going to find this to be a meaningful project. One that offers you a bright future."

The ghost pushed off the wall and laughed. "Oh, sweet Adeline. I did warn yous. No one is who they say they is." He tsk-tsked, cut between Otto and me and crossed the room.

I let my physical eyes watch him when he passed by. Under normal circumstances I would have been terrified to acknowledge a ghost in the company of others. Let alone my former employer. As it was, I really didn't care if Otto thought I was crazy. In fact, that might just be my out. If Otto thought I wasn't a trusted resource then maybe he'd leave me alone.

"I think you'll probably far exceed my expectations. Your grandfather always did. And much of your talent is probably in your genes," Otto said.

Cold adrenaline skirted through my insides, my body gave a little shiver.

"Speaking of your grandfather, and on a related note, your father—I think I may have some leads as to where they may be."

I crossed my arms and lowered myself to the couch. My mother and grandmother had always firmly held the belief that Otto was responsible for my father's and grandfather's disappearance. For a long while I tried not to believe them, especially in light of Otto's kindness to me. But after the events of last year I could no longer deny who he really was: a thief and a murderer. With an ounce of common sense, I had to assume his involvement in my family's absence as well. "What do you mean?"

"I never really thought they were dead, you see. I've always thought their disappearances were the result of a terrible mistake." Otto's voice gentled when he mentioned my family to me, almost like he spoke to a child. He picked imaginary lint off of his pants and waited for my response.

"So, you think...my father and grandfather are alive?" I squinted at Otto, my protective shields doubled, but a flurry of unwanted excitement shot through me at the suggestion that my relatives might be alive.

"Oh, I'm sure of it. In fact, I think you and I would be the perfect team to bring them back. We could do all sorts of great things together. You've heard of the thirteen pieces of art that were stolen from the Gardner Museum in 1990, I suppose? Well, I may know where those pieces are. Unfortunately, they're mixed with a few forgeries—rather fine ones, I admit. I'd like your help to tell me which are the authentic pieces."

An unwelcome hint of interest stirred within at the thought of reading a Vermeer or a Renoir. "You don't need me for that. There are plenty of experts out there who would be happy to help you."

I tried to sit tall and solid, and to be unreadable. Like a statue. However, if I were being honest, I felt more like a small bird on the inside. Otto had that effect on people.

"I don't want them. I want you, Addie." Otto's head bowed slightly and his features turned dark, like the mask fell without his knowing. "I've fooled the experts with my forgeries for years. I knew I couldn't fool you. You are foolproof, aren't you? Assuming you are willing to use your gifts." He stood and the antique chair creaked.

I remembered the vision I'd gotten from touching Otto's desk in his office: His father yelling at him when he was a boy, telling him that his artwork held no creativity, no imagination. But his gift was in replicating others' work.

"I think it's time you realized that your gift has a place in the world. A profitable, meaningful, and enjoyable home. With me. With my...gift."

It seemed even he believed what he was saying.

"So you want me to help you discern the forgeries among the Gardner art. And then my father and grandfather magically find their way home? Is that how it works?"

"In a manner of speaking. I was thinking of more of a trade. You see, there is a whole world of stolen art out there, just waiting to be bought and sold to willing buyers at a premium. The biggest obstacle to winning at this game is to know which pieces to buy. Forgeries, as you might have gathered, flood the market. So the trick to being successful is to know how to pick only the authentic pieces."

He was, as Blake had said, trying to replace Carolena. Blake's mother. Someone who had the same kinds of gifts I did. Someone he once loved, someone he once worked the black market with, and made a small fortune.

"So my father and grandfather return to their lives, but I lose mine?"

"I wouldn't say that you lose your life. I'd say that your life finds the meaning and the expression you've been searching for. And I'll make sure we bring your father and grandfather home. Alive and well. I would be happy to do that for you. I'll even make sure that Blake continues a safe existence."

His threat swam like venom through my veins. "How can

you be so certain that they're still alive? Or that you could bring them home?"

Otto's well-manned impatience delivered itself in a sigh. "Long ago my father taught me that nine-tenths of being successful is first knowing *where* you can be successful. I took that advice very seriously and now I have something of a knack for knowing ahead of time if a venture will work out. Or not. Kind of a sixth sense, if you know what I mean?"

I nodded slowly and decided this knack he spoke about had more to do with picking the right prey.

"So if I tell you I'm certain that an endeavor will work out, then I'm certain." Otto's eyes twinkled with the excitement of a secret well kept, and the power of being able to control another. "We'll work together on these two projects, Adeline."

I tried to take a breath but my lungs were flattened like cement to the back wall of my chest. What he claimed about my family was implausible and reeked of bait. Still, some little something said that he knew where they were. "If I say that I don't believe you and refuse your offer?"

Otto's signature smile broadened like I had just complimented his tie at a gallery opening. "Well, I suppose you've lived long without the men in your family. Perhaps you've gotten used to the arrangement. Or maybe no men in the family is the Montgomery tradition you'll carry forward."

"Blake," I whispered.

Otto cocked his head, raised his eyebrows and nodded once.

I forced myself to breathe calmly. "So, if I help you, you'll return my father and grandfather. Is that it?"

"I'm certain we could bring them back."

"You'll also stay away from Blake?"

Otto shrugged. "If we worked together, I'd have no business with Blake."

There was no reason to trust him."What sort of insurance do I have that you'll keep your word?"

"Read me." Otto turned his palms up. "I'm telling the truth. Work with me and I'll keep my word about your father and grandfather."

"And Blake."

"And Blake." He nodded.

"I'd need a few days to get on my feet. To regain my health."

"Very well, then." Otto reached into his front pocket when he stood, then produced the key he had apparently used to gain unhindered access to me. He waved it in front of me. "I'll leave this with you." The metal key clinked against the glass coffee table and I stared at it.

He walked across the room, deliberately precise, like stalking. I felt the hook he'd placed in my cheek with the reference to my father's and grandfather's whereabouts.

"I'm looking forward to working with you," he said and arrived uncomfortably close to me. "We'll make a powerful team." He lifted his hand toward me and I took a step back, afraid he would place his hand around my neck as a threat, a little promise, a taste of his intent. Like a toxic dance he stepped forward to my retreat, and ran the side of his index finger against one side of my exposed collarbone, and then the other, his touch nauseatingly tender. I shuddered.

"Oh." Otto backed up into my line of sight again. "If I don't hear from you soon, I will come for you."

I stared at the key, unable to move, and tracked his movements through the townhouse. His shoes ticked slowly against the foyer's marble flooring. Then the heavy door shut behind him.

I thought of the dream I'd had before we left for France. It wasn't a normal, random dream. My father and grandfather knocking on some proverbial door of my awareness. They certainly seemed alive to me.

Otto's enticing remarks were beginning to feel like validation to my suspicion. They did make a kind of sense. My own father and grandfather had died and I'd never seen them after the fact. I had seen every random dead person within 100 miles of me. However, I'd never received any messages from my own family. They'd never visited.

Because they couldn't. Because they must be alive?

Maybe.

Then why couldn't I feel them?

If they were dead, why couldn't I reach them? I could communicate with dead people. But not them? Nothing made sense.

Mental pro and con columns formed in my head. If I helped Otto, I potentially helped my father and grandfather. Of course Otto would then take me away from Blake. The man I'd searched my entire life to find, and finally had.

First I needed proof that my father and grandfather were alive. Assuming he could provide that, then what? I shook my head at the lack of clear answers. "I'll figure this out after I find Mitch."

Frank, the ghost, passed in front of me and blew a breath of cold air forcefully enough to blow my hair.

"Can I help you with something, Frank?" I gritted through my teeth.

The ghost stepped back and gave a hefty exhale, the liquor on his breath hit me in the face like a wet rag. "I like this feisty version of you when you're around Otto."

"Blake warned you not to harass me, Frank. What do you want?"

Frank circled me once, then twice, slowly and in an even pace. "What do I *want*? I want my payback. I want the score evened. I'm entitled to my revenge." Insanity raged in his glassy, dead eyes, his liquor-scented breath made my stomach pitch. I spun off the couch, moved across the room.

A seething burn rose inside. I'd been pushed too far, manipulated too much. "Why not go after Otto? He's the one who killed you."

"Yes, but you're the one he values most. Well, almost."

"Get out of my house, Frank. I've been threatened enough for one day."

An image of a woman with thick chestnut hair and wide brown eyes appeared to me. She was a softer, rounder version of Frank, sharing his features in feminine form. He was the boy she worried about, the man his mother still missed. She wore a flowered dress when she drove through the neighborhood and called his name when he was young. "Francis! Francis!"

She'd warned him to stay away from a certain crowd. A group he ultimately called his brotherhood, the mafia. Now she's older, prays the rosary and worries for him in a different way.

"Francis," I said, listening to her voice more than I listened to my own.

"Don't call me that! No one calls me that." Frank circled me like a wolf with bared teeth.

"I see a woman who resembles you, she's searching for you. She called you home at the end of the day. She still searches for you, she knows you're not at peace, Francis."

"Don't—"

"Fran-cis..." I crooned on the breath.

"Don't talk about my mother. You're one of those...a freak." He pressed toward me.

"*Right*, Frank. Of the two of us standing here in my home, *I'm* the freak." Frank's rage poured through me. "You gave Blake your word that you wouldn't threaten me anymore," I said.

Frank backed away at the mention of Blake's name and took a sip of brown liquid from an etheric rocks glass.

"Help me," I said with a balled fist at my side. "Find a way to get Otto out of my life, or stay away from me. Otherwise I'll call Carolena and tell her to kick your ass to the Other Side. And if that's where you end up? Prepare yourself. Last time I checked, karma had an awfully long memory."

## 6

Carolena put her evening glass of wine on the side table, then she reached beneath and pressed the hidden button. The bookshelf parted from the wall to finally reveal access to its secret treasures. She stepped inside, flipped the light switch, and gallery-style lighting illuminated the former museum pieces that hung around the room.

There were three in all, and each of them were gifts that she had taken from Otto's private collection. They weren't the most expensive pieces they'd stolen from her former employer, The Metropolitan Museum of Art. Although she knew these Wentworths were a few of the ones Otto valued most. He didn't know she had them now.

He'd kept them locked up in a spare room of her home when she and Blake lived in New York City. Blake had been only three or four then. When he asked innocently about these curious paintings that held so much allure for his father, Otto told him they were special paintings that could transport you.

Carolena felt the circle of peaceful quiet around her

when she studied them. She stared at their magic and she fingered the vintage ruby and diamond engagement ring that Otto had given her on the day their child was born. Though Blake was not the name they'd given him then, it was the name he used for himself now, to keep Otto from knowing his true identity as his son.

A lifetime had passed since she and Otto parted, but she still thought of him at least once every day. She tried not to. However, the memories burned too brightly for her to turn away completely. Remembering him was either going to be her fatal flaw, or what her soul needed to stay alive.

The knock at the door gave her a start, and for a long moment she stood frozen. She never received visitors except for the occasional repairman. Too dangerous. Too risky.

Carolena turned out the lights, slipped out of the private room, and slid the bookcase into its proper place against the wall. Then she stared at the backside of the front door. Another knock would not come. She knew it. Because she could feel that whoever had knocked on the other side of the door was not there. At least not anymore.

She let her awareness scan the outer area, she didn't find a lingering presence. Still, whoever had knocked on the door knew she was inside. She could sense that, too.

She took a steady breath to calm herself, then stepped slowly toward the front window that she kept mostly covered from the outside with tall, flowering bushes. From the corner of the window she could see the front porch. She lifted an edge of the silk curtain and peeked outside. There were two, large black cases propped against the front brick of her home.

## 7

F rancis finally left after I poked a finger into his icy chest to make my point. It irritated me to no end that he, Otto, and anyone else for that matter, could get to me any time they wanted.

Locked doors and U.S. federal marshals wouldn't help me.

Out of habit—and for protection—I sent my psychic sight through the house to make sure Otto was gone, and to see if I could sense Mitch. The hairy edge of a panic attack was prickling at my heart, taking stock of my surroundings would help. I found no one, which didn't help me to feel safe at all. Because Mitch was supposed to be nearby.

I called Blake. No answer.

I sent him another text: Call me. Please.

I tucked my upper lip between my teeth and I made my way toward the door, one slow and deliberate step at a time.

Mitch was gone, I could feel it. I stood on my side of the door, bare toes twitching on the cold, Georgian marble, my sixth sense wandering up and down the empty hallway on the other side of the door. Searching.

He wasn't there. No one was there. I didn't need to open the door to check.

But I did.

First I leaned against the door with both hands and searched through the fisheye peephole I'd had installed before I left town with Blake. Unless Mitch was hiding at the end of the hallway, no one was there.

I searched the hallway, half expecting to see Otto standing there. My psychic sight wended down the hallway and around the building. No one there. With my sight wide open I scanned the area where I left Mitch and unexpectedly noticed a few tiny white sparkles in the space. The outward sign that energy work had just been performed.

One little sparkle. And then a few seconds later there was another one. And then another. Tiny remnants of magic held in the air. Adrenaline sprinted along the wires of my nervous system.

Otto had pushed Mitch to leave his guard. I was alone.

After I closed the door, my hand hung on the doorknob. A heavy gust of Otto blew through me. He must have left his own hand on the knob long enough to leave an imprint. This would be my chance to fact check him, and to see if I could find out what happened to Mitch.

As if I could slow the pace of information by limiting the amount of hand I used, I limited my touch on the door knob to two fingers. Quick as lightning, a vision of Otto stood before me in my home. His thick, tanned, manicured hand held on to the knob, turning it all the way to the right with a gentle creak before closing the door so as not to alert me.

He was confident that Mitch was out of the way. Cocky that he had me all to himself. Didn't even remotely feel pressed for time. I didn't know what he did with Mitch, but I knew he wasn't coming back. I was on my own.

The loose key poked out from his other hand, his eyes brimmed with plot and poison while he searched for me, planning his surprise approach. He anticipated my reaction the way a vampire dreams of the first taste of new blood.

Otto's eyes moved coldly across the rooms laid out in front of him. He searched for me, with a singular focus to prey upon my weaknesses, my vulnerability. I followed his footsteps to keep in touch with his energetic trail.

With the stealth of a leopard he stalked me through my own home, then stopped at the doorway to my bedroom. Then the me of an hour ago took a deep breath while I laid in the library, and Otto's eyes shifted in the direction of the noise. When he was certain he hadn't been seen, he finally moved. He walked like a thief in the night, taking no chances, and then rejoicing at his fate that he should find me alone, asleep and eyes blanketed with a washcloth.

He stared at me for a few eternal moments. Then he took my phone and keys with him to his seat on the other side of the room and the action began. Essence of Otto pulsed through me, body, mind and soul and was akin to the effects of rat poison in my morning coffee.

He studied the library like he visited an old friend. And then he did it. He thought of my father and grandfather. He didn't remember them. He thought of them, and wondered how they were doing. Not affectionately, but curiously.

The living room was one clean area he hadn't visited. I sank into the ivory couch there to stay out of the way of Otto's presence which still hung in the air. His trail drifted through my home like a steam of polluted water.

The marshal was gone and he wasn't coming back. And my father and grandfather were alive. Or at least Otto believed them to be.

I had to figure out what to do next and how to do it now that Otto was free.

## 8

B lake felt the pain in his head raging against the inside of his skull in fast, metered beats. Then he noticed the small, sharp gravel against his cheek. Lying down. Why was he lying down? Something was dead wrong.

If only he could open his eyes.

A biting wind sailed across his uncovered head, sent its frigid fingers down through his body. The icy pavement beneath him called next. One sensation at a time, he was gaining new awareness.

He willed his hand to move and found it unreasonably heavy and awkward. When it finally reached his face, he used his thumb to physically lift one eyelid. Nothing was familiar.

A police siren sent off a warning somewhere behind him. The courthouse. *Right.* He was at the courthouse.

Blake pushed himself to a sitting position and leaned against the courthouse building behind him, his eyes still uncomfortably closed. He was supposed to be inside this building and giving his testimony. The cold from the wall seeped through his jacket and Blake shivered.

"Have to get to Addie," he said.

Blake felt his pockets for his phone, but it was missing. He rolled onto all fours and reached for the wall. Instead his hand landed on cold glass.

"A window," he said. He banged on the glass with the heel of his hand. As the muscles in his eyelids worked again, he stared at the face of a wide-eyed young Asian girl who opened the blinds on the other side of the courthouse basement window.

"Help," he said and hit the glass again. "Help."

## 9
---

Huddled in ear muffs and a heavy, down jacket against the cold and the wind, I stood next to the endless stream of cars and horns that rushed past Alexa's apartment building. I felt oddly brave. Completely free. Rather numb. Otto's freedom had killed the hope I had for Blake's and my future.

I waited under the green awning with two Starbucks cups in my hands, and my box of treasured possessions at my feet. The fact that I hadn't yet spoken to Blake about Otto was a missing step. I assured myself that he was okay. That he would call as soon as he could. Though nothing would take me forward until I could hear his voice, know that he was all right and tell him what happened.

Lex wasn't answering her phone, either. I let my awareness drift up to her apartment for the twentieth time. I knew she was in there. I'd left several messages and decided to stand out on the bustling New York sidewalk.

Considering Otto's access, I figured I was safer in public, around so many...witnesses. If Otto was going to drive up in his black limo and yank me into the back seat, maybe someone would call for help..

Chills ran down the upper part of my back, the standard sensation I felt when someone watched me. I searched the area but only saw the usual New York City street crowd—a random mix of every representation possible. None of them seemed to be looking in my direction. At least not for more than a moment or so.

My phone rang and I cradled one coffee while I dug my phone out of my jacket pocket. "Elizabeth, Hi."

"I just heard about Otto on the news," Elizabeth said. "Are you all right?"

Elizabeth and I had developed a close friendship when I worked for Otto. She was the Director of Acquisitions for two departments at the Metropolitan Museum of Art and the only person in the art community who was willing to show me the ropes. We hadn't spoken to one another since Blake and I left town six months ago.

"Oh, Elizabeth," I said. The cab next to me slammed its screechy brakes. "He got out of it. It's unbelievable."

"Where are you?"

"Standing outside of my sister's apartment, waiting for her to buzz me up."

"Did you testify today?"

"I was supposed to tomorrow. Not anymore, obviously." I drank a long gulp of coffee.

"Addie, you need to be careful. Otto holds grudges and he would know that you were in line to testify against him. Can you and Blake leave town again for a while?"

I decided to just blurt it out. "Otto says he knows where my father and grandfather are. He did something that made me think that he may be right. I can't really leave until I know for sure if he's telling the truth." A horn blared nearby and I clenched my eyes shut. I could feel every inch of Elizabeth wanting to tell me not to believe him.

"Remember it's his trademark to lead someone down the primrose path. You know you can't trust him. And I assume he wants you to do something for him in return for his telling you where they are?"

"Work with him on some project." I decided not to mention the Gardner art.

"Which, I would guess, is illegal," she said.

"I don't know."

"Because Otto is at the center of it. I don't think you should believe anything he says. I know that telling you what to do isn't going to do any good. So just be careful. Otto ruined my career because I wouldn't testify for him. I can't imagine what he has in mind for you since you were prepared to testify against him." Elizabeth puffed an audible sigh.

"He ruined your career?" I asked.

"After I declined Otto's attorney's offer to testify as a character witness, I was told by my boss that I was going to be relocated to a more suitable position within the museum. It came down from the board of directors."

"And you think that directive came from Otto."

"He has a long reach," Elizabeth said.

I nodded and surveyed the sea of cabs that had become prisoners of traffic, while throngs of New Yorkers moved along the sidewalk. The pedestrians lived their lives—they pushed strollers, carried coffee cups, talked on their phones. My life it seemed, was caught at a crossroads.

"Tonight I have to go to the Beyond Fashion exhibit," Elizabeth said. "I'll spend the entire event wondering who is a friend of Otto's. This is my last fete before I'm shuffled off to God-knows-where. Sorry, this call was not supposed to be about me."

"No, it's okay. I'm sorry you're caught up in all of this."

"You too, sweetheart. Let me know what you decide to do or if you need anything. I'm here for you."

Elizabeth and I were at similar crossroads. Both of our lives had been capsized by Otto and we had to figure out what to do next. Elizabeth and I made plans for drinks, but I knew I wouldn't be able to keep the date. I'd either be running for my life or enslaved in service to Otto.

A chill fluttered down my spine. Things were going to get worse, before they got better. I could feel it.

Cameron, the thin, Irish doorman with the slight limp finally appeared from wherever he'd been. "Miss Addie! How lovely to see ya, dear. Are ya lookin' for your sister, now?" He blew into his cupped hands and rubbed them together.

I turned slowly from the end of the covered sidewalk, picked up my box, and walked toward the front door, almost as slowly as if I'd had a glass of wine or two. I did feel a little drunk. The kind of tipsy you felt when you thought things can't possibly get any worse, and you couldn't quite feel the ground beneath your feet.

"Hi, Cameron." I balanced a Starbucks cup in the box. "I am. Would you buzz her for me, please? I've called but she didn't answer."

"Of course, my love. Come with me." He lifted the box from my arms and carried it to the semi-circle cherry desk on the side of the lobby. Then he picked up a landline and called Lexie.

Cameron had developed a crush on Lexie the moment she moved into the building. He was puppy-dog cute with slightly shaggy reddish-brown hair and a sweet ever-readiness about him. Lexie barely noticed him, but he kept hope alive.

"She may still be sleeping, Miss Addie," he whispered. "Or something. She came in rather late, and with a handsome mister." He twisted his face into a comical "don't tell her I told you, but..." expression.

"Ah." I winked in return. "That explains it."

On the fifth call Cameron gave up. "I'm no' supposed to do this, Miss Addie. But seein' as I know ya. And Miss Lexie should probably be checked on. Don't tell her I said that to ya'. There's jus' a lot o' strange people in the world these days."

"Thank you, Cameron." I gave him a hug.

He walked me to the elevator, blushing fresh crimson while he relayed a few details about Lexie from the night before. "She must o' forgotten about the cameras in the lift. Would ya' please mention them to her? I do' think I could."

I told him I would.

"If that recording should—could, get lost, perhaps?" I suggested.

"I'm already workin' at that, Miss Addie." Cameron stood taller, like he plotted to rescue his princess.

When I arrived at Lexie's floor I stood outside the elevator and felt the energy of the area for a moment. There was definitely someone new on the floor. Someone I hadn't read before.

Hers was only one of two apartments on the floor and sensing the energy of someone new wasn't difficult. An unfamiliar energy was sort of like the scent of an unfamiliar food wafting through the air. It was hard not to notice it.

This particular fragrance made the hairs on the back of my neck stand on end. I wasn't sure why. Something was off.

I knocked again, Lexie finally answered, wearing an oversized white T-shirt.

"What are you doing here?" Alexa inspected the hallway, then grabbed my arm, jerked me inside. "Are you okay?"

A statuesque 6 foot 4 inch male passed in the background. When he caught us staring at him he smirked and waved.

"I need your help." I reached into the box and handed her a cup of coffee.

"I didn't think you were supposed to be out?" Lexie took the coffee and locked the door behind us. "Why didn't you call me? I would have come to you."

"I did call, Lex." I walked into the living room and put the to-go box on the floor. The curtains were open, revealing one of the nicer views of New York. I rested my hand against the couch. Sketchy scenes of their night before put on a show.

Lex had a long history of mistaking attention for love. Love was always what she wanted. I didn't think she was going to be happy with the way this relationship ended.

I looked out the window and wondered if Lex had closed the drapes from the day before.

Alexa rubbed her hand across her forehead and glanced around the room. "I'm sorry. I don't even know where I put my phone. Are you okay?"

"So, that's tall, blond, and handsome? He's 'the one'?" I asked. The shower turned on in the background and I tried to figure out how to tell her what was going on with Otto without flipping her out.

Alexa tossed a few pillows around and discovered her phone buried beneath the couch cushions. "Yes. That's Todd. His sister owns the gallery that's doing my show. I can't believe you're here just...out in the open, that's insane. I thought you were staying hidden away until after the trial." Alexa shot over to the wall and closed one half of the drapes. "What if he sees you?"

"Speaking of being seen, you shouldn't do anything in front of an open window that you wouldn't want on YouTube. And Cameron asked me to remind you that there are cameras in the elevators." I tried to be delicate, but with Lex sometimes direct was best.

She stood still for a silent moment, surrounded by a puddle of winter sun. Her thin legs stretched long and lean beneath her T-shirt and she appeared as she did when we were about eight. Headstrong and naive, and with lots of smarts that yielded a false sense of security in the world.

I drank a long gulp of coffee and waited for the news to sink in.

Lexie finally nodded and shrugged, a blush climbed up her neck and beyond. I could tell her newfound feelings for the boy were scrambled with her common sense. His energy had engulfed her in a bubble and she seemed content to live there, even without knowing how she really felt about him. She liked being liked.

"Are you sure about *him*?" I nodded toward Todd's general location.

Lexie stared at me with her mouth open, as if I'd just asked a blindly stupid question.

"Because I think he's hiding something," I said.

"You think *everyone* is hiding something." Alexa waved her hand.

"Well, I'm not usually wrong about that." Lexie's defenses rose up. Her green eyes, which were soft and moony when I arrived, took on a sudden sharpness. I decided to skip ahead, rather than engage.

"Otto came to the townhouse this morning. Actually, he

came *into* the townhouse, while I was there. I can't find Blake and I really need your help."

With those words my worry hit fever pitch and I decided I'd had enough coffee for today. Caffeine, like any other drug of choice, only gave a certain amount of respite from the things that needed to be figured out.

"Can I get some water?" I asked. "Or mineral water, if you have it?"

"Yeah, of course." Alexa stood distractedly, like she'd been a hostess remiss and she headed to the kitchen. She also seemed happy to have a minute to process what I'd said.

A slightly parted bathroom door allowed steam from the shower to carry the perfumed scent of soap and shampoo throughout the apartment, as well as Todd's rendition of The Black Keys' *I'm Howlin' For You*. I decided not to say anything else about Todd even though I didn't like what she was getting herself into. Something about his vibe really stank. Like he could be bought and sold to do just about anything. I'd warned her. That was all I could do.

Cocoa, Lexie's little cinnamon-colored maltese-yorkie pup, ran into the room and jumped up at my legs. When I scooped him up, he climbed my torso and snuggled into my neck, his fur smelling of tea tree and lavender. It mixed uncomfortably with his breath, which smelled of soured beef. He burrowed closer, obviously knew with his canine intuition that something was wrong and that I needed comfort. I bundled him against my heart while I dialed William's number with my other hand.

Blake had given me William's number some time ago in case of emergency. I'd never called it before but I thought today qualified.

Voicemail. "Um, William, this is Addie. I see that Otto is

out and I can't find Blake. Call me at this number, please, if you know where he is. Or just have him call me. Thanks."

Alexa handed me bubbly water. The soda's effervescence spritzed against my face with welcomed coolness and I took a few much-needed sips.

"What do you mean you can't find Blake?" Alexa asked.

I told her how I'd opened my eyes from a rest to find Otto in my own home, blackmailing me to join him in his Gardner art scheme because he said he could return our father and grandfather, and I hadn't been able to get in touch with Blake.

Lexie sat with her mouth agape for a few moments then audibly clanked her teeth shut. Without making a noise she popped off the couch and walked a circle around the room. Then she sat on the couch again, leaned on her knees, her hands wrapped around her coffee cup.

I clicked my thumb and pinky nails against one another.

"How did he know you were there?" Lexie asked.

"He had to have had someone watching me." I felt supremely stupid and slightly sick for being one-upped by Otto.

"I can't believe he got off." Alexa stared into the corner. Otto's sinister presence was palpable in the room.

"I'm worried that something has happened to Blake. He would have called me the minute he knew Otto was getting out."

"Of course he would have," Alexa said. "Who else can you call that might know where he is?"

"No one. I've called William. I don't know any of the other people on the art crime team. Should I go to the courthouse? Blake asked me to stay away from there, but—"

"I'll go with you. Let me throw some jeans on." Alexa smoothed her hair. She grabbed my hand and dragged me into her bedroom. One of the windows was open an inch and the crispness of winter filtered into the recycled heat of the inside. Alexa was never without fresh air if she could help it, a fact I appreciated. I situated myself next to the breeze to staunch the nausea my nerves brought on.

"We'll find him, sweetheart." She ripped the shirt over her head and tossed it, then rummaged through a neighboring chair full of clothes. Cocoa made a nest out of the recently worn shirt on the floor. "Why would he say that he could bring Dad and Grandad home? Did he really think you would fall for that?"

I bobbed my head back and forth. "Well, I did do a reading after he left and I saw where he thought of them as if they were alive. So...of course I could be wrong, but if they're not dead, that *would* explain why none of us have ever heard from them."

I lobbed the possibility out gently. It was farfetched, I knew. And Alexa wasn't typically keen on entertaining potential solutions that she didn't like. She was apt to flick them away like ants at a picnic.

Alexa was somewhat dazed, maybe from the news and perhaps from too much champagne the night before. "It's hard to read things accurately in a situation like that," she said. "Don't you think this is just a trap to punish Blake for setting him up?"

"Yeah, could be." I searched for an empty spot to place my glass but there wasn't one.

Alexa read my face and gave me a worried smile. "Blake is probably just in with William. Don't worry, we're going to find him."

"I'm sure you're right. Or his phone is dead or he's held up in a room with the FBI while they overanalyze everything. Most likely both," I said to assure myself.

Alexa wrestled her jeans and jumped three hops to help them up.

"Can you see anything about where he is or if he's okay?" I asked.

Alexa rolled her eyes. "No. I'm sorry. Long night."

Lex was never more ineffective than when she'd had too much to drink, too much boy, and not enough sleep. She might as well be drugged.

"I don't think they're alive, or that Otto could have them, because, where would they be? I mean, twenty years is too long to keep someone hidden away. Unless they're trapped in some New York apartment somewhere." She selected a thin tank and hazelnut brown sweater from the pile. "I don't mean that, of course."

The haunting, Stephen King-like scenario ricocheted around my mind: our father and grandfather held up in some dark room, bound by shackles.

"Even then, someone from our family would be able to sense their whereabouts," I said. "So, that theory doesn't work."

"Okay, so if they're alive—and I'm not saying that they are. Just, if. Then my question is why? Why take them? Maybe they found out about the forgeries, and then Otto does what? Locks them away so they won't tell anyone?" Lexie slid the sweater over her head and static electricity crackled, making her hair stand on end.

I shook my head. "I don't think Otto kidnaps someone to keep them from talking. If you're Otto, and the secret is big enough, you *kill* them to keep them from talking." I thought about Frank, closed my eyes at the horror that the same thing might have happened to my family.

"That doesn't work, either." Lexie lowered her voice and moved next to me when the shower turned off in the background. "Because if they're dead, how does he keep us from interacting with them on the other side?"

I didn't think Lexie fully realized it but she was beginning to defend my side of the point.

"Maybe he's able to put up some energetic barrier in a way that we don't know about?" Lexie brushed through the knots in her hair.

"Nothing completely adds up," I said. "That's the problem. Though I do think he knows where they are."

The vivid dream I'd had months ago of our father and grandfather knocked on my mind's door. I heard their voices, felt their emotions run through me. I reminded Alexa of it while her new boyfriend bustled in the background, dropped change, and jangled keys.

"And you're sure they weren't ghosts?" she whispered surreptitiously.

"I...don't think so." I'd seen ghosts all of my life. This was a question I should know the answer to. I swallowed a bit of panic that crawled up my chest when I thought of our father and grandfather lost somewhere beyond our sight and awareness. Not the walking dead, like Frank. Maybe close. I shook my head and tried to make sense of the riddle. "It's like they're neither here nor there."

I made my way toward the door, across the cascade of linens and clothes. Cocoa hopped up and pranced behind me.

Alexa tied her hair into a low braid and lifted it to the front left side of her shoulder. "All right, I'm ready. Let's go."

Even after a long night Lexie was still one of the most beautiful women I knew. Her green eyes appeared to be lit from within, and the warm tones of her complexion looked air-brushed. The reasons why she chose to settle for someone as sketchy as Todd were as textbook as they were for any little girl whose dad had disappeared too early in her life.

"Oh, hi," Lexie said with a smile when she peered over my shoulder.

Todd had entered the room.

"This is my sister, Addie." Alexa gestured toward me. Neither Todd nor I made a move toward one another, but we both managed a near-impolite nod and slight smile.

With stars in her eyes, Lexie was ready for a hug and glided closer toward Todd, but he stood with his hands on his hips.

"I've got to get to the gallery. Piper needs my help with a few things." He nodded toward the door.

"I'll walk you out." She smoothed her hair and sweater when she followed him, tested her breath in her palm, and made a face.

My phone buzzed and I read the screen. My heart took off.

It was William.

"Hello?"

## 10

Two security guards and an EMT guided Blake into a small office where William Condon of the FBI's art crime team barked at two other men. Blake's grip on one of the guards was tight for balance and for strength to remain upright. Whatever they stuck in his neck kept him stumbling and dizzy.

William hung up a call, seemingly before it started. "Well, you finally decided to show up. Where have you—" His words halted when Blake was fully in the room. He assumed the pallor he felt must have been visible, along with drops of sweat that rolled down his cheeks. The guards eased him into the red leather chair that was closest, and he tried not to pass out from the pain that battered his head.

To his annoyance his strength was returning at glacial speed. He tried to ask William for a phone to call Addie but only a gasp escaped from his dry throat. The tall man with ultrashort, reddish-blond hair responded quickly from across the room. He opened a bottle of water from the side table and handed it to Blake. The EMT removed Blake's jacket and shirt and took his vitals.

"We found him and Marshal Roxy Dalton on the west side of the building, Mr. Condon. He says they stuck Marshal Dalton and him with something. There's a needle mark on the side of his neck. Here, where the blood is." The security guard pointed to Blake's neck. William and the EMT leaned in for a closer inspection.

"They took Marshal Dalton to the hospital—she was unconscious."

Blake lowered the half-empty bottle from his mouth. "I need a phone." The words came out far slower than they had repeated in his mind.

"Thank you, Lewis, Donald. We'll take care of him," William said, and the guards left the room.

Blake managed to sit on his own now, though he leaned back for support. He took a few deep breaths for the EMT who listened to his heart. His lack of resistance made him appear cooperative, but really he was using the moment to reclaim more strength. As soon as he could, he would grab someone's phone and call Addie.

The EMT hung the stethoscope around his neck and ripped the blood pressure cuff from Blake's arm. "His vitals are improving, but I think you should go to the—"

"I'm not going to the hospital." Blake tried to stand and walk toward William, but sat in light of the dizziness that nearly dropped him to the floor. "And you can give me your phone, or I'm going to walk out that door and grab one from whomever happens to be closest."

Blake lowered his head and leaned on his knees to steady himself. The lack of enough stamina to walk across the room infuriated him.

William nodded to the EMT who packed up his equipment. When he was gone he addressed Blake. "Addie called earlier. She left a voicemail and asked about you. Apparently, she's been trying to reach you. I was calling her back when you walked in. Tell me what happened, and you can have the phone." William held his phone out of Blake's reach.

Blake exhaled with frustration then drained the rest of the water from the bottle. "I got here two hours before the trial was scheduled to start, like we agreed. I took three steps from the car and two men stuck a gun in my side, took us down the side alley, then injected us with something that knocked us out."

He put his hand out for the phone.

"Considering the weather, you're lucky you woke up when you did." William put the phone in Blake's outstretched palm. "We had to drop the charges against Otto."

"What?" Blake yelled, and the pain in his head increased accordingly. "Otto's free?"

William stuck his hands in his pockets and took a step backward. His lips thinned with the familiar anger and resignation of someone who fought within the system.

"No!" Blake buttoned his shirt as fast as the strange numbness in his fingers would allow. He needed to get to Addie.

"No one showed up. Not one witness." William nodded across the room to the lean, muscular man who had brought Blake the water. "Ryan was finally able to get ahold of three of the witnesses. Seems some of Otto's mafia friends suggested that they needed to choose between their families' safety or testifying. They were told they couldn't have both. This morning each of them had a car parked down the street from their houses. A reminder not to attend the trial."

"Tell the judge. I'll tell him what happened to me and we'll get a new trial." Blake rubbed the soreness on his neck where he'd been stuck, and fought the intense but dwindling surge of illness.

"I have told the judge. The defense is saying Otto didn't have anything to do with it. It doesn't look like any of Otto's former clients are willing go up against the mob. When they were just testifying against Otto for stealing their art, they were all in. They had nothing to lose. Now they do. So even if I get a new trial, I don't have any witnesses. Without them, I don't have a case."

MY PHONE SCREEN, which had just shown me William's caller ID, was now blank. William had called, but the line went dead when I answered. I dialed William's number again and his voicemail clicked on. So I hit redial. I would stalk him until I had answers.

"Where are you?" Blake answered William's phone, his voice tense and raspy.

"I'm—I'm at Alexa's."

Blake breathed a heavy sigh and relief carried through the phone. "Otto's out, the charges were dismissed—"

"I know."

"You know?"

"Otto came by my townhouse, I was there—"

His temper hit an all-time high and his emotion struck me in the stomach. "Are you okay? What were you doing at your town house?" He sounded half-choked with panic.

"I'm okay. I've been calling you all morning are you—?"

"Something happened to my phone. Stay put. I'll come get you."

"Okay," I said.

Blake sighed. The kind of deep exhalation that signaled

nervous relief. Whatever had happened to Blake today, it felt like we were both dodging bullets.

"I love you." Blake said like he might never have the chance to say it again.

"I love you, too." I hung up and held my phone at my chest for a moment. I inhaled a deep breath. Alexa and Todd kept on with their good-byes in the hallway, and I flipped on the TV for noise and distraction. A moment's break.

Unfortunately, a previously recorded courthouse step scene of Otto and his family, including his wife and sons, Philippe and Nicholas, appeared on the screen of the local news coverage. Nicholas was a young replica of his father. It showed in the frame of his face, the ready tan on his skin, and even Otto's body language repeated in Nicholas' stance and movements.

Philippe was cast more from his mother's lineage, with side swept brown hair, soft, rounded features and large, earthy-brown eyes. He had been my favorite playmate when he and Nicholas and Lexi and I roamed the firm as children.

Today Otto's family stood in support of him as a free man, and my heart plummeted to the pit of my stomach with a sick thud. "This is why I don't watch TV."

"Earlier today the charges were dropped against Otto Albrecht as the prosecution failed to produce its witnesses. Albrecht's attorney, Chris Menger, had this to say in a statement to the press."

The stocky, bald man in a slick suit stepped to the microphone and adjusted his tie. I'd seen his face in the papers when he defended aging mob bosses. "Justice was served here today when the prosecution's witnesses apparently had an attack of conscience. I'm happy to say that due process took its appropriate course and my client is a free man once again."

Chris Menger patted Otto on the back while shaking his hand. Otto smiled like an innocent man, though more confident than surprised over his victory. His family members stood on either side of him, like a matched set of reluctant winners.

I thought of Frank and his other mob relations and I figured that was how Otto got out. Frank's mob family probably bought the judge or threatened to kill every witness if they showed up to testify. Otto moved to the mic, shook his fist in the air, vowed to overcome the wrongs that had been committed against him and his firm. He said he'd rebuild his reputation.

The front door closed with a heavy *thunk*. Cocoa jumped off the couch and ran to see who is was.

"Are you ready to go?" Alexa asked, and scooped up her dog.

"Blake called. He's on his way to pick me up."

"Oh, thank goodness." She dropped on the couch and sighed with relief.

"Yeah, he said something happened with his phone. I guess I'll get the whole story when I see him." I drew in a deep breath and knew that none of us were safe now that Otto was free.

"Good. Good." Alexa leaned back. "Wait, what's the matter? Why are you looking at me like that?"

"I think that if I'm a target for Otto, then you're in danger as well. You need to be careful."

## 11

The man made his black baseball cap sit so low that it almost touched the top of his black sunglasses. It wasn't his normal presentation, which was the point. If he wanted to be recognized he wouldn't have worn the hat. Baseball wasn't his thing. No sport was his thing. His passion was art.

He sat in his car which was parked near the loading entrance of the firm, and he held the screen of his phone in front of him like he was reading a text or checking email. Behind the sunglasses his eyes searched his surroundings. With the recent press coverage around the case, reporters around the world were bound to try for a picture or an interview. He didn't want either right now. Which was ironic, because at any point in history he would have welcomed the attention.

The driver's side window was cracked and his hearing was primed to hear anyone who might approach. No one had. He lifted the ring of keys from his jacket pocket and filed through them one by one until he found the two he needed. Then he quietly, quickly approached the locked door and inserted the keys, one at a time. When the locks opened, the alarm sounded. He punched a code on the keypad, then relocked the door. And listened.

The building was filled with a particular kind of thick, heavy quiet that only abandoned spaces could create. His soft-soled shoes made the slightest squeak when he walked steadily down the sloping hallway toward the stairwell. He assumed Ellen would have shut them down. He paused at the elevator bank and pushed the button just to see if they were working. They didn't respond to the call button.

Satisfied, he tugged on the heavy door that opened onto the stairwell. He listened into the darkened silence of the vertical hallway to make certain once again that he was alone, then he began his quiet descent. How many times had he been up and down these steps? Not once did he ever think the firm would cease to exist. It had been a monument in the city for half a century.

He exited into the tiled foyer that led to the vaults. Yellow police tape lay on the floor and he shook his head when he walked by it. Historically, he'd felt pride at knowing that the firm's vaults held secret treasures. Now they were nothing but vapid reminders of how the firm had been exposed and lay in ruin. It was nothing but a shell of its former, glorious self.

When he arrived at the unobtrusive gray door he took the keyring from his jacket pocket again, and selected two new keys. He unlocked the door, pushed it open with some effort, then made sure he locked it behind him. A cool breeze blew against his neck and he raised his shoulders against it. The drafty origin lay with the ancient, rectangular windows that lined the ceiling of the mostly open room. If they hadn't been blacked out, he knew he would see boot-covered feet and small sweater-wearing dogs on leashes passing by. And if snow weren't gathering on the sidewalks he would hear their steps more distinctly. As it was, the endless honking from cabs and other cars that littered the New York landscape was ambient noise.

Certain that there weren't any cameras around, he removed his sunglasses from his face and stuck them on the back of the cap. He stood with his hands in his pockets and surveyed the room he hadn't visited in years. The street-level windows, which let in too much weather and noise, were the only reminders that he was no longer in the firm. He was now in the bottom-level room of the building next door. To his knowledge there was only one other entrance than the way he came in. It had been designed that way.

Someone had been in here, though. Against the brick walls were several old ladders and paint cans with dried, colored drips on their exterior labels. Ellen probably had maintenance leave them here, and now they'd been forgotten. He tried to sense if anyone else had been in here recently, but didn't find any energetic traces to speak of.

He directed his attention to the left, where one-quarter of the room was completely bricked. The walls were probably several layers thick. If he couldn't access the other way in, he would knock the walls down to get inside.

## 12

Carolena gazed at the three new pieces in her art collection and admired their beauty. They were nothing less than awe-inspiring. She had touched them several times, with the ring finger on her left hand—the receiving side of her body—to read them one more time. It had been a very long time since she had touched a genuine masterpiece. These did not disappoint. She'd placed a folding chair in front and had enjoyed them for nearly an hour.

She stared at her phone, which sat on the small, three-legged table she'd positioned beside her. It also held a glass of red wine, so she could have her private viewing with relaxation. Though the phone had not yet rung, it would. Soon. And she knew who was calling. She could feel him thinking about her, she felt the call coming. She gave a labored exhale into the silence of her secret room. It had been a mistake to ever let him make contact with her. Old habits didn't die just because they should.

Carolena left her private art gallery and moved to the

black upholstered couch positioned in front of the fireplace. She curled up on one end of the sofa, and took a long, therapeutic sip of wine. Her phone rang. She gave it her best disapproving look, one that had been honed over years of mothering.

"You are breaking our agreement," she said when she finally answered.

He laughed. "Is that all I get after giving you such priceless gifts?"

Her lips turned up in one corner. "I suppose I shouldn't be surprised that you found me."

"Probably not," he answered.

Carolena read his energy before replying. "Perhaps I am more disappointed than surprised. I have stayed hidden for a reason, you know."

"Well, if I hadn't found you, then you wouldn't have the best privately-owned art collection in all of France. Maybe even all of Europe."

"Hmmph," she said, overtly skeptical of his motives.

"I can take them back if you don't want them," he said.

"Yes, I am certain that you could." Carolena's voice was calm but her breath came quick. "If I keep them, I suspect that you will tell me you need something in return. I am right?"

"Yes, you would be right. I've never lied to you," he said, his voice smooth and steady.

"And this is where you say that the same thing can't be said about me?"

He was quiet for a few minutes before he reluctantly answered. "I understand now that you did what you had to do. You had to leave."

"You realize that I will simply disappear again? And this

time we will not speak—ever. My past must stay in the past, for everyone's sake." For a moment Carolena remembered that she didn't know the location of her caller. Maybe he sat in a car outside of her house.

"I've decided to open the secret room we discussed," he said.

Carolena waited before answering. "And you want...?"

"I have to have one of the special paintings that you took with you when you left. In case what I need isn't there."

"I don't know what you're talking about." She stood and paced the floor.

"Carolena...I know you took them when you left. I'm just asking for one. You can have it back when I'm through with it."

"How did you find me?"

"I followed you after our last meeting."

"I knew that was a mistake."

"I'd hate for you to think that," he said.

Carolena ended the call and closed her eyes against the ache in her chest. She would have loved to invite him in and talk about the old times they shared. She knew she couldn't do that. Too dangerous.

That he had found her would start a wave felt around the world. She'd allowed the meeting, in a quiet but public place, and only for a few minutes. Long enough that she could hold his hand and see for herself how he was doing. Because he was strong as nails outside, but precious few people knew what he kept on the inside. He would always have a home in her heart.

Carolena returned to her private gallery and surveyed the paintings he mentioned. She focused on one of the framed pieces, the images seemed to move before her eyes.

She could feel herself wanting to leave her problems behind and lean in to it, accept the escape it offered her.

She shook her head to break its trance. These paintings had the power to transport, just like all good art. But these were unique. And powerful. And dangerous in the wrong hands.

## 13

"Everyone okay, Miss Addie?" Cameron tipped his hat when he opened the front door of Lex's apartment building. His expression told me he hoped for information, but I didn't have the time for that today.

"Yes. Thank you, Cameron."

Blake emerged from the back seat of the town car parked in front of the building and I rushed into his arms. His embrace was possessive and I exhaled relief.

We scooted into the back seat and I put the box of my things on the floor near my feet. When he shut the door behind us, I expected him to vilify me with endless streams of "why didn't you stay in my apartment?", but he didn't.

He rubbed my sleeved arms just gently enough that when I opened my mouth to tell him about Otto, about his scheme to involve me in the Gardner art, and how my father and grandfather must still be alive, that Otto was using them as blackmail—I took in a deep breath, instead.

The subtle scent of traffic exhaust wove through the

heated air. Blake drew me close to him and we held one another.

He poured us each a glass of scotch. "It's been a heck of a morning."

We clinked our glasses together, toasting my survival, I guessed. By the third sip, the warmth ambled through my body.

"You're okay." He said it as much as he asked it, and rubbed his thumb along the top of my hand.

"I'm okay," I said.

Blake exhaled an imperceptible breath, then shared how he and the marshal were knocked out long enough to miss the trial, how Otto also managed to get to the witnesses—or his mob friends did, anyway—and how no one showed up to testify against him.

Although somewhat slowed by the scotch, unwelcome adrenaline moved in all directions of my body. "Are you sure you're okay? Have you seen a doctor?"

"I'm fine." He squeezed my hand and exhaled a sigh that was heavy with the ache of failure. The courage that had shone bright in his eyes this morning was now replaced with a dullness that only defeat could bring. "William needs the clients' testimony to make the charges stick. Right now no one is willing to testify. So they probably aren't going to have another trial."

"I'm sorry." I was sorry enough for the both of us. "It shouldn't be this hard to put someone as evil as Otto in jail."

"The more heinous the criminal, the longer they take to fall," he said. The clear realization hung between us that our nightmare had come true. Every success we planned had failed. Every threat we guarded against had risen against us.

I shot the rest of my drink. Then I spilled the story of Otto's visit, his proposition about the art, how I'd told Otto I was sick, and his threat to come for me if I didn't respond soon enough. I told him about Otto's touch, and quickly realized I shouldn't have. Because the concern in the car shifted into fierceness.

Blake closed his eyes briefly, his hand squeezing claw-like around his glass. "We have to leave. This is moving more quickly than I anticipated," he said. He poured another two fingers of scotch into each of our glasses.

"What do you mean you anticipated?"

"We knew that his coming for you was a possibility." Blake's eyes locked square with mine. His jaw set. "I've known Otto for a long time, and he's predictable about many things. Timing isn't always one of them."

He was right. And had I not already known one other piece of information, I would have agreed. "I'm not sure I can." I braced myself for Blake's response.

The muscles on the side of his jaw worked.

"Otto offered up a little motivation, an incentive in case I decided to refuse him. He said he could bring back my father and grandfather, that they were alive."

I took a few more sips of scotch to cushion the nerves. I knew what I was saying must have made Blake think that I'd lost my mind. When he left me this morning we were on the same team, ready to commit Otto to jail for the rest of his life.

Now here I was, saying that I was going to work with the man. I knew it was a possibility that he would use me for the Gardner project, and I wouldn't get any information about my family. Frank and I could end up being bodiless room-mates in my townhouse. But I couldn't ignore this first chance in twenty years that might lead me to find my family. Otto did seem to think they were alive.

"I see." Blake's eyes went cold and he became unreadable, as he had the ability to do. "You realize he's playing you. You remember what he is—a liar, a thief, a murderer."

"I know. I know who he is. But what if he really knows where my father and grandfather are?"

"He still wouldn't help you find them."

I stared at the empty glass in my hand. "No, I suppose not. If I got close enough to read something of his though, I could learn where they are and how to bring them back."

Blake stared at me, I assumed he was waiting for me to say something else. Anything he could refute. A part of him had left the conversation. He was planning. Plotting. Moving pieces around on his mental chess board, much the same way I had seen Otto do earlier in the day.

Carolena was right. In many ways, Blake was just like his father.

"He's holding a card I need," I said.

"You don't know that." Blake took my face in his hands. "I can't let you gamble your safety for a hollow promise. Otto knows what you want to hear."

I edged away from him and ran my hand along the leather seating, there was a cushiony layer of sealant that Blake left intact. The one that kept people from reading the energy on things he'd touched. "You chose to tangle with Otto to free your mother. You are the one person in the world who would understand why I need to do this."

Blake gave a subtle nod and glanced at my hand, his eyes dark with hatred. "That's different."

"How is your situation any different from mine?"

He scoffed. He mentally jumped from one potential argument to the next, unable to find one solid enough. "You don't have anything to prove here. It's not your fault that your father and grandfather disappeared."

"I am not trying to prove anything. And this isn't about fault—I want to help my family."

Blake and I stared at one another. I sickened at the thought of having to partner with Otto. But I was resolute. "Because I think they *need* my help. I know that you of all people understand my situation."

"I do understand, better than anyone," he began. "More importantly, I understand the evil you're facing. He's playing you. You don't have a guarantee that Otto has any information about John and Campbell. Otto wants you—your gifts. He wants to punish me and he would dangle anything in front of you to make that happen."

"I know that—"

"Before he was arrested that he promised to take you away from me. That's his game. Getting you to walk away from me *willingly* is part of his goal."

Blake's life was in danger. As was mine. And, I believed, my father's and grandfather's. So now I had to choose who would get saved and who wouldn't? Otto had to know he'd put me in this situation.

"I can't forget that dream I had about them before we went to Paris. They reached out to me. They were warning me, and there was something about their demeanor that made me think they needed my help. If this is my last chance to help my father and grandfather, and I miss out on that? I'll regret it for the rest of my life."

"You can't do this." Blake sighed.

"Why?"

"Because if you work with Otto, he'll make sure you lose everything: your freedom, your family, your life...us."

"He's on his way to doing that anyway."

Blake ran his hand through his thick hair. "Knowing that is supposed to motivate you to stay away from him—not work with him." He stared out the window. The familiar lines of his face did nothing to comfort me as they usually did. I wasn't used to us being on opposite sides of such an important issue.

"What if I contacted William to help me with this? I might be able to locate the whereabouts of the Gardner art while I help my family. He would protect me."

"Addie, this is a bad idea."

Blake's searing stare burned. I turned away, raised my hand to the window until the cool chilled my skin. "I know what I've seen about my father and grandfather is right."

"It's too risky." He was resolute.

I leaned back onto the soft, cool leather of the seat, and tried to tell myself that Blake was protecting me. "I won't ignore my family when they need my help. Any more than I would ignore you if you needed my help."

We stared at one another, at an impasse.

I hadn't felt this far away from Blake since before we'd met.

THOUGH I THOUGHT we were on our way to Blake's apartment, the car stopped in front of the building where his gallery was located. The streets were quiet at this time of day, in this area of the city.

"I need to pick up some papers," he said and dodged my glance. "We should stay together. Just in case." He looked out all windows. And then finally at me.

My mouth opened, but I couldn't find the right words to say.

"Let's hurry." Blake moved away from me and out of the car. Once inside he avoided the elevator bank in the lobby and we climbed several flights of stairs. He unlocked the front door of his gallery and we headed down the marble hallway toward his office in silence.

"Put that down," a woman's voice said from Blake's office. We hurried down the rest of the hallway.

"What are you doing here?" Blake's tone was edged with frustration.

Anya, his assistant, turned to face us. The front tips of her raven-black hair graced her collar bones. Her hair did a breezy dance when she tossed it with a confident shake of her head, and she cast a cool and familiar once-over at me. Blake rushed over to kiss her cheek and jealousy gave my heart a death squeeze. I crossed my arms and conjured a smile.

"Just organizing some things," Anya said. "I was too worried to sit at home."

"I told you not to come in. You're going home." He crossed the room to the corner. "You can have those, but be careful with them, buddy. They could be valuable one day."

"What do you say, Tristan?" Anya's voice rose an octave.

"Thank you," a tiny voice finally said. The words sounded big in his mouth.

I walked across the room to see who the child's voice belonged to. Blake picked up a dark-haired young boy of about two years. He wore blue jean overalls, and held baseball trading cards tight in his grasp. He and Blake were nearly a mirror image of one another.

No one got those light blue eyes unless they were gifted genetically. And the child's genetic donor appeared to be right there in the room with him. I couldn't believe Blake hadn't yet told me.

"You should see a doctor," Anya inspected his neck and

stroked it with her thumb. "I don't know what we'd do if something happened to you."

"Go home and stay there." Blake kissed Anya again, then ushered her toward the door.

"You know where to find me if you need me." Anya's heels clicked noisily down the hallway.

"Is that Anya's son?" I asked quietly.

Blake nodded with a smile and waved good-bye to them. The little boy waved over his mother's shoulder in return.

"The child has your eyes," I said.

"He has good genes. Anya is my sister. Half-sister." Blake rummaged through a filing cabinet.

"Your sister," I murmured. "She's not related to Otto, is she?"

"No. Thank God." He grabbed a folder, stuck under his arm. Then he opened a drawer, collected a ring of keys, and shoved them into his front pocket.

The puzzle pieces snapped into place. Blake's omnipresent affection for Anya: a brother protecting his sister. Anya's surly manner toward me at the gallery were of a sister protecting her brother.

As usual, I was Queen of the Half-Story.

"Carolena decided that if she couldn't be close to me in New York, that she'd have a representative who would." Blake still managed to avoid looking directly at me.

I felt a prickling on the back of my neck and rubbed at it.

"Anya's a good person, but she's overprotective." Blake jingled the keys in his pocket. "Let's go."

"I guess it travels down the family tree," I said.

The sensation on my neck intensified and a cool breeze brushed across my cheek. I turned just in time to see Frank drift toward me with an etheric glass of whiskey in his hand.

My chest tightened ran a cold finger across my neck, then stood in front of me. His eyes were two dark slices of night. The result of no conscience.

"Lovers quarrel, huh?" Frank asked. "I see Otto is working his magic between the two of you." He reached forward, I leaned away.

"Back off, Frank." Blake walked between us.

Frank glided away. He stood with his hands on his hips, his grin rife with secrets. "You're about to get a visitor."

## 14

_____

Several pairs of shoes beat a swift pace against the marble floors of Blake's gallery. My body jerked hard at the energy that preceded them.

"It's Otto," I said.

"Sit down." Blake pushed me energetically and my body did as it was told. He stretched across his desk and grabbed a gun from the rear drawer, then spun to the front edge of his desk and sat casually, the gun at his side. We exchanged a glance—he exuded impossible calm in repose. He gave me a low hand signal to stay put and keep it together.

The footsteps slowed when they neared.

Blake's expression was simultaneously alert and steady.

Otto appeared in the doorway.

The terror within me nearly broke free at the sight of him.

"Blake." His voice was all silk and cordial, like he'd been invited. "I hoped we might catch you in residence."

"Otto." Sharp-edged instinct filled the air. Blake moved nary a muscle.

They faced one another like alpha wolves.

Otto cast a quick and malevolent glance around the room. First to the gun, then to me. I sat stock-still on the couch.

Two men edged around either side of Otto, guns in their hands. Blond curls twirled from under the cap of the man who faced me. The other man had long dark hair that was slicked straight back. He fixed his eyes on Blake.

"That's far enough." Blake pushed them energetically when the men attempted to spread across the room. A bit of their strength and intent disappeared. They stopped and assumed the fig leaf position—a wide stance, guns resting in front.

Otto pushed Blake to back down as hard as Blake pushed the three men to drop their guns and leave. No one moved and the tension in the room stretched taut. Like two hands from the same body pressing against one another, Otto and Blake were equally matched.

Otto studied Blake with narrowed eyes. He didn't know that Blake was his son. Neither did he seem to know that Blake had the ability to push. I thought Otto might clue in to the latter after today. Otto swiveled to my direction. "I guess you're feeling better, Addie?"

I forced myself to meet and hold Otto's stare. Even though it left me weak and hollow.

"I don't know if she mentioned it, but Addie and I ran into one another this morning. She's considering an offer I made her." Otto's eyes locked on mine. There was no doubt in my mind that he planned to leave here with me. His prize, his trophy. The only question was if he would let Blake live.

"She mentioned it," Blake said.

Otto pushed me to walk over to him, and the need to meet him across the room compelled me. It seemed the safest thing to do. For me, for Blake. I stood, like a string lifted me up. I caught myself and my body lurched forward. I looked to Blake for strength. His eyes had regained their steely edge, and he was eager for a reason to shoot. I wished him to, but with two guns against one, that was obviously ill-advised.

"She'll be in touch as soon as she's fully recovered." His attention tightened on Otto but I knew he tracked the other men for the slightest movement. "Did you come for a reason? We have a busy evening ahead of us."

Otto sank into a nearby leather and gold armless side chair with a sigh. He crossed his legs and inspected at his fingernails. "Two reasons, actually. First, I was concerned about you. I thought I would see you at my trial this morning. You didn't show." His socially trained air of disappointment was disarming. It was a complete front for the pride he really felt over Blake's disappearance. "Lots of people didn't show, as it turned out. And here I thought my trial was going to be the event of the season."

"Sorry to hear that." Blake's tone was solid strength.

Otto opened a dark place within Blake where secret fears mixed with rage and grief. The reckless combination snaked through the room.

"The other reason..." Otto's eyes gleamed with amusement. "I have the funniest feeling that you might stand in the way of our sweet Adeline's decision. You see, her father and grandfather have been sorely missed by her family. I'd like to help reunite everyone—I think it would mean a lot to her. I know how protective you can be when it comes to the women in your life."

Otto paused for Blake's reaction and my breath hitched.

"I thought she might need my help," Otto said, a shadow fell over his eyes.

I felt the end coming.

"She doesn't need your help."

Quicker than light, Otto's bodyguards took aim at Blake, their guns cocked and ready. Blake aimed his gun at Otto in return.

I leapt to my feet and screamed, "Stop!"

Otto smiled. "Maybe now would be a good time for you to give your answer to my proposal, Addie."

Frank leaned against the wall next to me like he enjoyed a matinee, and I felt his excitement. "Might want to take him up on his offer, hon. Or it's bye-bye, Blake."

Blake aimed his gun with confidence at the center of Otto's body mass. He wouldn't miss. My eyes shifted between Blake and the two guns pointed at him. They wouldn't miss, either.

Blake's fear for our safety rivaled my own. His instinct was typically an invisible barometer that gave good feedback on any situation. But today it gave me no comfort in terms of what might come next.

I calculated the outcome of several potential scenarios. If I left with Otto, how quickly could Blake get the police to arrive? Or, if I left willingly with Otto, how could I be sure he wouldn't hurt or kill Blake after we left? If I stayed, what were the chances that Blake could kill both of these armed men, before one of them killed him?

There was no magic way out of this. It was two against one.

"You can't win," Blake said, his expression as smooth as steel. "Even if one of these guys manages to shoot me, my finger will still pull this trigger. You'll be dead before I hit the floor. Is that the deal you want?"

Otto's smile widened on a sinister laugh, and he patted his crossed leg. "Did you really think you could call the shots with me?"

"I could ask you the same question." The hatred Blake held for his father burned with such violent rage, I thought something in the room might spontaneously ignite. Carolena had been dead on about these two men—they were too much alike. One was going to kill the other.

"Stop," I said. I squeezed my nails into my palms. There was only one way out. Though Blake might never forgive me for it.

"Why don't we let Addie answer your question? Is this the deal you want, dear? Would you like to see me dead at the expense of Blake's death? Or would you rather keep him alive and see the return of your beloved father and grandfather?"

"Don't do it, Addie," Blake said.

"What's the matter? Afraid she won't choose you? Let the woman make her own decisions."

With the loss of the sun, the room had gone gray. Everything in it seemed to have lost light and warmth, stolen, perhaps by a man who sought only to destroy.

Otto cast his clear blue eyes in my direction. He ran his ring finger along his well-trimmed eyebrow.

"I'll do it," I said softly.

Blake never moved but a silent bomb of his fury detonated and hit me in the gut.

"Gentlemen, I believe the lady has given her final answer. You've made a wise choice, Addie," Otto said. "I knew there was no real reason for concern. Now we'll set about to bring John and Campbell home." The corners of his lips turned up in the enthusiastic smile of a child who had been given his favorite toy. He stood and extended his hand for me to come to him.

My body gave an involuntary shiver. I bent slow and stiff, picked up my purse and crossed the floor to Otto.

Once I stood with him, Otto gave the hand signal for his bodyguards to claim Blake's gun.

Blake released his gun to the blond bodyguard, then he cocked his head toward me. His expression was a mixture of sadness and rage.

"I'm sorry," I mouthed. I didn't think either one of us would recover from what just happened.

Blake shook his head and looked away. I felt the dagger in his heart.

"If you'll give us just a moment to say good-bye," Blake said to Otto.

Otto's eyes bounced between Blake and me.

Blake's lack of reaction watered the sting of Otto's victory, and confusion beset the aristocratic features of his face. It was the first time I had seen Otto genuinely surprised.

"Say good-bye, Addie," Otto said. "Then," he said to the dark-haired man and nodded in Blake's direction.

"No! What are you doing?" I yelled. "I said I'd go with you. You promised me this morning that if I went with you, you would leave Blake alone. If you hurt him I won't help you."

Otto studied me.

"I'm serious," I said.

Otto waved to the dark-haired man, who moved away from Blake.

Blake raised a finger to me as if to say "just a moment." "Privately," he said to Otto.

Otto's eyes narrowed. "You can have your private good-bye, with the door open. You have one minute. Check the room, Tate," he said to the blond one.

I hung at the top of my inhale as Tate lumbered around the room, opened the closet and then the bathroom door, pressed and knocked on walls, and searched for secret exits.

Tate took his time, then shrugged and returned to Otto.

"It's just a good-bye," Blake said. "I might be able to make your relationship with her a little easier, if you'll give us a private moment. Three minutes, alone and behind a closed door."

Otto scowled at Blake, then took his own tour of the office. He searched the drawers, under the desk, and ran his hand against the walls. Then he waved the bodyguards toward the door.

"You have one minute. And it began thirty seconds ago." Otto and the other two men stepped just outside the door and closed it behind them.

I rushed toward Blake for what I thought might be our final embrace, at least for a long while. "Blake—"

He laid a finger across his lips, grabbed my hand, and we scrambled to the rear of his office. The door in the back right corner of the room was invisible to the eye, hidden behind the full and gathered end piece of tapestry window coverings.

There was no doorknob. Only a button on Blake's key fob that released the latch and popped the door open. It was so short and narrow that we had to turn sideways and duck to fit through the corner opening. Blake reached back through the opening, fluffed the thick curtains behind us to hide the door again, then quickly punched a code on the noiseless, digital keypad on the interior wall. The door closed and sealed again.

We took a collective breath in the solid quiet.

"Shoes off," Blake mouthed and pointed to my feet.

I did as I was told, put my hand through the shoe straps, left them dangling around my wrist. We tiptoed to the end of the hallway to another door. Blake tapped a code on the soundless keypad then placed his hand on the scanner.

A neon green light slid across the screen from left to right. The door popped open to a spiral staircase. The interior walls were ancient, exposed brick, the staircase was made from shiny, black iron. New iron. No dust in sight. The stair steps were padded with linoleum, which kept our movement secret.

Blake texted nonstop while we descended floor after floor, winding in a dizzying circle. We reached the bottom and he sent another text while we held up just inside of a vaulted door. He tapped a code to the keypad, and the door popped ajar.

He grabbed my hand and we ran at a breakneck pace toward a moving limo.

Tires screeched from another level in the parking lot.

## 15

B lake called Anya to warn her, then he called William to let him know that Otto tried to kill him and kidnap me. William said we should go to Blake's, since his apartment had the most security. Then he said he would send agents to stand guard outside until we had our next move organized.

Streetlights dimmed when we passed through the double gated entryway. We drove several levels down, and finally stopped in a darkened corner at the back of the garage.

Blake scanned the area before opening the door. He studied the camera perched inconspicuously in the eaves. "Let's get inside."

I crawled out of the limo, trying to do so elegantly. But Blake gave me scotch to quell my nerves, and now I felt like an elephant crawling out of a clown car.

Two men in black FBI jackets stood on either side of a low-profile black door. They met us halfway and escorted us to the door. The keypad next to the external door required a five-digit code and a handprint scan for entry.

"Does every resident have to give a handprint scan to get into their home?" I asked.

"Only if you're using this door, which would mean you were trying to get to my apartment," Blake answered.

He placed his hand on the scanner. As before at the gallery, a green light scanned his palm then a latch released. He searched the area one last time, then opened the door, and shut it promptly behind us.

A short hallway laid out before us and a silver elevator stood open on the right. Once inside the elevator, Blake entered another code, then placed his thumb on a scanner. A signal beeped from the device. There was but one button on the panel: PH. And it illuminated immediately after the tone.

Blake let out a deep exhale. It was the first time I'd really seen him breathe since before Otto appeared at the gallery. Silence was so thick in the tiny elevator that it pounded at my eardrums.

I wondered if Blake was using the quiet ride to lower his heart rate.

"Was this security here when you bought your apartment?"

"Mostly." Blake took his eyes away from the rising numbers on the illuminated display and glared at me. When I saw the emotion in his eyes, my stomach dropped

"Don't ever hand yourself over to Otto like that." His tone was hemmed in anger.

I wriggled my hand loose from his. I had never been on the receiving end of his anger before, and it was vicious. "You were about to be killed—"

"He would have backed down," he said.

"Otto had us outplayed—"

"I had him outplayed!"

Blake's blue eyes burned with heat.

"Had I not have been willing to give in, you wouldn't have had a move."

"Did you offer yourself to Otto because you believed he could help you with your father and grandfather?"

My heart beat hard against my rib cage. "I didn't offer myself to him. I did what I thought I had to, to save you from being shot."

The elevator door opened, and I walked away. I stood in a service hallway. There was one nondescript door on the right, and another at the end. Both had a keypad and a scanner. Blake passed me then stopped at the closest door, input a seven-digit code, then placed his chin in the groove for the eyeball scan.

The handleless door released and we stepped inside.I threw my purse on the kitchen counter and it landed with a heavy *thud*. I shoved the swinging door and entered the main salon with its light cream walls, large, carved mantel, and rich, upholstered seating. Glints of gold were at every turn.

Blake stormed past me.

"You have a funny way of showing gratitude when someone helps you," I said to his back.

He paused against the loggia, the last of the day's light poured in behind him. I was struck by the resemblance between him and Jack. Not their appearance—eyes excluded. Their pose. Their energy. On the inside, he was the exact replica of the man who had made regular, life-long visits to my dreams. The feeling that we'd shared a past life together was as present between us as it had ever been. That hidden connection had never left us.

"I did the only thing I could—to protect you," I said. "And I'd do it again."

He stormed toward me, slow and fierce. When we were only inches apart he grabbed my shoulders and I braced myself for whatever he was about to say. But then he drew me close. So close I thought we might melt into one. And somehow, that felt more right to me than anything I'd ever known.

When he finally pulled back, he held me by my shoulders again and stared at me intently. "Don't ever...hand yourself over to Otto. Do you understand me?"

Something terrifying danced behind his crystal blue eyes, something that mimicked what I'd occasionally seen in Jack's eyes. Whatever it was, I wondered if it was the reason he'd come back for me in this life. If it was part of the reason we felt so frightened to lose one another.

"Okay," I said.

He pulled me to him again, holding me close.

I buried my face into his neck, and inhaled the sweet vineyard scent of his skin.

WE LAID TOGETHER on the couch and watched the sun disappear. Blake's heart beneath my ear, strong and powerful, and I considered just how indescribably much this man loved me.

He opened his eyes as I raised my head.

"Come on, my sweet Sassy." He stood. "This way."

"Where are we going?"

He tossed a thick robe to me from a bench in the loggia and placed his hand on a door that led to the rooftop deck.

"There's snow on the ground," I said.

"The water will warm you," he said.

I changed into my blue one-piece swimsuit and quickly

put on the robe he'd given me. When I came out of the master, I found Blake in a matching robe, his hand on one of glass-paned doors. We went outside where the air was cold but tranquil. He dropped his robe and lowered himself into a large, square hot tub, separate from the frame of the pool. He sighed and coasted back a few feet between us.

I tossed my robe on a chair and descended the steps.

"I added it when I bought the apartment." He put his hand out when I took the last step, the bubbling water currents gliding between us. He wrapped me in a hug and we floated together. An entire unspoken conversation, rich with hard-won intimacy, streamed between us.

True to his promise, the water warmed my skin, and comforted me. It tore away all the remnants of the day, including all the memories of Otto and his band of thugs.

Knowing I was behind so many different security systems left me feeling safe for the moment. Though, like a teenager who escaped parental view, I knew my haven had an expiration date.

Because we still needed a plan. Blake had no interest in supporting mine, which was a problem because I believed that Otto knew where my father and grandfather were, and how to get them back. I didn't have any proof—just the reading I'd done. I also had my gut. Which wasn't scientific but it was rarely wrong.

"The idea of losing you, of losing us, drives me to the brink." His voice was tender, but weary. He stroked the length of my hair.

I rubbed my hands along his neck and broad shoulders, I felt his muscles relax.

"I only agreed to go with Otto because I thought if I didn't he would kill you. I mean, I've never seen you shoot before, but...it *was* two guns against one." I laughed a little.

Blake finally gave a slow wink.

The sacred femininity of the full moon bathed our bare skin. Silence fell between us.

I leaned back and gazed at the star-scattered sky. Blake, my anchor in a world of chaos, held on to me.

The expression on Otto's face when he sat across from us in Blake's office reappeared. Confident, cocky, calculating.

"I don't think anything will ever stop Otto from hunting me down," I said.

"He's always been that way with Carolena. He'd do anything to get his hands on her again."

"Then I think we need to find a way to stop him."

Blake cocked an eyebrow. "Not by working with him."

I opened my mouth to respond, maybe to object. Then I thought better of it.

"We're safe here, for a while," he said. "We'll plan our escape tomorrow."

I agreed and his lips unfolded into a grin.

I lost myself in the depths of his eyes, and I realized I'd known them for longer than I could remember.

"I've never stopped loving you," I said. "Not even when I couldn't remember you. Does that sound strange?"

His grin widened into a full-fledged smile. "Past life hangover. They're impossible to cure." He pressed his lips to mine in a kiss that held the promise of forever.

## 16

Once inside again, we laid on the couch together, surrounded by the warm flicker of candlelight. Clothed in Blake's thick, white robes, we sipped brandy—cognac that had been aging longer than I had.

I stared at the door to the left end of the room. A pulse emanated from that room, Like it was the place in his home where Blake had spent most of his time. My hand traveled along the woven grooves of the upholstery and I checked to see if Blake had placed a sealant there.

He hadn't.

Of course.

The sealants in his office were there to keep Otto from seeing his true identity. That he was Otto's son. And that he had come to New York to put Otto away forever.

Secrets were here for the taking if I wanted them. So I took a tiny taste of whatever would offer itself up to my fingertips. Blake ran his fingers through my damp hair while Bessie Smith crooned through the tiny but powerful speakers. Letting my fingertips graze across the textured upholstery, I searched for information. Anything interesting. Anything at all.

Scenes of Blake working late at night, pictures of him and Anya talking. He held her hand at one point, hugged her when she cried in another scene. Another woman sat on the couch with Blake. Beautiful, older, graceful, protective—his mother, Carolena. I was surprised she had been in New York. Maybe she had just been on the couch, wherever the couch had been at the time.

Blake tipped my chin and kissed my lips. Soft. Loving. Demanding. "Where did you go?"

"Not far." My wine glass clinked against the top of the side table when I replaced it. My fingertips danced over the green marble and I wondered for a moment why the framed pictures weren't sitting atop. It seemed the perfect place for them. The energetic groove of the captured memories spoke to me as my fingers traced the veins in the marble. Deep abiding love complicated by life.

"What do you see?" Blake pulled me back to recline on his chest.

"Secrets. Always secrets. Anything people keep tucked away or ruminate over." Exhaustion gathered at the corners of my mind, and I let the tiredness sweep my body into a lull.

"Do you see my secrets, Sassy?" he asked.

"I see your secrets," I answered confidently. The truth was that he could still hide whatever he wanted from me. It was possible for Blake to throw some sort of energetic shield around himself and I'd never be the wiser to what he held in the quiet. "I know you used to keep framed photographs here. They're missing now."

"Impressive." He stood, opened the drawer from the side table and lifted two photos encased in silver frames. One of him and Anya, they sat with arms around one another at the edge of an infinity pool. Gorgeous mountaintops and an ice-blue lake were in the background. The siblings' deep familiarity with one another and their special bonded love was evident in their wide smiles.

The other photo was of Carolena and Blake, in jeans, cream-colored sweaters, and hiking boots, resting against a lush mountainside. She hugged his arm and laid her head on his shoulder. He looked as happy as I'd ever seen him.

"And yet in spite of the secrets you've discovered about me, you're still here," Blake said.

"Love has a funny way of requiring trust as payment for its continuation," I said, facing the photos. I thought of Carolena'a advice that people were like faceted stones, many sides. Not all of them positive.

The firewood crackled and popped.

"How did you learn about sealants?" Blake hugged me, then squeezed me close, bringing my attention back to him. Back to us.

"My grandfather. Who learned it from his father. He worked in intelligence during the war. My grandfather told me that energetic sealing became more widely know after WWII. Hitler had been afraid that gifted spies would learn his secret plans by touching his personal belongings. So he hired shamans to place energetic sealants on his things. The energy in the sealant was misleading, so spies would see only what Hitler wanted them to see. How about you?"

"My mother. She said she learned it from a friend and taught me how to create them. You never know who's watching." He elbowed me and I laughed.

"Why didn't you cover your pocket watch in a sealant?" I remembered touching his watch a long time ago and found that it was the only object in his office that hadn't been sealed energetically. Blake's and my hands twined together, and I decided I ought to read the watch more fully at some point.

"Sometimes I get impressions from it, and the sealant would keep me from reading it clearly," Blake said.

"Do you keep any more secrets from me?" I tried to ease the question into the space. "I mean, I just wonder. There have been so many secrets."

Blake inhaled deeply. "Not intentionally, Sassy. Though there may be one more. We can talk about tomorrow."

I AWOKE IN THE DARK, and fumbled around the side table until I found the clock.

3:00 a.m.

The time when all those susceptible to things unseen were awakened. Otto's voice echoed in my head, along with memories of our narrow escape. Knowing I wouldn't go back to sleep, I ventured into the kitchen.

I poured a glass of water, leaned against the marble countertop, and thought about next moves. With Blake's resources it would be easy to get out of town. We'd have to disappear for a decade or more. Blake would have to work out his departure with William, since he was still under contract to help find the Gardner art.

I considered contacting William directly to offer my assistance, with the condition that I receive his in return. I did think it was possible to help find the Gardner art by working undercover—Otto would lead me right to it. In the process I would find out where my father and grandfather were.

This could work. It wasn't like Otto was ever going to

leave me alone anyway. I thought it was better to meet the snake head on. Blake would have to understand. I wasn't the only person under this roof who needed to protect their parent from Otto.

I walked to the salon and paused in front of the dark-stained wooden door. A strong energy pulsed from the room. The heart of his home. Inside was something significant. Maybe the last secret Blake wanted to share with me once the sun had risen.

I put out my left hand and tried to read whatever was on the other side of the door, but couldn't. I didn't want to wait that long.

I turned the antique brass doorknob. It wiggled from loose screws and creaked gently. It wasn't locked. The moon was full and bright. Its glow suffused the handsome study enough to reveal picturesque, art deco glory. The room wasn't large, but the power that emanated from it made me catch my breath. Much like the rest of the house this secreted room was drenched in rich, textured tones, deep leather hues, and cream-colored walls that felt thick and insulated from the real world.

Its pulse threaded through every fiber and wood grain, and it awakened a part of me to respond. It brought me into perfect measure with a life that only existed within these four walls.

A decanter of scotch caught the moonlight. It sat on an antique glass beverage cart near the window, and I glided toward it, not quite feeling my legs beneath me. The glass decanter was cold and thick and heavy like they used to be. Its grooves were surprisingly familiar, and yet I felt the same ache of loneliness I often felt after Jack faded from my dreams.

A glitter of gold jumped into the corner of my field of

view, and I expected to see something typical of the era. A mariner's scene or, better yet, the unexpected—like the Canalettos I'd heard Blake reference several months earlier. Instead, the portrait over the hand carved mantle made me gasp. It was a painting of a woman. A woman whose slight smile was at once familiar.

My eyes fixed to the painting. It drew me to it, to touch it, to know its story. I studied her blue eyes with the tiny white starburst around them. They stared back at me as they had my entire life. The woman in the portrait sat poised in a blue Delphos silk dress, just as I had in the dreams that began all those years ago. My blond hair was styled differently now, but it was light like her own. There I was, myself from another life. Yet looking remarkably the same.

I inched closer to it, examined her hands. They rested in sophistication on her lap, and there it was. As it appeared on my own hand today.

Her ring.

My ring.

A cushion cut sapphire nestled in platinum. My past life and my current life were tying one into the other. Like loops of the same bow somehow bringing my lives closer to one another. No matter how I fought or craved it, it had its own momentum.

What was and what would be were simply coming for me.

## 17

G race tipped her head toward the wolf moon and bathed in its reflection. The ocean's gentle waves poured onto the grassy edge and washed her bare feet. She could feel the course of the tides when they responded to unseen forces, just as clearly as she could sense Otto's next move.

"He's gunning for Addie now, and with a ferocity I haven't seen before." She leaned back into the arms that wrapped securely around her. While their relationship had at one time been illicit, in the years since John's disappearance, he stood with her and by her. His presence both calming and complex. She'd always felt it like a mosaic of tones that leant comfort and strength. It spoke to places within her that no one else saw. And despite the fact that his appetite for risk far surpassed her own, he was still an unexpected comfort in this era of her life.

"Which means he's not getting what he wants," he said.

"I have very few moves left to help my own granddaughter."

"You have one," he said. "I've hung the Monet. From what you've told me I think she'd be—"

"No," Grace interrupted. "It's much too dangerous."

He nodded and kissed her gently at the temple. "Come on, then," he said and guided her back toward the house.

## 18

Ellen slipped the key gently into the lock. Though she knew at this hour no one listened or watched, and Otto had told her that Addie and Blake were held up at Blake's apartment, there was still the illicitness of breaking into someone's home and that was best done as quietly as possible.

She moved quickly inside and locked the door behind her and thought, oddly, of a poem her son had written in elementary school about marshmallow toes. The verses were his teacher's effort to help the kids to walk quietly through the hallways. And now, years later, that's how she walked through Addie's townhouse—on marshmallow toes.

She'd wrapped the letters and pictures, as usual, in a blue satin ribbon that wrapped around all four edges of the papers. This time she included an envelope on top that was labeled: Read Me First. Because he needed to be made aware of what Otto planned next.

"Take heed," she whispered, then kissed the small bundle and placed it inside the front cover of the book.

Then she disappeared into the moonlit night as softly as she'd arrived.

## 19
------------

Unsure of what I'd see, I hesitated only slightly. Then I lifted my hand to touch a bit of the elevated paint on the lower right hand corner. I prepared myself in case it was similar to the horrifying story I'd seen inside of Blake's pocket watch so many months ago. Its history, her story—the one whose imprints I felt determined my future, was inside this painting.

There wasn't an energetic sealant on the painting. Just its raw story, and I tumbled into an onslaught of images and their conflicting attachments.

A warm breeze gently caresses my face with the fragrance from the roses that climb the wall of the house. Jack and I sway in one another's arms to the beat of a small band in the distance, the rounded tan and white gravel crunch beneath our feet. Deep green hedges have been crafted into geometric shapes and are large enough to hide us from the rest of the party.

"Our train leaves in forty-five minutes." Jack snaps his pocket watch shut. "It's time to go. Did you get everything you need? We won't be back."

"I have everything I could ever want right here." I kiss him soft and slow, the taste of forever is on my mind.

Jack leads us through the side entrance of the house. The painting of me wearing sapphire-blue silk hangs on the wall to the left. "It's too bad we can't take it with us," I say.

Jack squeezes my hand. "We'll have another one painted. Come on, let's leave through the kitchen." He picks up two brown suitcases.

"Or maybe we'll just stay right here." A man bursts through the open doorway with two large men in tow. His black hair is slicked in a severe side part like his mother forced him to style it that way. His dark navy suit owns the man, a dire effort to appear respectable.

"Gary," I say, my stomach hollowing at the sight of him.

He raises a gun, then walks to the beverage cart, and pours himself a shot of whiskey. He taps his gold ring against the rocks glass three times. "Where have you been, doll face?"

"I was on my way home." I press a hand against nerves that jump in my stomach.

He nods to the suitcases in Jack's hands. "Seems like you might have had the decency to tell me if you were taking off somewhere."

"Jack is going out of town. I was saying good-bye."

"I see. You're next." He points a finger toward me.

"You're first," he says, and fires a bullet into Jack's thigh.

The hard-bodied suitcases thud to the floor and Jack gasps in pain. A red blotch spreads on the leg of his cream-colored suit.

"Jack!" I scream. I run toward him but one of the men holds me in place.

"I've waited a long time for this, Jack. You screwed

around in my business, and with my girl, and now..." He waved the gun.

Jack swallows visibly, his face is red from the pain. "Gary, we can work this out."

"I've already worked this out." Gary Walker bites the words out.

I know that most of the joy he gets from killing someone comes from toying with them ahead of time.

"Gary, don't!" I struggle against the heavy hands that keep me anchored, captive. I fight the panic that claws at me and I try to come up with a plan. "He's nothing to me, baby. Just let him go and I'll come home!"

"Oh, *now* you'll come home, Sarah? Or shall I call you Sassy? Isn't that the nickname he gave you? Sas-sy," he mimics in a child's voice. "After today you might wish it was you who died instead of your...lo-ver," he says the last word in his flat, sociopathic way.

Jack opens his mouth to speak and raises his hand to stop him, but Gary just smiles. He'll not only deny the man the rest of his life, but also his final words.

The gun fires a deafening blast.

"NO!"

There's a laugh from the man holding me back and I fight him. Jack falls to his side, red blood leaking a wide stain onto the carpet.

"Jack!" I cry.

Gary strolls to where I stand, his rage visible only in a cruel sneer. "How about this, doll? I'll not let him go and you'll still come back to me."

His fist hit my cheek, and the pain and the shock of it hurts today as it did then.

"Give me twenty minutes to get out of here," Gary says to

the bodyguard. "Then bring her to me. Clean up the mess." He waves his hand toward Jack's dying body.

Gary lights a cigar and glances at me. "You should make better choices." Then he leaves and I hear the gravel crunching beneath his fading steps.

Gary's bodyguard finally releases me.

"Don't leave, don't leave. Jack!" I yell for him through his fading consciousness, and cradle him gently on my lap.

"You are mine, always, Sassy." He chokes and blood spatters across my dress. It stains his lips.

I lower my lips to his and kiss him gently. "I don't want to be in this world without you."

"I'll come back for you, Sarah. I promise." His breathing slows, and gurgles. His eyes fall open.

"Jack!"

## 20

S obs welled up.

I released my contact with the painting.

Jack's death happened at least a lifetime ago, but the grief I felt was raw and fresh. The deep ache was not unfamiliar. It was a fear of loss that had always been with me, a shadow that came and went over the years. Now it raged with a new life.

It felt silly to cry and yet I couldn't stop. I put my head on my knees and let the tears fall. They were uncontrollable.

"You read the painting." Blake said.

I gasped and sat up.

He kneeled next to me like shelter, like a safeguard against suffering.

I pointed to the portrait. "This painting has been in my dreams all my life. She's the mirror image of me and—you realize that's my ring?"

Blake wiped the tears from my cheeks, "I do." His smile was calm, comforting. Unflustered. As usual he was ahead of me.

I stared at him, then up at the painting and back to him again. "Was this the secret you were going to show me?"

He nodded, and pushed a lock of hair behind my back.

There was a shift in the silence. Like peace. Like a perfect fit. Like the painting sensed we were together again.

I pointed to the portrait again. "This is how you knew me, this is how you recognized me when we first met."

"It is," he said.

"You know the history in the painting?" I asked.

"Carolena has read it for me many times over the years."

I drew in a deep breath, and shared what I'd seen. And though we'd talked about the history of my lifelong dreams with Jack, I cried when I described Jack's murder.

A GLASS OF SCOTCH EACH, we stared at the portrait. It watched over us from above the mantel, the same portrait that had watched Blake's death in another life. Sassy appeared peaceful, elegant, regal.

Jack's murder was still raw in my mind, but his death had a far less triumphant ring now that Blake and I were together again.

"How long have you had it? Where did you find it?" I couldn't take my eyes off of my former self. The painting gave such validity to the dreams that had called to me.

"I found it at a Paris flea market when I was about thirteen." His eyes narrowed slightly like he remembered the day. "It was a real gift after a tough time."

Blake sipped from the glass and winced as he swallowed. "Carolena was unhappy back then. And we had a few close calls with Otto. Finding the portrait was, to me, anyway, a sign that I had a better future ahead of me. It gave me hope."

Blake met my lips for a lengthy kiss, and I curled into the nook he made for me.

"This isn't exactly a standard purchase for a thirteen-year-old boy," I said.

"It is standard for a future art dealer."

"Good point. So, if you were thirteen, that means I would have been...twelve. And that's exactly when the dreams started."

"The dreams with Jack," Blake said thoughtfully.

"The dreams with you." I caressed his face, and scratched my nails along the fresh, dark stubble. "I would wake in the morning, all dreamy-eyed, lovesick and unable to eat, and I'd tell my mother and Grace about my dreams of Jack. They would say I was remembering my future. That a love as profound as ours didn't stay in the past. It drove what was yet to be."

"Nothing could have kept me away from you. Not even death," he said.

## 21

My eyes opened into the cool stillness of the dark bedroom, and the scent of hot coffee and warm bread fills the air. I headed toward the kitchen then I unexpectedly detoured at the open door to Blake's study. I found my portrait again.

I studied the room in the portrait, the one that served as the backdrop for my sitting back then. There were bookshelves in the background, slightly blurred in the distance. There was also the edge of a mantle and hearth.

It wasn't the same angle, but that was the same room where I'd seen Jack get shot and where he had lay dying on the floor. That must have been Jack's home, and he had been noticeably in charge of it.

I realized, that in my dreams, this was the room where I had seen the portrait hanging over the mantle. If only the artist's eye would turn, I was sure I could see Jack again. He must have been there during the sitting.

I ran my fingers through my hair. Something tickled at the back of my brain. Something I'd seen earlier that morning. Something I'd missed. So I reached up and touched the painting again, this time I touched a different section of paint.

My heart skips a beat when I land in the library where Jack was killed. Coffee in hand, and wrapped in a navy satin robe, I spin my sapphire ring around my finger and admire it. I watch Jack—still alive and pacing back and forth with a candlestick phone in hand. His hair blond and cut short, fading up to a longer top, it is styled with a light tonic. It is the opposite of the greased, flattened appearance of Gary's hair.

"All right then," Jack says loud and distinct. I surmise the connection is not clear. "Draw up the papers and I'll be by to sign them. Time is of the essence, Knox. I'll be by at noon. Good-bye."

He straightens out the long, thick tail of the telephone wire, and returns the phone to the corner of the desk.

"My sweet Sassy." He uses one finger to lower the paper I'm reading and he leans down for a kiss. My eyes stay closed for a moment and I swim in his love for me.

"Anything interesting in there?" He asks.

"Maybe a little something," I say, and point to a black-and-white photo of Gary. "It doesn't look like he's going to be convicted."

Jack frowns at the paper and shakes his head. "Judge Cross. He's as crooked as Gary."

Gary's face hits me like a curse, and it jolts me back to Blake's study in the current day. I stepped back from the painting and clamped my fingers over my mouth.

"Everything okay?" Blake asked.

I turned and found Blake standing in the doorway. He sipped espresso from a glass cup.

"He—He's Otto. Gary, from that life, he's Otto—today."

"Are you sure?" Blake asked.

"I'm sure. It's him." I walked a wide circle in Blake's study. "Yours and Otto's possessiveness toward me makes more sense now. Also my feelings that Otto is unbeatable."

"He doesn't win this time," he said.

"No, he won't," I said. "Once was enough."

My thumb reached to spin my ring as I had on the day I'd just seen. My ring wasn't there.

I looked at my hands then back to the portrait.

"The ring, it's on my *left* hand in the portrait. We were engaged when this was painted."

Blake's eyes narrowed in focus at my painted ring.

"That's why he killed you. I belonged to Gary in some way and you and I must have been planning our future. Our escape." The realization of what I'd said kicked me in the gut. "Oh, gosh, just like today. It's all repeating."

"No. It's not. What's next is ours. Plus you don't belong to him." Blake led me out of the study. "You need coffee."

The kitchen counter was laid out with a basket of croissants, fresh berries, and sliced meats and cheeses.

"When did we get all of *this*?" I asked.

Blake took a green shake from the fridge, peeled the saran wrap from the top of the glass and offered me the juice, but I refused.

"Nothing green before coffee," I said.

"Anya made one of the agents bring it to us this morning."

"That was nice," I said.

Blake pushed the button on the espresso machine to make espresso. It rumbled and the water steamed. And though Blake wouldn't admit to it, I felt the pulse of fear course through his system. He was as rattled by this new information as I was. We probably both wondered why Carolena hadn't told him this sooner.

"We have to be careful how we plan our next steps." We took our breakfast to the solarium on Blake's rooftop. "Past life events create imprints and tendencies. If we're not careful, that could lead us into a trap."

I scanned the skyline and, as usual, tried to sense the location of my father and grandfather. I found nothing. Otto knew where they were, and he could probably bring them back—if, like he said, I would help him with the Gardner art.

Of course Otto could have been lying and my father and grandfather might have already died. My dreams about them could have been the result of how much I wished they were still here. I could've asked Otto for proof of their existence, but that was risky. I didn't want to get one of my father's fingers in the mail.

I cleared my throat.

"We could do the French countryside again." Blake layered multiple pieces of cold meats and cheeses inside of a fresh baguette.

"Have you talked with William?" I asked.

"We spoke this morning, He's up to speed."

"What are his expectations on your help in finding the Gardner art?" I knew it was a loaded question.

"No matter where we are, he wants me working and following leads."

"Meaning he doesn't want you to leave."

"He doesn't want me to leave." Blake put the makeshift sandwich down and met me square in the eye. "I will anyway."

I chewed the inside of my bottom lip, then said, "If we run, we'll be running for what—ten, twenty years? What if we let William know that I have a new connection with Otto, and that he's willing to take me right to the art? We could set up a sting."

Blake shot his espresso, then dropped the porcelain cup into the saucer. "I said roughly the same thing to Carolena several years ago."

I picked at the bread on my plate. "This is where you tell me that didn't quite work out the way you planned."

Blake stiffened, his crystal blues became sharp and clear.

"Maybe this is different. Otto needs me, he needs my gifts. We would be going to a specific destination, a place here in New York where he has the art hidden. I could wear a tracking device or a wire. And William's team could be close by."

"It's a bad idea to position yourself as bait for Otto," Blake said.

"I think it would be better to face him directly than spend the next ten or twenty years running from him."

"And in exchange for helping him, you think Otto will tell you where to find John and Campbell? "

"Not...necessarily. But if I could put my hands on something he owns, I might get the answers for myself."

"What if he doesn't give you that chance? What if you read the art and he sends you the way of John and Campbell, anyway? Or worse, Frank?" Blake's eyes turned cold and serious.

"He probably wants to use my gifts too much to kill me. At least not right away."

Blake threw his hand up in the air then slapped the table with a loud smack.

"This could work—and it would help my family at the same time!"

"At what cost?" Blake asked.

"Our freedom is already requiring a really steep price."

"Addie. I know what it's like to need to help a parent. But you don't know what he's capable of.."

"Otto kidnapped, and maybe killed, two members of my family. I know what he's capable of. And this isn't only up to you, Blake. I have to make my own call on this."

Blake's chair screeched across the floor and he stormed to the wall of the solarium that overlooked the city. A plane rumbled overhead in seemingly slow motion. Everything between us was off kilter. Like an irregular heartbeat.

When he finally faced me, he was quiet and steeled.

My teeth set against one another, my decision firm.

"When I found your portrait, I had only a few immediate impressions. One, that we had a passionate history. Two, that we would meet again. Three, that I'd lost you because I failed to protect you," Blake said. "I won't...make that mistake again."

"I have to make my own decisions," I said quietly.

Blake strolled halfway to the table, hands in pockets. "I want you to have your father and grandfather home, and I believe you when you say Otto had something to do with their leaving. But I don't think you're being honest with yourself about why you're willing to risk your life and everything we have together."

I pushed away from the table.

"I'm sure that my fear of losing you is a past life hangover," he said. "I have no doubt that my possessiveness is an imprint from another time—"

"I just need to do the right and best thing for my family. This is my first chance to help them."

"There's usually a pattern to Otto's possessiveness," Blake said calmly.

"What do you mean?"

"He did it with Carolena. First he destroyed her career by implicating her in art thefts at the Met. That he orchestrated, I would add. Then he isolated her, kept her from having access to the outside world. Lastly, he threatened her."

Blake sat down, crossed one leg over the other.

"He told her she'd never see me again if she didn't help him with the black market purchases."

I stared at Blake, unable to speak.

"Do you have a career?" he asked.

I didn't answer.

"Are you isolated?" he asked.

I still didn't answer.

"And you've been threatened," he said.

I felt myself deflate.

"Otto's an old dog with old tricks."

We stared at one another.

The text alarm on my phone dinged and I looked at the screen without moving my head:

*Would be best if you came home for a few days. We need to talk. I'll make sure you're safe while you're here.*

"It's from Grace." I exhaled. She had been my rock and my guide for as long as I could remember. "She wants me to come home for a little while."

The text alarm on my phone dinged again. And though I should have expected it, seeing Otto's backlit name made me choke on the spot.

*How are you feeling? I'm sure seeing your father and grand-father again would help. I know they'd love to see you, too.*

*It's too bad you had to leave in such a hurry. I thought we had an agreement. If you're not back by the end of the week to work with me, then you'll never see your father and grandfather again.*


MY HEART CAROMED in my chest.

Blake peered across the table and read the screen.

"He's putting his plan into motion," he said.

"I see that." This was just as he had done with Carolena. "Why didn't he just kidnap me when he had the chance at my townhome?"

"Because he wants you to choose him over being with me. It was one of the last threats he made to me before he was arrested."

"The past repeating," I whispered.

"He's dangling the carrot of your father and grandfather to encourage you."

I stared at Otto's message on the screen and wished he had never been born. "What do I do? If they're still alive, I want to help them. And I think they are alive."

Blake's contempt for Otto hardened his features. "You can't help them by working with Otto."

"I don't want to work with Otto, I hate him every bit as much as you do, but I have no choice if I want to help my family. I don't have access to them otherwise, and I can't abandon them if they need help!"

Blake studied me for a moment, then nodded.

"I'm going to take a bath," I said.

"Then we'll go see Grace and Isabella." Blake followed me from the solarium to the master bath. He started the bathwater, poured in bath salts, then left and came back with a glass of Prosecco for me.

He turned the water off and studied me.

Otto-inspired anxiety had crept into my inner world and Blake seemed to know.

I had no words and no clear answers.

If I went with Otto, there was no guarantee I'd get my father and grandfather back. The FBI wasn't trustworthy. They could fail us and who knew what Otto would do to me once he had me?

If we ran, I would miss out on what was probably the only chance to find out what happened to my father and grandfather, and, to help them. Otto would be in pursuit of me for the rest of his life. He wouldn't stop until he killed Blake and had me forever under his thumb.

Neither option was a good one.

Never lacking for strength or insight into what I needed most, Blake said, "Let's just not worry about it for a minute." He closed his arms around me.

"It's like I'm walking a tightrope, and no matter how many careful steps I take, the journey never gets any easier."

Blake hugged me closer, his protectiveness surrounded me.

His kisses were comforting and sure, his lips soft and loving.

In one another's arms, we fell hard into total surrender. For a long while we were lost in each other,. His heartbeat was strong enough for me to feel it in my own body. And then, it pulled my own heart into its cadence. I yielded to its strength.

The healing I'd sought, I'd found. The assurance I'd wanted, he'd given. And the sense of direction I'd craved alighted on me like a feather.

"You always bring me back to the best part of me," I said.

He turned his head to meet my eyes.

His luscious mouth curled into a smile that made my heart jump our partnered rhythm.

"Because I know you, my love. No matter the lifetime, I know you."

## 22

Grace and I spoke directly and she assured us we'd be safe while we were in Savannah. I didn't know how she could promise that, but I knew better than to underestimate her. She also insisted that Alexa come with us.

Blake told William that Otto had the art stored in New York, so William had kept near round-the-clock surveillance on Otto's movements. Then William ordered agents to escort us to the private airport, agreeing it was good for us to get out of town for a while.

I fought the urge to have my own conversation with William about next steps. I'd promised Blake we would talk with Grace before we made a final decision as to what to do —engage the William or run. I think we were each convinced that Grace would take our respective side.

Blake's chartered jet climbed toward the clouds on its way south to Savannah, and I stared out the tiny window. When we reached our cruising altitude I exhaled fully. The physical distance from Otto gave an undeniable relief. Too, there was a sense of peace that always accompanied home.

"You're glowing," Blake whispered into my ear. He laid a kiss on my temple, left his lips there just long enough to make me smile.

"If y'all are going to do this for the entire trip, I'm going to move," Alexa said from across the wood top table. We both turned in her direction.

Lex's presentation was more plain than usual. Her beauty was usually the focal point in any room, like an extra presence that demanded all of the attention.

"Fine." Lexie picked up Cocoa. She huffed and moved to the second seating group, as far behind us as the environment allowed.

"I thought she was seeing someone," Blake said.

"She is." I was puzzled at her behavior. Usually she was the incurable romantic. I watched Alexa re-situate herself with indignance.

"By the way, it's rather a lot to have all of the female members of my family under one roof at the same time."

"I'm used to it," he said.

"Not like this you aren't. I mean, I know Carolena is gifted, and I don't know about Anya, but Isabella and Grace —well, they don't hold much back. If they're seeing it, they're saying it. And they see way too much."

"I haven't had a private thought since I was born." Blake poured merlot into two glasses. Welcomed, velvety nuances of raspberries, plums, and apples wafted into the air.

"Right, me either." We clinked our glasses in a toast. "I guess what I'm saying, is... That I can't be responsible for my family. Or what they might say. Or do. I adore them. But there is a reason why I moved to the opposite end of the eastern seaboard. And of course there will be a jab or two in my direction about how I never use my gifts enough. Or well enough."

Blake smiled. His blue eyes were keen and sparkling, which made me relax.

"I can handle it," he said.

"Every woman in that house will have an opinion about my situation. A strong one. Which means we'll have a plan in place before we leave. Sort of like making a diamond from carbon in forty-eight hours. I hope Grace is right in that she can keep Otto from seeing where we are."

"Other than the pilot, the FAA and your family, no one knows where we're headed. But I've learned not to underestimate Otto. So I think all we can say is that I hope Grace is right."

The memory of Otto breaking into my home was fresh.

"Oh! I have something for you. Almost forgot," he said.

"For me?" I asked and held my eyelid stable with my fingertips.

Blake searched through the contents of his computer bag. "Why do you call Grace and Isabella by their first names, but not your father and grandfather?"

"Grace left for a while when Lexie and I were kids. She took some world tour, never said good-bye. She was gone for a few years." I clicked my thumb and fingernails against one another. "Then after our father and grandfather left, Isabella became distant for a while. A long while. I guess that created a rift between mother and daughters, and grandmother and granddaughters. We started using their given names after that. It stuck."

"Here it is." Blake took out a small clear bag with a photo of my painting in it. He held it in front of me at eye level and shook it such that the small, multi-colored, irregular shapes at the bottom jumped around.

"What are these?" I took the bag and examined the thinly-sliced pieces.

"Chips."

"Chips?"

"I knew you didn't yet want to part with your painting," Blake said.

"My painting..." I clasped the bag to my chest.

"Those are a few pieces that came off with time. I saved them. You should be able to read those, right?"

I hugged and kissed him. Then I hugged and kissed him again.

"Thank you," I said.

~

"Hey, Lex," I said.

Cocoa stood and wagged her tail long enough to get a few scratches. Then she curled up again in Lex's lap.

Lex brushed her ash-blond hair away from her face, gazed out the window. Her green eyes were watery. I put a glass of wine in front of her and took a seat.

"Thanks." She took a sip, then wiped the side of her mouth with her thumb.

"What's going on?"

She took my hand in hers and squeezed it. "I'm ruined."

"What do you mean you're ruined?"

"My career. My reputation in the art community. My show at the gallery. Everything I've worked for. I think I need to talk with the both of you," she said. "Together. And I'm really sorry."

We walked back to the front seating group. Blake and I sat together at the table and waited for her to speak. She stared at her hands for a long time. The jet engines provided enough background noise to cover her silence, but I couldn't stand it any longer.

Not wanting her to suffer alone with whatever this burden was, I wrapped my hand around the emerald ring Alexa wore on her left hand and I searched for the source of her suffering. Immediately the blond boy from her apartment came into view. I watched him look over his shoulder surreptitiously at Alexa, who was curled up and asleep on the couch. Only her ring watched the action from her finger. He took something from his soft-sided briefcase and placed it on top of the armoire in the corner. Then he connected a wire to a small box on the floor and out of sight.

"What did he put on the armoire?" I asked.

"Who's he?" Blake's glance ping-ponged between Alexa and me.

Alexa and I stared at one another in silent communication. Just as when we were little, I would often get the entire story out of her psychically so she wouldn't have to say it out loud.

"I knew something was wrong with that situation from the moment I stepped off the elevator," I said.

"What elevator?" Blake looked to me.

"What was on the armoire?" I asked again.

Alexa took her hand away. "You know, Isabella is right. I can be incredibly self-obsessed sometimes."

"What was on the armoire, Lex?"

She sighed hard, reached into her orange hobo bag, and took out a tiny camera with a long, black wire attached. She placed it in the middle of the table. "This."

Blake and I stared at it as if she'd just placed a snake in front of us.

"I know it's a camera, but I'm not sure how it works."

"It's a motion-activated video camera." Blake turned the device over in his hand. "It turns on automatically when motion is detected in the room and records everything, including the audio. This is a wide angle lens. This long wire would have been connected to some kind of Internet connection, so that the images and the audio could be received at a distance."

"Like this?" Alexa held a small, black portable wifi box.

Blake nodded.

"*When* did you find this?" I asked.

"I'm not *exactly* sure how long it's been in place. I found it yesterday. The cleaning lady knocked it over when she was dusting the top of the cabinet. I think Todd put it there."

Blake examined the black box. "I guess he didn't think you would find it up there."

"I have a German cleaning lady and she's relentless about perfection," Alexa said.

"Who's Todd?" he asked.

"I thought he was someone who cared about me. But people who care about you don't install cameras in your home without your permission. Do you think he's some perv who's selling our time together on the Internet?"

"What about the cleaning lady? Could she have had something to do with it?" Blake asked.

"I don't think so. I was in my studio when she came running in with it. The wire was dangling from the camera, and she was screaming about how people were spying on me. She comes every week, dusts everything in and out of sight, so I know it was placed there since she came last. And the only person who's been in my apartment this past week besides Addie, was...Todd. He's the brother of the gallery owner who's doing my show."

Blake rubbed his jaw. "Mind if I keep these? I have someone who might be able to download the images that were captured. At least then we'll know when the camera was placed and what they caught."

Alexa shrugged. "I wish you wouldn't." She drank a long gulp of wine. "I'm...so gullible."

"No you're not, Lex." I burned with fury at Todd. He'd seen her one weak spot and exploited it in the worst way possible. "Have you tried contacting him?"

Lexie's eyes welled up. "He hasn't returned my calls."

For the first time in a long while, my social-over-achieving sister seemed very alone and vulnerable.

"What about his sister, Piper, who owns the gallery? Do you trust her enough to reach out to her about this? Maybe she could run an intervention?"

Lex made a face and inspected a tiny piece of thread on her sleeve. "I called her with a few questions about my show. She hasn't returned my call either. Which isn't like her. She was really excited to have my work at her gallery."

"Would whoever is on the other end of this video feed have seen her housekeeper disconnect the equipment? I mean, do they know that this thing is disconnected?" I asked Blake.

"At the very least he would know that the equipment's not transmitting anymore," Blake said.

"So, he knows the jig is up," I said.

"Most likely," Blake said. "Whatever he had planned for the footage, he's probably already doing it."

## 23

The wide dirt drive to my childhood home was long and extended beneath two long lines of live oaks. They braided their branches over us in a protective arch. Spanish moss swayed like tinsel in the breeze and gave the impression that the hundred-year-old trees were bewitched. Like the trees might lower their bend and sweep unwanted guests away at the command of their caretaker.

"Nonsense," my grandmother said when I suggested as much. But the gleam in her eye made me think differently.

Born and raised in the shelter of Savannah's elite, Grace Campbell Montgomery was the daughter of one of the city's more notorious mayors, Sanderson Campbell, III and as such she was a debutante at sixteen, educated in the city's finest private schools, and dated the state's wealthiest boys.

She was also the daughter of Adelise Baudin, a woman of unexplainable mystical talent and French beauty, whose psychic gifts flowed in Grace's veins. Those same gifts were passed freely to her children and grandchildren.

Home appeared as it always had—a cloudless vision from a dream. White columns and two wraparound porches, one on each of the first and second levels. Over-grown magnolias and water oaks grew wild around our pre-Civil War property that lined the ocean. And a forest of pine trees and dogwoods flanked the wide yard.

"We used to have Easter egg hunts on the front lawn," I said to Blake. "Everyone in town would dress in their Sunday finest and bring their children."

"Daddy always hid a few eggs just for us on the South-eastern side, right under those bushes." Alexa pointed to a wide, leggy hedge beneath the porch railing.

"In the shade of that maple over there Grace would have a table of deviled eggs, sliced ham, and..." I stopped and looked at Alexa.

"Hot biscuits," we said together in slow reverie.

"Those things are a buttered slice of heaven," I said and my childhood Southern accent peeked through.

"I swear, Stan Parker ate twice his weight of those biscuits every year. Ruby had to make an extra batch just to cover his appetite," Alexa said, and we laughed.

Blake nudged me and pointed out the window at the dead Civil War soldier who leaned against the wide trunk of an oak tree. He sipped from his canteen.

"Wouldn't be home without a few of those," I said and we drove past him.

Grace descended the brick steps that stood rock solid between two wide, deep green palms in Grecian urns, and both Alexa and I sat up a little straighter.

Her ankle-length, navy dress with subtle pattern and sparkle flowed down her thin frame. She wore a long, double strand of pearls, the epitome of early 1900s elegance. Her bright silver hair was secured at the nape of her neck and illuminated her fiery blue eyes that missed nothing. She waited at the edge of the circular drive while our limo approached, the gravel crunching beneath its tires.

Though the windows were tinted and she couldn't see us physically, I felt the impact of her reading each of us, one by one.

"Whoa," Blake said. He sat up straight.

"She is a force," I said. I watched Blake while my Grandmother's energy honed in on him. He was not unprepared for the force of it, but still visibly impressed.

We exited the car and Grace took my hand, but she spoke to Blake first.

"I see you have finally shown up," she said, not referring to his arrival in Savannah. "Blake, is it now? Addie was worth the wait, I hope."

"She was," Blake said confidently. He kissed the back of Grace's hand.

Grace was also visibly impressed.

Like the good son of a gifted psychic, Blake stood in front of Grace with his defenses down. He allowed her to read whatever she wanted about him. He knew she'd see his secrets, if not now, soon enough. Hiding was futile and not worth the effort.

Grace kissed Lexie and me on the cheeks, eyed our faces closely, then kissed us both again. "Fret not, girls. The battle may be won, but the war is far from over. Spin around right quick and let me snap a picture of the three of you."

We gathered together and smiled, not entirely certain who the picture was for.

"Ruby has a late lunch ready for you on the veranda." Grace gestured toward the open front door.

Our heels clomped on the ancient confederate blue boards that were the front porch, and I felt a cool, shielding sensation that poured over and around me. I did an about-face to the direction we'd just come from and saw the reason why—a gel-like, concave wall with static running through it.

"That's new," I said.

Grace opened her mouth, shut it, then opened it again like she debated whether to explain it or not. "Actually, it's a timeworn technique, and it will keep Otto or anyone else from being able to see that y'all are here. At least for a little while. You could have learned to do this." She elbowed me.

My breath caught at her dig about my gifts.

Blake and Alexa squinted into the distance, unsure of where to focus.

"What is it?" Alexa asked.

"A sealant," Grace answered. "To keep your whereabouts quiet as long as you're here." She narrowed her eyes and focused on the edge of the bubble.

"Huh," Alexa said and walked toward it. "Is it over the entire property?"

"No, it does best with an object at the center. Creates a hiding place. In this case I used our house as the center."

"It ends just at the far side of the drive there," I said and pointed.

I looked at Grace. "I would like to learn how to do this>"

Grace's eyebrows lifted with surprise, her smile broadened in admiration. "I'll teach you."

"How long does it last?" Blake asked.

"Depends. A few days, usually. Then I redo it," Grace said.

"And you think Otto can read people or places at a distance?"

"I don't think Otto can, no. Though he tends to surround himself with people who can do a lot more than he can. So I don't take chances." Grace ushered us through the front door. The warmth and smells inside the house were welcoming.

"I need to make a few calls." Blake held up his phone.

"You're welcome to use my husband's study. Or you can pace out here in the drive if you like. As he often did." Grace had a faraway glimmer in her eye like she could still see her husband mark off his steps with a phone to the side of his head.

"I'll pace," Blake said.

"Suit yourself. We'll be on the veranda in the back when you're ready. Make yourself at home." Grace smiled and clicked the strands of her pearl necklace between her fingers.

Alexa and I dropped our luggage at the foot of the grand staircase and gazed over the large family room that held so many of our childhood memories. Vivid, warm images of our family gatherings throughout the years played before me. Our brightly lit Christmas tree in the background, Alexa atop her brand new pink bike with training wheels. Grace dared her with one stern glare to ride the bike inside, while Grandpa encouraged her to do just that.

Me on the couch with my roller-skated feet propped over my father's legs while in a fierce competition of Go Fish. Isabella placed a tray of cookies and eggnog on the table, then kissed and bear-hugged her husband around the shoulders.

"Come on, let's go eat," Alexa said and broke my visit to the past.

I waited for the familiar heartache of my father's and grandfather's absence to ebb, then followed Lex to the back veranda which overlooked the water. Grace enclosed this best-loved room each winter to keep the elements out and the warmth in.

Two dolphins played in the deep water sound just a few feet beyond Grace's docked boat like they came to celebrate our return. Alexa and I took our usual seats at the same glass and iron table we'd occupied since we were in high-chairs. Without the extra leaf, there were six chairs at the table, enough for each member of our family.

"So, as we discussed on the plane, you're starting the conversation, right?" I whispered to Alexa.

"I will," Alexa said. "Though I'm not telling Grace about the recording equipment. I'm hoping I don't have to tell anyone about that. Where is our mother?" She noisily scooted her chair toward the table.

"She's on her way back from Atlanta, sugar. She didn't expect you in until later this afternoon." Grace made her way to the head of the table and gave Lex a raised eyebrow for scraping her chair against the floor.

"Sorry," Lex said.

"We had an opportunity to leave early and we decided to take it," I said.

"Considering how Otto's pursued you lately, I'd say that was wise," Grace's southern accent emphasized the long I in wise. She strengthened any word she felt was most impor-tant in the sentence.

Out of habit I stopped my breath on the top of my inhale and waited for the *I told you so*, I feared was on its way. This time it didn't come. And when I exhaled more audibly than I meant to, Grace's light blues landed on me.

"Some things can't be avoided, sweetheart." She gave my arm a loving squeeze. "Sometimes the challenges of life have to be worked out by traveling the path. They won't resolve any other way." She let go of my arm but not before giving me her signature triple pat. It always spelled out I

Love You. Sometimes she said it along to the beat of those three words. Sometimes the pat said it for her.

There was no *I told you so*, she didn't fuss at me for going to work with Otto like both she and Isabella had originally. Everything was just easy.

*Too easy.*

I studied my grandmother's face while she sipped her chilled white wine, and listened to Alexa chat about her art. Grace's face had very few lines and wrinkles, and even fewer brown spots. Like age had decided that ten or twenty of her birthdays should simply go uncounted. I guessed this was thanks in part to her wide-brimmed, Southern hats and a general aversion to the sun.

Today, as always, beneath that smooth exterior, pulsed information just out of my reach. Something she held back. Deliberately.

Grace gently returned her wine glass to the table, and I reached out and placed my hand over the fifteen-carat emerald engagement ring my Grandfather had given her. I hoped she would be so engrossed in conversation with Alexa that she would absently hold my hand, which would allow me a little time to explore beneath the surface.

Grace slipped her hand from mine.

"Don't go fishing for trouble." She wagged her index finger back and forth just once, as if she could cast a spell with it.

"I just..." I felt her push my probing energy back. "Sorry."

"We need to talk about next steps for you as soon as your mother arrives."

"Yes," was all I could manage to say, and tried to arrange my thoughts in logical order.

Cocoa yipped excitedly when the front door opened,

and my mother, Isabella, made a grand entrance as usual. She rushed into the room with Blake on her arm, her ginger-flavored hair, thick with a light wave, still long and youthful. She often was mistaken as Alexa's and my sister, an error she not only welcomed, but encouraged.

"This is who I found outside! Isn't he just *beautiful*?" She emphasized the last word with three distinctly pronounced syllables. She kissed Blake on the cheek before he went to his seat, then did the same with Alexa before she made her way toward me. She kissed each of my cheeks once, then first cheek again. "My darling angels are home again." She beamed at Lexie and me with pride.

Isabella had left Great Britain when she was just a girl but shades of her British accent remained around the edges of her words. She refused to give up her accent entirely, and often said she simply liked the way the British pronunciation of things felt in her mouth.

Her floral perfume, a subtle mix of sandalwood and irises, left its trace in the air. I brought the side of my collar up and breathed in her leftover scent, just as I had done throughout my first day of elementary school.

"You're just in time, Isabella." Grace poured her daughter-in-law a glass of wine. "Ruby has made a delicious late lunch. Or maybe it's an early dinner, I'm not sure. Alexa is telling me all about everything, except what's really on her mind. And sweet Addie here is quiet as usual and fishing for my secrets. See? Nothing has changed. You've not missed a thing."

Alexa and I exchanged a glance then pleaded with wide eyes to our mother for help.

"Grace, you make everyone feel like they live in a gold-fish bowl," Isabella said. Then she took her seat at the end of the table opposite of Grace, which had historically been our grandfather's seat. She was the only one to break with the traditional seating order.

"Mmmm, Ruby, I don't know what you do to a hush puppy to make them turn out this way, but I'm glad you do it," Alexa said with a mouthful.

"I'm happy you like them, sweetheart, and I'm glad you're home." Ruby leaned down and gave Alexa a red-lipped kiss on the cheek. "You should come home more often." She gave Alexa a little shove with the side of her hip, then carried Cocoa out to the kitchen with her.

Grandmother Grace lowered her fork, then scanned me with her light blue eyes like an X-ray.

"Okay," I said to the unasked directive and gave Alexa a raised eyebrow, a cue for her to kick off the conversation.

"No," Grace said. "I think I'd rather hear it from you."

Alexa tossed the last half of the hush puppy in her mouth, and smiled an almost tight-lipped-chubby-cheeked smile, thrilled to not be on the spot.

She and Isabella and I had already spoken at length about Otto since I'd called them before we left. They knew about Otto's threats and Grace said she had sensed as much. I told them I was unsure of our next steps, and wanted their help.

Today I shared my story of how my father and grandfather—Grace's son and husband respectively—had visited me in my dreams just before Blake and I left for France. Then I told them how I felt they weren't dead, that somehow, some way, they must still be alive. Not just because Otto said he knew where they were, but because I'd seen how he thought of them—like they were alive.

I suggested my plan. I would involve William and the FBI, set up a sting whereby I would have access to Otto and his things, find out where my father and grandfather were, and locate the Gardner art for William. Because this was better than a life of running.

Then I waited.

At the very least I expected a slew of questions, as well as their insistence to be involved behind the scenes. At best I hoped for their outright support, then for Grace to calm Blake's objections and recruit him to our team. Instead I received nothing but quiet. Grace and Isabella each glanced at Blake who silently twirled the stem of his red wine glass.

We all sat quiet for a moment, and missed the men we loved. I glanced at the water and saw the Civil War soldier place his gun and knapsack in the shade of a large live oak tree. Then he sat and leaned against its trunk and drank from his canteen.

"If they were alive, I, or any of us, would be able to sense their location," Isabella said with a note of finality.

"They're dead, honey." Grace patted my hand quickly, then took it away. "If they came to visit you in your dreams, then you're the first of any of us to feel their presence, and you should be glad about it."

"It wasn't a normal visit from the other side. I've seen hundreds of other people's dead relatives before. This wasn't that," I said.

Grace and Isabella exchanged a glance.

"What was different about it?" Isabella asked politely.

"When someone comes to me from the other side, they're decidedly...gone. They no longer have a presence here. They're dead. Trust me, I know dead," I said and cast a quick glance at the soldier in the shade. "And ghosts are dead but just not yet gone. Dad and Grandad were...neither. I'm not sure how to explain it except to say that I was left with a feeling. An impression about them that hasn't dissipated."

I could tell by Grace and Isabella's solemn expressions that I wasn't convincing them. Old childhood frustrations of being discounted rose up.

"I'm not imagining things," I said, and fingered the stem on my wine glass. "I know what I saw."

"If they're not on the other side, then...where are they?" Isabella asked.

"What if they're some place between this world and the next?" Alexa said. "And they can see us?"

Isabella placed her wine glass loudly against the table. "Alexa, please."

"It's too coincidental that he brings them up and I've had this recent experience where they've reached out to me," I said.

"Sometimes it's hard to read things accurately in the moment. That was a terribly frightening morning for you. So you might have misread how he thought about them. And you don't know that they were reaching out to you," Grace said. "At least not for help. You miss them, sweetheart. It's hard to be objective."

I sighed loud and hard and stared at the soldier who was now cleaning his gun. "I don't know anything about the state of their being. But I have my gut, and my gifts, and trusting both is something you've always encouraged me to do."

Grace's lips thinned. "Working with Otto in any form is a bad idea. He took my husband and my son, he'll take you, too."

Blake nodded in agreement with Grace, and I wanted to punch him.

"I've been thinking about this," Blake leaned forward onto the table. "And I think we have to examine all the reasons why Otto wants you with him. First, there's the

Gardner art. Second." He extended his index finger to match his thumb. "He wants to punish me for setting him up and for taking you. Getting you to voluntarily leave is the best way to do that. There is a third reason. And I don't know if Otto even realizes it himself."

Blake ran his hand through his thick, dark hair, then shifted his glance to Isabella. I knew what he hesitated to say in front of my mother and grandmother.

So I said it myself. "Carolena." I grimaced at the thought of it. "I think it's safe to say that he's never stopped loving her. I know he's never stopped searching for her. We think he sees me as his final chance to replace her."

"In what way?" Isabella asked.

Grace slid her thumb along the side of her left index finger. "All ways, probably. Makes sense."

Isabella shook her head.

"Addie's able to do many of the same things she can, psychically. While he says he wants her to work on the Gardner art, beyond that, I think what he really wants is to re-enter the black market with her as his partner," Blake said.

The wind rattled the porch windows. I caught a whiff of Otto's feelings for Carolena and a sickly sweet sensation coated my stomach..

"He wants to own her," I said.

Blake touched the end of his nose, then pointed at me. "Bingo. He'll own you if he can't get to her."

I remembered the one touch I'd accidentally placed on Carolena's bracelet and thought about the scene of the two of them dancing, holding one another. They seemed so in love. Perhaps it had been real at one time. Though she'd left him for good reason.

"It's what he does. He surrounds himself with the best of

everything. Art. People," Grace said.

"The best of the best." I remembered Otto's favorite catchphrase. "It doesn't matter if it's an imported coffee bean, a piece of art from one of the masters, or a human being. His goal is to simply have the best."

"His goal is to simply *own* the best," Blake emphasized.

"He's a psychopath," Alexa said.

Grace turned to me. "So, it's settled. You won't work with him."

Anxiety flowed through my chest and tightened all the muscles. "I don't disagree about anything you've said about him. I don't. But what if this is our one chance to get a real lead on where our family is?"

"Your father and grandfather are not accessible to you. They're gone. If anyone could have located them it would have been me." Grace put her wine glass down.

I eased back into my chair. There was the "I told you so" I'd been expecting. It was subtle but it was there. She was saying that I should have used my gifts the way she and Isabella had.

"I think the point is that Otto is a man without a conscience," Blake said. "If he has you within his grasp, there's a very good chance you'll disappear the way your father and grandfather did. And there isn't anyone at this table who wants that to happen."

"You went against Otto," I said.

Blake leaned in. "And I lost, didn't I? The odds are not in your favor on this. I won't lose you." He extended his hands across the table and invited me to put my hands in his.

"Addie, please. Don't do this," Isabella said.

I felt trapped. By the people I loved most in the world, and those who I knew were watching out for my best interest. But I was trapped, nonetheless.

"I can't walk away from my family. You didn't see them the way I did." I pushed away from the table. "I need to find a way to help them. *We* need to find a way to help them." I looked at Blake. "I really thought that you of all people—someone who has spent his life protecting the one he loved most in the world—would understand that."

I waited for a response but everyone at the table stared at me in silence. I scoffed and shifted my attention to the outside. The Civil War soldier startled when he saw that I had seen him. He quickly gathered his knapsack and ran.

I wanted to turn and run, too. I thought I would have had Grace and Isabella's support on this. Apparently, this situation was no different than any other in my life. I'd have to go my own way. As much as I didn't trust our government or any three letter agency, I knew I could get a deal with William. He already knew that Otto threatened and tried to kidnap me. Now I'd just have to show him Otto's text, make my offer.

Isabella and Grace, however, would lose their tempers. I could get over that. Blake would probably try to convince William not to involve me. Then he'd try to persuade me not to do it. He'd just have to get over it.

I faced them. "I have to do this my own way."

Blake's jaw muscle worked. "I'm not against you on this —in fact, I think this house is full of people who love you and want to protect you."

I held the bag of chips from my painting and shook it between us. "No matter where I turn—last life, this life, childhood, adulthood—Otto takes my most precious loved ones away from me. I will not...let him...continue to do that. I'm not running from him anymore.

With or without your help I'm stopping him this time."

## 24

The building was cold. He never liked it cold. Ellen turned off the heating system when the firm shut down. All of the clients removed their art from the vaults, so there was no longer a need to maintain a temperate climate anywhere in the building. She'd probably turn it back on when the weather heated up again. Just to prevent mildew and whatnot.

He ripped the yellow police tape from the wall so he could pass through the narrow hallway. All of the vault doors were left open, and he glanced inside each one of them when he passed by. They hadn't been this empty since the firm had its grand opening almost a half century ago. Hard to believe.

When he finally reached the end of the hallway, he stood quietly in front of the door that had been sealed for several years, and he took a folded piece of paper from his pocket. Written on it were five possible combinations to the old-fashioned dial lock on the door. At one time he knew the combination by heart, but so much time had passed, he had forgotten it. He probably should have written it down.

He tried the first three combinations, but none of them worked. Same with the next two. He thought about talking with Ellen—she would still have the combination. He also knew she wouldn't want him to do what he was about to do. So she would lie and say she didn't have it.

Today, he was in a hurry. So, he'd have to enter the room from the other direction.

## 25

I placed one foot on the cool, inky-black step, then cautiously felt for the next step before placing my weight there. In the dark of this moonless night the stairs were nearly invisible to the sleepy eye and I wasn't in the mood to fall.

Three more steps to the landing, then four steps to the floor, I counted.

Blake was still upstairs. Sleeping blissfully, purring a little, actually. My mind was awake and sprinting from thought to thought like a gazelle connecting the numbers on a dot-to-dot drawing. The end result? A picture of Otto that popped me off the bed and sent me in search of calm-inducing, chamomile tea.

My family was right. Each of them was right. Otto was a soulless creature who shouldn't be trusted. For that very reason I had to put a stop to him. Same went for helping my father and my grandfather, and I wasn't going to run from that, either.

I placed my foot on the cool, wooden floor, and I heard a teary-voiced gasp that came from the direction of the library.

I paused mid-step, gathered my old terrycloth robe around my neck, and tip-toed through the family room. Grace stood in my grandfather's office across the way, near a walled bookshelf with her fingertips to her mouth. She read from a yellowed piece of paper.

She wiped tears from her cheeks with the back of her hand, audibly smoothed the crinkly letter, and placed it in a box before tucking the box in the bottom left drawer beneath the shelves. She lifted a fresh piece of stationery from a letterbox and penned several lines. She then slid a thin, navy book from the shelf, placed the letter inside the front cover, and returned the book to its home.

I kept to the shadows of the darkened family room until Grace returned upstairs and disappeared from view. When I heard the faint click of her door, I padded silently to his office. It was damp outside, a condition that gave the room a stronger than usual book smell, one of my favorite scents. When I got close enough to it, I saw that the navy, hardback book she'd touched held little sparkles around it. That was the sign that energy work had been at play.

But on a book? What was she up to?

I inspected the book more closely, and recognized it as F. Scott Fitzgerald's *This Side of Paradise*. When I reached for it, a tingling of electricity ran up my arm. I retracted my hand, and it lessened. I reached toward the book, and the sensation intensified. There was also a funny scent, an acrid burning.

I abducted the from its home, a faint crackling filled the air. When I opened the front cover I was surprised to see that the letter Grace placed there was gone. I held the book by its front and back cover and shook it, expecting the letter to float free. Nothing fell out.

I *had* seen Grace put the letter in the book. I scoured the bookshelf to see if there were other books that were navy in color. Perhaps I'd taken the wrong one.

This was the only navy-colored book in the area where Grace had been.

I flipped through the pages in case the letter was wedged tight near the spine and I stopped at the front, inside page where it was written in black script:

To Grace,
    Who embraces the epitome of her name.
    With luck and compliments,
    F. Scott Fitzgerald

Grace and my grandfather had several antique and first edition books. How clever that they found one with her name in it. Just like my grandfather to celebrate her in that way, he did the same for all of us.

I returned the book to its home on the shelf. The sparkles remained. Like the intermittent ringing of both sides of a large bell, one sparkle illuminated, and a moment later another one would appear on the opposite and lower side.

My hands rested on my hips. Why would Grace do energy work on a book? To make it absorb her writing? Make things disappear? A chill sprinted up my spine and generated a shiver. Honestly, I wouldn't put anything past Grace. Magically, that is. It seemed there wasn't anything she couldn't do.

The outside lights were on tonight. Through the 100-year-old window-paned glass, I watched the rippled view of water oak branches bend in the wind. A shadow passed in the distance. The soldier, most likely.

The wind howled, the house creaked, and I froze where I stood. In a house this old I never could be sure which noises to attribute to weather, people without bodies, or people who still had their bodies. I hoped it wasn't Grace. I really didn't want her to see me down here snooping.

After a while I was satisfied that Grace remained safely behind her bedroom door. I breathed a moment of relief.

Slowly I opened the deep drawer where I'd seen Grace place the box. It glided open to a halt, a whiff of unfinished rosewood climbed from the drawer. There sat the silver and blue enamel box that had been my grandfather's. When he used this office, the box sat on top of the round side table in the corner. Tonight it was hidden in the middle of this drawer.

I knew that my grandmother might magically appear at just the wrong time, so I left the box in the drawer and opened the lid. The hinges were tight, and it squeaked slightly, then stood on its own. Just as I had when I was a child and searching for treasures, I peered inside the box.

Yellowed letters were folded in half and stacked neatly in two piles, side by side. The bundle toward the back was tied together in a white, satin ribbon. Gently I unraveled the ribbon and started at the top of the pile. Letters written from Grace bore the current date, but they were yellowed and deeply creased. I turned the brittle paper over, and found another letter written on the other side.

A slight breeze seeped through the aged windows but that wasn't what chilled me. I recognized the handwriting.

The stiff, yellowed paper crackled when I unfolded it:

. . .

DEAREST GRACE,

Love and greetings!

Travel by plane is still quite unregulated and no one keeps to a schedule here. Last week we spent an entire day in a cornfield in rural New York, waiting our turn to fly to Savannah. There were about ten of us, I would guess, and each of us carried enough cash in our pockets to get to our destination. Travel is too slow by train and not according to our custom.

Do let us know if you'll be in New York again soon.

Love,

John


MY GRANDFATHER HAD PENNED this letter.

"Need company?"

I jumped and turned. It was Blake, sleepy-eyed, boxer-clad, and standing in front of me. He pulled on a t-shirt.

"You scared me." I pressed my hand to my chest. My heart banged against my fingers.

Blake walked over to the desk and frowned at the pile of antiqued letters. "What's this?" He placed his hand against my upper back, his thumb stroking gently.

"Letters from my grandfather. To Grace."

"Old love letters or something?" Blake yawned and scratched at his wild hair.

"These were written during the time that he and my dad have been gone."

Blake stared at me, incredulous. "Are you sure?"

I picked up a stack of letters. "Holy cow, the last letter was written two days ago." I pointed at the date Grace had written in elegant longhand in the upper right hand corner. "And these two were written just last week. She lied!"

Blake took the two letters I handed him. "Effectively, too. I believed her. Why are these so yellowed?"

"I don't know," I said, and told him how I'd seen her place a handwritten letter into a book, and how I couldn't find it a few minutes later.

"Which book?" he asked.

I handed him the F. Scott Fitzgerald book and he shook it just as I had, flipped through all the pages, then searched for a pocket on the inside of the covers.

"You're sure it was *this* book?"

"Positive," I said.

"Is she asleep?" Blake asked.

"She's in her room. And she has a way of popping up when you least expect her."

Blake peeked out the double doorway of the office and searched the shadowy layout of the main floor. "Let's take these upstairs." He lifted a stack of the crisped letters like he handled a hollowed Easter egg, and handed them to me. "We can come back for more after we've read these."

"Good idea." I tucked them into the front pocket of my robe and patted them twice.

I walked behind Blake while he led the way up the wide stairway. If Grace were to pop out from around some corner, I'd rather he be the front line of defense.

We stepped into my old room and placed the letters on the quilt that was folded on the end of my bed. Then I locked the door behind us with the brass skeleton key that rested in the antique mortise lock.

"So, you realize," Blake said, leaning in close with that heart-stopping smile of his, "that there's no reason for you to work with Otto if Grace knows where Campbell and John are."

An unexpected wave of relief washed over me and left

me near drunk with happiness. A giggle burst free. "They're not dead." I snuggled against him and gazed at the array of letters in front of us.

Blake pressed me close to him and swayed, just a little.

"For the first time in twenty years I have proof, and in their own handwriting. They're alive." I pressed my hand to my chest.

## 26

After reading all of the letters, and a fitful night's sleep, I retied the satin ribbon around the letters. I showered and dressed, and tucked the letters safely into the pocket of my long jacket.

I met Blake in the hallway and together we headed downstairs.

With every step I rubbed my thumb over the fold of the letters. I would have to confront Grace about what she knew. She was a force, and she didn't take kindly to confrontation of any kind. But my father and grandfather were alive.

The rest of us had a right to know where they were. Because, I believed, they needed our help.

The last step squeaked when my bare foot hit it. Grace set her coffeecup audibly into the saucer. My heart did a triple thump, a little dance of dread.

Blake must have known because he placed his hand on my shoulder.

"Mornin', sugar," Grace said, and bowed her head to see over her frameless reading glasses. "Sleep well?"

"Mostly. Lot on my mind."

"I understand." She returned to her paper.

Alexa dunked a glazed doughnut into an extra large coffee cup. Her hair was piled high on her head. She lifted her eyes from her phone screen and winked at me.

"Let me get you both some coffee," Isabella said, and kissed my head when she passed by. "Espresso okay with you, Blake? Or cafe americana?"

"Espresso is fine." Blake's smile warmed the room.

"Lex, love, do you want anything?" Isabella tied her hair together in a braid and fastened a brown elastic to the ends. She and Lexie looked like two variations of the same model.

"Yes, please," she said with a mouthful, and tapped her cup.

"I'll help you." Blake followed Isabella into the kitchen.

My father's and grandfather's energy shot up from the letters and through my palm. My pulse rocketed. "Grace, there's something I need to ask you about."

She folded the newspaper and placed it in front of her. Her smile was kind, but there was a fierceness to her eyes and for a change, I took it as a challenge.

I placed the letters on the table between us. Like the unveiling of a secret weapon.

Alexa's eyes glommed onto the letters.

Grace stared at them, too.

The seconds ticked by.

"I see you've been through my things," she finally said. Her cool blue eyes met mine and adrenaline shot through my system.

There were many undeniably feminine characteristics about Grace. Her figure. The way she wore her hair, her exquisite jewelry. The way she held a glass of wine.

But when she was angry, she became less feminine. More creature-like. And it scared me.

She forced a closed-lipped smile and I half expected to see the tips of fangs peeking beneath her upper lip.

Alexa put her coffee down and a chunk of doughnut floated in the cup.

I touched the edge of one letter for comfort.

"I wasn't snooping. I came down for tea last night and I saw you. You were upset—I wanted to know why. I wanted to see if I could help."

Alexa cleared her throat.

"You don't know what you're getting into here. This isn't what you think," Grace said.

"You know where Dad and Grandad are. And you've kept it from us," I said.

"What?" Alexa gasped.

"Kept what from you, love?" Isabella reappeared from the kitchen and placed a cup of freshly made espresso in front of me. The platinum band of her square cut diamond engagement ring chimed against the cup.

"Letters from Dad and Grandad," I said. My throat convulsed a swallow.

Isabella followed my line of sight to the letters on the table and she stopped cold.

Blake walked behind me and sat down. His cup and saucer clinked when he placed them on the rosewood table.

I placed my hand on his knee for strength.

"How did you find those?" Isabella asked.

"You know about these, too?" I asked and felt my face color.

"From Dad and Grandad?" Alexa stood partially and peeked at them.

"Current-day letters," I said to Alexa.

"We were protecting the both of you." Isabella crossed

her arms in front of her and fiddled with her engagement ring.

"From what? Our own father and grandfather?"

"They're alive?" Alexa's voice shook.

I leaned toward Grace. "And you told us just yesterday that they were dead. How could you do that?"

Grace placed her hand in front of me on the table and I moved the letters a little further out of her reach. "Addie, honey, this is not what it seems. It's complicated—"

"And dangerous," Isabella said. She crossed her arms a little tighter.

"It's a lie is what it is. You told us that our father and grandfather were dead. When in reality they're alive and well and corresponding with the two of you!"

"It's not quite like that," Isabella sat down across from me. She glanced at the letters, then to Grace, then back to me. "It's hard to explain." Her head twitched a tiny shake.

"Try me. You'll find me to be oddly bright and sufficiently capable of understanding complicated and dangerous."

"You need to trust us when we tell you that we *are* protecting you and Alexa." Grace clicked the pearls of her necklace against one another.

"You *had* my trust," I said. "Now I need the truth."

Grace's teeth were clenched behind tightly closed lips, her nostrils flared slightly. It was a far more intense version of the look I'd received as a child whenever Alexa and I had ruined something of hers—furniture, a party, plans for the future.

"I can't believe you've done this," she said.

"You should be happy. Because if you know how to get to Dad and Grandad, then I don't have to partner with Otto."

She opened her mouth to respond but a loud knock on the front door prevented it.

Grace's shoulders stiffened, her chin jutted out slightly. With steady eyes on mine she snatched the letters, and headed toward the door.

Grace returned with a package and laid it on the table.

"It's for Alexa," she said.

I felt the energetic scent coming off the small package and my heart kicked up its pace.

"It's from Otto," I said. I reached out with my left hand and touched the package with my fingertips. "It's not good." My heart fell hard and flat.

## 27

"It's bad," Alexa said when she opened her bedroom door. "It's everything you said it would be kind of bad."

"I'm so sorry." I gave her a hug. "I was afraid that something like this would happen." No hug was returned and all I felt was the internal wall she put up as I leaned into her.

"Why do you say that?" Alexa asked. "Because I didn't keep myself out of the dating world like you did before Blake came along?"

I was sure I heard the sound of a needle ripped off of a record.

"No. I'm not blaming you," I said.

"I know what you're thinking. That if I had been more like you, and if I hadn't slept with Todd that this wouldn't have happened."

"No, I'm not—"

"No, I can see it, I can see the judgment. It's a sex tape, like you predicted. And since I'm not some kind of a reality star, this is not going to help my popularity." Alexa crossed her arms and hatred fired in her eyes. Everything she had worked so hard for—her career, her reputation—swirled down the toilet. Thanks to Otto.

"There was a letter in the package." Alexa grabbed a piece of paper off the bed and shoved it at me. "He says that a copy of this has gone to the gallery that was supposed to do my show. He says if you don't work with him that plenty of other galleries will get a copy as well, and he'll make sure that I never work again."

"I'm sorry—"

"You should never have gone to work with him in the first place. I told you not to do that!" Alexa stormed to the window, then stared back at me. "You've not only ruined your life, but now you've completely destroyed mine. I think we've found your real gift, Addie. Who's next?"

I folded my arms across my stomach to shield myself. "Lex, I'm sorry about all of this."

"You really didn't think about anyone else, did you? You took that job because that's what you had to do for yourself. Everyone else can fend for themselves."

"I wasn't thinking that way. I was at the end of my rope when I interviewed with Otto. I needed a job—"

"And now I've lost mine. My career—"

"Alexa!" Isabella said from the doorway. "Addie didn't do this to you. If you want to be angry at someone, be angry at Otto. Don't let him destroy your relationship with your sister."

Alexa shook her head and faced the window.

Isabella closed her eyes for a painful second then ushered me out into the hallway where I found Blake leaning against the stair railing.

"What's on the tape?" Isabella shut the door behind her.

"I haven't seen it. Apparently Todd, this guy she was seeing..." I focused on the floor and ran my hand through my hair. This was not the news anyone wanted to give a mother about her daughter.

"Tell me so I can fix this," Isabella said.

"He planted some video equipment in Alexa's apartment and filmed them while they were...together."

Isabella pressed her fingers over her eyes. "To blackmail you into working with Otto, I guess?"

"Yes." My stomach twisted.

"I had a friend trace the location of the Internet connection that received the contents of the video. I'll send you what came in earlier today," Blake said. "I'm pretty sure it leads to Otto, or at the very least, Todd—who's apparently working for Otto. You could get an injunction against the video's release, which will limit how far the video travels. It will keep it out of stores and off of online sites. Unfortunately, it won't prevent Otto from sending it to a few galleries. I'm sorry."

Worry lines creased Isabella's forehead and she traced them with a finger. "Thank you, Blake. Grace already called her attorney and he's working on the injunction." She squeezed Blake's arm then held mine. "Give her some time." She disappeared into Alexa's room and closed the door.

## 28

W hen I reached the bottom step I smacked the top of the newell and my hand stung.

"Grace will get the injunction filed," Blake said from behind me.

"Even if we can prevent wide distribution, there's nothing to stop Otto or Todd from sending a copy to more gallery owners who might have helped Lex with her career. That's where the real damage is." "Lex is right—this is ultimately my fault."

Blake stepped in my path and squared off with me. "No. This is Otto's fault." His face was stern and battle-ready, the result of facing-off with Otto too many times before. His eyebrows raised in a "got it?" kind of fashion. "He wants you to feel guilty. So, don't."

"All right." I said. Though I did feel guilty.

"He's at the middle of all of our problems right now. Not you. And sending out sex videos like this is illegal. There may be one more thing I can try—I'll be right back," Blake said. He dug through his pocket, took out his pocket watch, wallet, and phone. He held on to his phone and left the other items on the side table.

"What are you going to do?" I asked.

"Going to try to call in a couple of favors with some friends on the FBI's Internet-related crime division. I'll see what I can do." He brushed by me and headed toward the backyard.

I yanked my fingers through my hair and tugged. Lexie was suffering and there wasn't anything I could do to help her. Not immediately, anyway. Otto had a sick gift for destroying lives. I picked up Blake's pocket watch, stroked the smooth, cool surface, and glanced outside at him. Even pacing through a grassy backyard he was official and gallant. Though I knew it was driving him nuts not to have something on Otto that would put him away. He worked that pursuit for years, only to come up with nothing.

The vision sputtered at first, in competition with my other thoughts and focus. I started to put it down. Then the memory found an unreasonable strength and lifted fully from the watch.

Alice peels the blood-soaked dress from my body and places it in a bag so I won't have to see it. Or smell it.

She puts the bag behind the French rattan chair to keep it out of sight, out of mind. She has wiped most of the blood from my face and neck, has washed my hands and arms in the sink. Still, some remnant stains of Jack's blood tints the hot bath, and I fixate on the pink water.

Twice she drains the cast iron tub and refills it, until the water holds clear. She washes my catatonic body with a soft yellow cloth and rose-scented soap while she hums *Take Your Burden to the Lord and Leave it There*.

My burden is lodged just beneath my heart by virtue of Jack. Originally, I thought the Lord had placed that burden there as a gift. Though just now I don't know how I am going to handle it.

"Oh, Miss Sarah," Alice says when I rub my hand absently over the slight protrusion on my belly.

My tears fall with a new purpose. "I'm pregnant with Jack's baby, Alice. And now he's gone, and we're alone. I have no way to take care of myself or this child."

Alice's lips draw thin, her eyes narrow, her accelerated breath through slightly flared nostrils the only sign of the building rage I know she reserves for Gary.

"He said he wouldn't kill me. But for this I think he just might. I can't let him kill Jack's baby."

She hoists me out of the tub and wraps a white towel around me. "Get dressed, Miss Sarah. Get dressed, darlin'." She points to the clothes she's laid over the vanity bench.

A crystal vase of white roses from Jack sits on the vanity, fresh and scented like they've not yet been told what has happened to him. Even though Jack's pocket watch rests to the side of the vase, and my bloody fingerprints are on its cover.

"I'm going to call Mr. Knox," she says. "Mr. Jack's attorney should be able to do something." She disappears through the bathroom door.

I reach inside my towel and rub my palm over the swollen area where the tiny butterfly wings flutter inside of me. I'm surprised by joy.

"What's the matter?" I heard Blake say.

Still caught halfway between here and there, I couldn't quite make out Blake's appearance. But I knew he was there.

He took the pocket watch.

I pulled up the photo of my portrait on my phone. It was mostly indistinguishable to anyone who didn't know, cloaked by the loose fabric and style of my dress. But if you read the portrait closely enough, and only because my fingers rested below it just so, you could see a small swell of my abdomen. I wondered if Jack knew before he died. Knew that I was carrying his baby.

"I was pregnant when you died. When Jack died, I mean. I was carrying your baby—his baby." The fluttering sensation had been so vivid when I read the watch, I put my hand across my own belly and expected to feel it.

Blake took the photo and focused hard.

"I wonder if our child lived," I said. "Or if Otto did away with it. Or did away with me."

"Probably not if he thought it was his baby," Blake said.

I cringed at the thought, and wondered if we would ever find a way to put him out of our misery.

Blake walked me to the kitchen and prepared two new espressos. I was quite ready for a new dose of caffeine, and anticipated the grounding.

"Any luck from your call?" I asked.

"They can shut down the sender if Alexa or one of the gallery owners can provide proof of receipt of the video. They can't do much proactively, though. Todd could just say she agreed to being filmed."

"By the time the galleries see the footage, the damage is done."

Blake nodded.

Otto had us once again.

"Thanks for trying." I kissed his cheek. Still grateful that we were beyond our last life, that he was alive and we were together.

A strange and sickly quiet had come over the house, the result of the tragedy that surrounded Lex. It made me feel small in the face of it. It was the same feeling that swallowed me whole when I was about ten, and learned that the people I loved most in the world could be ripped away from you.

The front doorbell rang and Grace's heels clicked across the marble entryway.

I peeked through the doorway and saw Grace in the foyer with a man I recognized as Fowler Townsend, her longtime attorney, family friend, and former client of my grandfather's.

His dark wavy hair, parted on the side, was perfectly coiffed with a bit of sheen. His strong southern sensibilities shone brightly when he kissed her hand. Like Grace, he was a dying breed, a blue-blooded Savannahian from a bygone time. He was powerful, yet the perfect gentleman, and Grace had always seemed smitten by his charm.

"I know him from somewhere," Blake said.

"The injunctions have been filed," Fowler said. An air of protection emanated from him and swirled around Grace. "And I've hired an online PI firm. If that video makes it onto any online site, they'll know about it and they'll get it down immediately."

"Thank you," Grace said. Fowler closed his arms around her and hugged her tight. Grace uncharacteristically rested her head on his chest when she hugged him back.

My mouth opened slightly. I'd never seen her let her guard down with a man other than my grandfather. And even then, rarely so. She was southern steel inside and out.

"The day I get my hands on that man is the last day he draws a breath." Grace pulled away, and she twisted and clicked her long strand of pearls between her fingers.

A subtle grin of pride bloomed on Fowler's face.

"Have you heard anything from John or Campbell?" he asked.

"They're back at home base." Grace took a letter from

the front pocket of her dress and handed it to him. "They're going to try to find one of the paintings in the basement of the Met. John made a contact who is willing to take them down there."

I elbowed Blake."They're in New York." My palms tingled with adrenaline, though it still felt irrational to get excited about seeing them. I wasn't entirely used to the idea that they were alive and well.

Fowler nodded while he read the antiqued letter.

"He was right, you know," Grace said. "No one there knows what they have in that collection. Not really."

"Of course they don't," Fowler said. A quiet moment passed between them.

"Why don't we try again?" He touched her arm. "We could try the Monet."

"I have to settle this with Addie. And now this with Alexa." Grace waved her hand upstairs toward Alexa's room. "I can't run the risk of being away too long. Could end up losing the rest of my family."

"Of course." Fowler lowered his head and rocked back on his heels in a way that said maybe he didn't entirely agree.

"Addie thinks she can help find Campbell and John if she goes back to work with Otto. Which would be nothing less than a death sentence." Grandmother Grace took the letter from Fowler, then spun her emerald ring around her thin finger. "She found several of these." She waved the letter and then put it in her pocket.

"Then she knows?" he asked.

"No. And she won't," she said in a warning tone. "She's aware that I know where John and Campbell are. She'll not find out any more."

Fowler put his hands in his pockets, his lips strained

with a thin smile. "Knowing Addie, if she knows that much, I don't think she'll give up until she knows everything. Why don't you just tell her? She could work with the Monet. It would keep her away from Otto. This new beau of hers could go with her."

"He knows *everything*," I said with a scoff. "And he's not even family."

"You of all people know how dangerous this could be for her." Grace's voice pitched with frustration.

"The Monet," Blake whispered. "That's it."

"What's it?" I asked.

"Fowler got that Monet at auction from Christie's. That's where I've seen him before."

"Of course you're right," Fowler said in a most gentlemanly fashion. Though the expression on Grace's face said she knew she didn't have his agreement.

"Well, let's get these signed." Fowler placed a stack of papers on the foyer table, and handed Grace a pen.

Grace's frustration was evident when she scratched the pen against the signature line. "I've spent most of my life protecting my family from this wretched man. And not very well, I might add."

Fowler flipped the page for her to sign again. "We'll think of something."

"One would think," she said.

A gaunt man with thinning gray hair entered the room behind Fowler and smiled.

"Oh, no."

"What's the matter?" Fowler asked.

"Allen's dead," Grace said.

"Miranda's husband?"

"Cancer. They just brought him home from the hospital last week," she said, and placed her hand over her chest.

"Allen, you're okay?" Grace asked the gray-haired man.

Allen smiled and waved his hand to encourage her to come with him.

Fowler seemed unsure of where to focus.

"Seems Grace has shared a few secrets," I said to Blake. I wondered if mine were still locked away.

Grace disappeared into her nearby study, then reemerged with her purse and keys in hand. "I won't be long, but I need to check on Miranda."

"Of course you do," Fowler said.

"Oh, the signature pages from the updated will," Grace said. "They're in the study, on my desk. If you would?"

Fowler ushered Grace toward the front door. "I'll get them. Go see Miranda. We'll get together tonight."

"Thank you, Fowler," Grace said and walked out the door.

I walked toward the foyer with Blake in tow. "If Grace won't enlighten me as to where they are, then I need you to make sure that Fowler will," I whispered.

Fowler, hi," I said when we reached the foyer.

"Addie, darlin'. We were just talking about you." Fowler hugged me with a kiss to the cheek. "How are you?"

"I'm fine. Doing fine. Fowler Grant, this is Blake Greenwood."

"Blake, good to see you, sir." Fowler shook Blake's hand. His welcoming smile warmed the room. "Grace tells me you have a successful gallery in New York City."

I felt Blake ready to push. But he didn't. "I do. Next time you're in New York, I'd like for you to stop by so I can show it to you."

"Why, I'll do just that. You know I am a bit of a collector." Fowler adjusted his tie.

"Now are you the same Fowler Grant who just picked up Monet's *L'Ile aux Orties* at the Christie's Auction last year?"

"One and the same." Fowler's smile broadened.

"You want to invite us for a private showing today, don't you?" Blake pushed so gently that Fowler moved along without resistance.

"I'd love to have you over for a private showing. Would today work for you?"

"How about now?"

"Now, sounds grand."

Fowler Townsend lived on one of the more prestigious squares of downtown Savannah. His historic red brick home boasted a wide porch and graceful archways under its roof. Tourists and locals alike would often take pictures.

"If you can get him off to the side to push him for information, I'll search his study to see if I can find anything. Grace usually meets Fowler here to discuss our family business, so there's bound to be something." I said.

"I hardly had to push at all for this invite. So I think he wants us here." Blake said.

"Based on what we just witnessed between the two of them, I would agree."

We stood on the front porch and Blake looked upward toward the second floor. "This house feels haunted."

I nodded. "Every house in Savannah has a ghost story. Sally Anne Hunter lived here with her husband in 1861. She caught him raping one of their slaves, and she shot his head off. Or most of it anyway. I think she's still here. What else do you think Grace has shared with Fowler?" The doorbell's melody carried throughout the inside of the house.

"Grace is also pretty shrewd, so it's hard to say," Blake said.

The front door opened.

"Mr. Townsend is expecting you, Ms. Montgomery, Mr. Greenwood. Right this way, please."

Smith, Fowler's butler, was a tall, thin man with creases at the corner of his eyes. They were a tad deeper than I had remembered. His classic British accent never failed to make me smile. Fowler's home was wall-to-wall finery. Anything less than an English butler was simply unimaginable.

Today my grin was a little wider than usual.

"Is that a toupee?" Blake whispered while we wended our way across Fowler's Persian rugs. "And is it blue?"

"Actually, I think it's so black that it appears to be blue." The shade really didn't fit his pale complexion and suggested a misfired attempt to recapture his youth. It was also slightly crooked on his head, and I fought the urge to straighten it for him.

"Ms. Montgomery and Mr. Greenwood, sir," Smith said when we walked into the library. Fowler stood near the warmth of the fireplace, with a scotch in one hand and a cigar in the other. Fowler had tied a yellow ascot around his neck and tucked it into his white shirt and black sweater. He wore a pair of round, black-framed glasses.

"Addie, Blake, how marvelous!" Fowler kissed both of my cheeks and then shook Blake's hand enthusiastically. Like he hadn't just seen us an hour earlier.

"Come in, come in," he said and adjusted his glasses. "The Monet is just here in my study."

The beauty of Claude Monet's *L'Île aux Orties* was breathtaking in its isolated position on the largest wall of

Fowler's study. The purples spoke first, followed by the subtle blues, and then the greens. In perfect harmony, the reflection in the water revealed itself next, drawing the eye to the blues of the water, then the sky and back to the purple blooms.

Color and light had always been Monet's crowning achievements.

Blake walked to the painting and eyed its various brush-strokes up close. I stepped toward the painting with him and ached to put my fingertips on the paint. I'd never read a Monet before.

"Exquisite," Blake said.

All I could do was take it in. Monet left me speechless.

"Addie, I've wanted to show you this Monet for some time, now."

"You have?" I remembered his suggestion to Grace that I could work with the Monet and that would keep me away from Otto. I had no idea what he meant.

"Eight million, was it?" Blake asked.

"Eight point one," Fowler leaned against the doorway, his now-extinguished cigar perched in the corner of his wide smile. "A bargain compared to the Picasso." He covertly checked the time on his watch.

"The Picasso?" Blake asked. He searched the walls for evidence of the artist.

"I keep it upstairs. In the sitting area between floors. Keeps things unexpected. Would you like to see it?" Fowler smiled, ever the gracious host.

"I would." Blake put his hands in his pockets and smiled.

Fowler was beating him to the punch at every turn, there was no need for Blake to push. I knew we both thought it odd.

"Make yourself at home." Fowler gestured to me, and across his office.

"Take your time," I said, and noticed that Fowler wasn't the least bit concerned that I stood so close to his Monet. Which was unusual for a collector with such an expensive piece.

Before he turned the corner with Fowler, Blake raised an eyebrow at me. I shrugged, then set out to find anything that might help me find more about my father's and grandfather's location.

Fowler's antique walnut writing desk with the green marble inlays stood guard in front of the picturesque, antebellum window, and I ran my fingertips along the wood grain to see what was there. Plenty of information relating to his law clients and art deals, some information about my family business, but nothing about my father and grandfather. His papers were stacked in short piles, sparsely placed. The drawers were locked.

I touched the upholstered high-back chairs, polished tables, lamp shades, framed portraits of his horses, and even lumbar pillows and flower vases, but there weren't any clues that helped me. Apparently, he didn't talk with Grace about these particular family issues in here. There were no personal effects lying around. Not even pens or pieces of pocket change. What I wouldn't give for access to Fowler's wristwatch.

Hopefully, Blake was getting some answers.

The late day sun shone through the window and highlighted a section of the bookshelf at the far end of the room. There wasn't any seating over there, so I thought it unlikely that any objects would have captured conversational details, especially if the front side of the office had not. I walked there, nonetheless.

Antique books were the backdrop for a littering of photographs of Fowler with prominent politicians and various celebrities. I stifled an urge to take one of the books from the shelf, crack it open, and take a deep sniff.

The crystal chandelier in the middle of the ceiling was dimly lit and gave the room a candlelit glow. His office felt to me like a tiny jewel box that was stuck in some better place in time. I dragged my fingers against the faded spines on the middle shelf. There was a chatter amongst the books, their stories murmured tidbits of importance. Storied were trapped on the pages. Each one of the books was anxious to be read.

This was so unlike the art I usually read, which imparted emotions first and then the stories that came through in pictures. I often sensed details about the artist, their history, and their intent for the art. *Usually*. There was immediate information about its authenticity, what the canvas absorbed or witnessed from its position on the wall, and on and on. The details I could obtain from a piece of art were simply endless.

I traced the gold titling that still shone bright against the muted fabrics of blues and greens. My fingers paused for a few seconds on one title before moving to the next. Like a record player's needle that read the spinning vinyl, each book responded to my touch and spoke its story with a strong voice. Authentic and clear.

"Of course the books would speak in words first," I said, and instinctively let my fingers scan for the strongest voice on the shelf.

I landed on a blue linen-grain cloth with its spine lettered in gilt. The book all but sang its story to the last balcony seat. I leaned forward and tugged the book from its home that was positioned near too tight between its neighbors.

"*The Great Gatsby,*" I whispered, and studied the familiar cover. The book made a cracking noise when I opened it. A first edition. Its value must have been close to $200,000. Maybe more.

It must not have been touched often because I could have sworn I felt F. Scott Fitzgerald's vibe coming off of the book. His mercurial nature and star-powered social life glistened in bright images, feelings, and sounds across my awareness. His laughter filled the room so loudly it startled me, and I fumbled the book. I quietly slid the book back to the shelf and resumed my tour.

A black and white photograph in a simple silver frame grabbed my attention from its far-corner. Two of the four people looked strangely familiar, and the scene appeared more intimate than the other publicity-type photos in the room.

There were two elegant couples who sat around a white-topped, ornately iron based table in what resembled a Parisian cafe. They drank and laughed and raised their glasses in a toast to the photographer. The first couple on the left was immediately recognizable. Their photos had been spread across the world for nearly a century. His center part, thin lips, and light blue eyes. Her wavy blond hair, almond-shaped eyes, and babydoll mouth. They were the most popular couple in literary history, and certainly throughout the 1920s.

They were F. Scott and Zelda Fitzgerald.

This wasn't the couple who surprised me. No, it was the other man and woman at the table. Her pearl necklace was looped three times around her neck. Once close to her throat, the second time just below her décolletage, and the third longest loop disappeared behind the table. His black hair was shinier and combed into a different style, one more befitting the era. It sported the same dark waves I'd always known him to have.

Grandmother Grace and Fowler Townsend sat closely, his arm around her back. Neither Grace nor Townsend were more than a few years younger than they were today. However, they were resplendent in mid-1920s fashion and partying with literary royalty.

## 30

Old demons rapped at the recesses of my mind. The same ones who leashed my gifts when I was about to see something I didn't want to. No longer because it would shatter some misplaced need for normal, but because I had that feeling that I was dancing too close to the fire.

"This doesn't make sense," I said. I released the latches from the back of the frame with a few clicks so that I could touch the photograph directly.

I touched the front of the photo lightly, and I wondered if this was an editing trick. Perhaps a party favor from a New Year's Eve party. But the energy rose up from the photo, the movie played, and there was no mistaking the fact that the four of them were friends. Old friends. As in, this is not their first time visiting with one another kind of friends.

I sat in one of the two high-back chairs positioned in front of the Monet, my fingers traced the photo again and again, and I tried to find some flaw in what I'd seen.

Problem was, the only story I could see was the one

where Fowler and Grace were old friends with F. Scott and Zelda Fitzgerald.

"Ha!" I laughed and shook my head.

I put the frameless photo on the small round table between the two chairs, leaned forward with my chin on my fingers, and stared at the Monet.

I walked through the history I'd read and tried to make sense of it. Though, sense wouldn't come because I couldn't find where this wasn't true.

Grandmother Grace was one of the most powerful psychics, if not *the* most powerful, I'd ever known. As a young girl she visited France with her mother and studied for years with a shaman, where she learned impressive energy work. She had always had a wealth of secrets. I'd known her all of my life, and I was still unraveling her mysteries.

I glanced at the photo again and realized that the old saying was true. Watched pots never boiled, and answers didn't reveal themselves just because you needed them to. Grace's smile gleamed. It was impossible to know if she was keeping yet another fantastic secret, or had managed to fool my gifts with some kind of trick.

I walked close to the Monet and eyed the brushstrokes, delved into the beauty and the colors. Anything to take my mind away from the photo. Even a short break would help bring clarity. Two pair of white gloves stretched neatly on the console nearby and I slipped one on. Like the scent of coffee beans at a wine tasting, a tiny touch of this master-piece would refresh my psychic receptors.

With one hand gloved and the other half so, I glanced at the photo on the table again. Fowler would be down in a few minutes with Blake, and I would ask Fowler about it. Placing it in front of him would be enough of a question.

With gloves intact, I stood in front of the Monet and studied the greens and lavenders. The scenery came alive. The movement Monet had created in the water currents and gentle breezes made me sway hypnotically. Energy currents jumped in arcs with Monet's brushstrokes like dolphins playing in the waves of the Atlantic.

The ring finger of my left hand laid on this motion, and Monet's story rose to my touch first. For some reason I thought he would be someone whose gift was more obvious, perhaps even burdensome as mine had been. Though it was more casual to him. His gift did as he commanded it to. Creating this image to appear like that and evoke the other. It was more like he was a child playing at the beach than a world-renowned artist creating a masterpiece. He simply did what he knew how to do. And he enjoyed it.

Unlike most artists I'd read, Monet wasn't interested in telling a story—his focus was to capture the beauty and the light. In terms of how precisely the painting matched the object, well, he was more intent upon creating an emotional expression for the viewers. As with any artist, he would bring himself into the painting. "No one would know," he'd thought as he painted subjective details here and there. "Besides, it *should* appear this way," he said and he added yellow where there was none on the landscape.

Coolness surrounded me, a light breeze that came from the painting. I opened my eyes and expected to see a ghost interfering with my reading.

Instead I saw something far more alarming.

## 31

I couldn't see my hand.

I wiggled my fingers and found that I could. They were there—I could feel the soft cotton glove.

There was also a tingling, like low-grade electricity, that crawled up my arm and created a drag. The force tugged evenly on everything it covered. It wasn't an entirely unpleasant feeling, except for the fact that the pull was stronger than I could resist, and my arm now disappeared up to my elbow. It disappeared into the painting.

I leaned forward and my head spun with a dizzying sensation, though I was certain that my feet were firmly on the floor. Because at least I could see those.

Perhaps this was a new type of reading my gifts were morphing into. A deeper reading. Or maybe it was the painting itself that offered more information. No, not offered. Led. It guided me to new depths of information. Normally, when I read a painting, the information simply lifted to my touch. Its story presented itself to me like words on a page or stars in the sky. This information, however, was drawing me into it like it wanted me to be a part of it.

I moved my hand back and forth inside the painting, and found a connection with several avenues of information. It seemed I could go in any direction I wanted with these different options, and I stepped forward so that I could see them better. All but my left foot buzzed with this electricity. Only a little bit of me remained in the house.

Laid out before me were all the options this painting had to offer, like hallways that lead to unique, historic worlds. There was Monet, the artist, and his life experiences. When I moved my touch, my line of sight shifted onto another pathway that told the story of the painting—everywhere it had been, what it had seen, essentially the life it had lived. There were other portals as well, seemingly endless ones that could take me in an overwhelming number of directions as they related to Monet, his life, this painting. The possibilities were exciting and readily available to me with only a slight consideration of them.

A cool darkness fell on the painting, like the sun went behind a cloud, and the interesting options were lost to an unexpected murkiness that blurred my vision. Sudden crosswinds blew through the area. The dark energies of Monet's more difficult emotions—hopelessness, self-doubt, and depression carried on these fierce winds and clung to me like I could offer them salvation.

His insecurities, indecision about his work, the disappointments of his life were like gale-force currents that sucked me deeper within its ominous grasp. I felt panic like a drowning victim, like I would not escape. The more positive avenues were gone, and there was nothing left to reach for, nothing to hang on to. I drifted further into the well-worn pathways of his deep sadness that were imbued into each brushstroke. I floundered and choked on wails that filled the air while Monet still mourned the loss of his first wife, and I felt them as my own. I felt, just as his depression insisted, that there were no answers.

Fully prostrate into the winds of the emotional storm now, I prayed for help. Reading art had always been my stronghold, the one way I could use my gifts that never failed. Now this betrayed me, too. I screamed in frustration then felt the top of my foot hit something cold and hard, like a railing. The frame. I flexed my foot against it, and—I held on for dear life.

"I think I will take that drink. Scotch, please. Yes, straight up." I heard Blake's voice from a long distance. Then I felt hands around my ankle.

"Addie!" Blake yelled.

It was a tug of war between the painting that felt it must hang on to me, and Blake's grasp, which was just as unrelenting. With a heave and a jerk, my body was ripped from Monet's emotional purchase, and I landed sunny-side up with Blake beneath me on the floor of Fowler's office.

"Oh!"

"Everything okay?" Fowler asked from the doorway with a glass in each hand. "Am I missing all the fun?"

Fowler placed the glasses of scotch on his desk then extended a hand to help me. Once upright my stomach felt nauseous, and my skin clammy. My eyes felt pasted wide, and I reached for the floor again. I wished it to stop spinning.

"Are you okay?" Fowler asked.

"I guess I lost my balance," I said stupidly, and climbed back onto my feet. Slowly, I smoothed and dusted my soft gray woolen pants, even though there wasn't anything to brush off. Blake hopped up on his own and raised a hand to refuse Fowler's help.

Blake squeezed my arms like he tried to prove to himself that I was all here.

"That was hideous," I said after Blake helped me to a chair. I cut my eyes to the Monet. Unsuspecting monster that it was. I smoothed my windblown hair. I figured I looked as hysterical as the emotions I'd just left. My body gave an involuntary shudder, and the grief Monet ingrained into this work began to leave me. Intentional or not, I'd never seen anything like it. "How could something so beautiful on the outside be so debilitating on the inside?"

Fowler handed me a glass of scotch, then sat in the highback chair I'd sat in earlier, and studied me with the most peculiar concern. His chest barreled on a deep inhale.

He leaned forward and studied me.

I pushed a lock of hair away from my face.

When he placed his glass on the side table, he picked up the photo I'd left there. Only his eyes raised to meet me, and a chill covered my back.

"I have a few questions I'd like answered," I said.

"As do I," said a stern voice I didn't expect to hear.

The three of us turned with alarm and saw Grace and Smith standing in the doorway.

"Ms. Montgomery, sir," Smith said belatedly. He intuited the tension in the room, bowed and scurried away.

Grace glided into the study with all the beauty and force of a deadly storm. Fowler smiled and stood to welcome her, the bob of his adam's apple the only sign of nerves. She paused next to Fowler, eyed me with care. Thenshe followed the energetic trail from the Monet to me.

I crossed the short distance to where she stood, took the photo from Fowler, and handed it to her. "What is this?"

"Something I would rather you hadn't seen."

"I never suggested she touch it," Fowler said.

"You put her in front of it," Grace said. "You wanted this to happen."

"It was worth a try." He raised one eyebrow at her.

A well-worn argument seemed to thread between them. It was now obvious to me that for as much as Grace didn't want me to experience the Monet, Fowler did.

"This may very well be an option. You have to keep moving forward on this," he said.

"Not at any risk." Anger leapt in Grace's eyes.

Though I'd always known Fowler as a man who could hold his own, I felt for him to be on the receiving end of Grace's temper. I looked at the pearls around her neck and the pearls she wore in the photo. They were arranged differently today, but they were clearly one and the same.

Blake walked over to us and Fowler took the photo from Grace's stilled hand, handed it to Blake.

"It's a lovely snapshot, don't you think? Grace didn't want the photographer to take it. Scott insisted and she's always had a hard time saying no to him. Haven't you, dear?" Fowler said.

## 32

"Tell me what happened." Grace turned the steering wheel hand over hand, and navigated her car around the old city squares.

"I don't know how to explain what happened." Actually I didn't want to explain. And I felt oddly weak and in need of food.

"Start from the beginning. You touched the Monet? Did you have intent when you touched it?"

"Yes," I said.

"Tell me, Addie." Grace's tone was sharp.

"I touched the Monet for an energetic break. I'd stared at the photo of you with F. Scott and Zelda Fitzgerald for too long. I wasn't getting any answers that made logical sense. So I was going to read Monet. For fun." I placed my hand on my stomach to quell the nausea.

"Tell me what I want to know and I'll give you something that will make you feel better."

"Really, Grace? Then how about this: you tell me what is going on with my family, that photo, and the Monet, and I won't go work with Otto." I'd never yelled at Grace in my life. This was a first. My day was full of firsts.

Grace's breath was equally measured on both the inhale and the exhale, and her lips thinned. "You don't know what you're asking for, Addie."

"I'm asking for answers, Grace. Answers about my own family. Answers you should want to give me so I can help them, not to mention protect myself. If you'd been straight with us a long time ago about Dad and Grandad, maybe then Otto wouldn't still be in our lives and threatening us. And it would be nice if you would help me for a change instead of working against me."

"All I've done is help you!" she growled. "And anyone else in this family who's gotten wrangled into Otto's world."

"You judge and criticize me for not using my gifts the way you want, you abandon us for years at a time without explanation, you keep secrets from me like I'm a child, but you don't help me."

Grace slowed the car to avoid the tourists who clogged the walkways on Bull Street. I watched her face and knew she was caught between what she'd held secret for years and what I needed.

"If I tell you I'll endanger your life," she said.

"My life is already in danger," I said. "Telling me couldn't make that any worse."

"You'd be surprised," she said.

We turned onto the dirt lane that led to our family home. We passed under the long threshold of live oaks and the car jostled back and forth, a gentle rocking I'd often found comforting.

Pea gravel crunched under the tires and Grace stopped the car in front of our majestic home. She sighed. For the first time since I'd known her, age crept into her features. Resignation replaced the usual sparkle in her eyes.

She pointed a long, thin finger at me. "I'll tell you. But first you'll tell me what you saw in the Monet."

～

WHEN WE GOT to the kitchen Grace made a tunafish sandwich. She cut the crusts off, cut the bread on the diagonal, and put a few chips on the side, just as she had done when I was little. "Eat this. It will make you feel better."

When I finished that sandwich, she handed me another. I waited to see if she would still slice and peel an apple for me, too.

But she stormed around the kitchen, instead. Slamming cabinet doors, and muttering mostly unintelligible things.

Lexie descended the back stairs, having showered and changed her clothes. Her swollen eyelids and blotchy skin told me the tears hadn't yet stopped. Not that I would have expected them to.

Grace kissed Alexa and gave her the triple pat just before she passed her on the steps. "Family meeting in ten."

"If she hadn't called it, I would have," I whispered to Blake.

"She's a lot like Carolena." Blake stroked the rasp of stubble along his jawline, and narrowed his eyes at Grace when she disappeared up the back stairway. "She doesn't see that the more she holds back, the more she puts you in danger."

Grace's perfume hung in the air—black currant, gardenia, and lavender peony notes—like blooms on a vine. "I don't think she'll ever cough up all of her secrets. Not entirely, anyway."

"Carolena, either." Blake said.

Lexie flopped into a chair next to me. She crunched into a small red apple, then swished the bangs away from her face.

"You okay?" I asked with a mouthful of sandwich.

"Isabella did some energy work on me while y'all were gone, and I feel better."

I patted her hand with my own triple pat. "Heartbreak is one emotion that won't be rushed. Take your time."

She took her hand from under mine and held my hand tight. "I'm sorry. I shouldn't have said those things to you." She swallowed the last of her oversized bite, then exhaled thick and heavy. Her face was tight with stress. "I was completely enchanted, literally, with his attention—how I thought he felt about me. He was so handsome and full of charm. I never took an objective minute to think about how I felt about him, or if this was a good situation to be involved in. I just ran headfirst, jumped right in. And destroyed my career."

"Most women would have gotten swept up in that charm. Sometimes it's hard to see those ulterior motives."

"Well...I'm sorry," she said. "I need to get my act together."

I squeezed her hand in return and felt the warmth between her heart and mine.

## 33

We gathered in the main family room—the four Montgomery women and Blake. Grace stood at the fireplace and adjusted a few family photos.

Grace and Isabella had met behind the closed double doors of Grace's bedroom before we convened. Now a plan seemed to be in place between the two matriarchs.

The door to the veranda was open an inch, and the cool, damp, salty air brought a thick seaside flavor into the room. Blake built a fire. Isabella and Alexa popped the corks on two bottles of red wine and filled five glasses halfway.

We all settled into our usual family seating order, while Blake occupied a historically empty seat beside me on the couch.

"Addie read a piece of art at Fowler's house earlier today. Monet's *L'Ile aux Orties*. I'd like to hear about this reading first, then Isabella and I have some things to share about John and Campbell."

"Did you have an intent when you went into it?" Grace asked.

"Well, it wasn't to go into it, I can tell you that. My intent was just to take a break from reading the photo of you and Fowler and the Fitzgeralds. I intended to read a few interesting facts about Monet and leave it at that."

"Who are the Fitzgeralds?" Lexie sipped her wine.

I slipped the black-and-white photo from my jacket pocket. Blake walked across the room with it and handed it to her.

"Holy..." Lexie's mouth hung open and she flipped the photo from its front to back side several times. "Is this real?"

"Go on," Grace said to me.

"It wouldn't allow me to just read it. It sucked me in, it wanted to..."

"Own you?" Grace said.

"Yes," I said, thankful that she understood.

"Why would a painting want to own you?" Lexie held the photo close to her eyes and inspected it.

"Because that's what people with unresolved grief can do—they grab ahold of whomever and whatever might rescue them. Or they might grab ahold of what distract them from their pain," Grace said.

"Initially, there were options," I said. "Like these hallways I could travel. I just noticed them and I felt I could go there. Then these crosswinds kicked up with all sorts of debilitating emotions. They attached to me and grabbed at me. If Blake hadn't caught me and pulled me out, I don't think I ever would have gotten out of that painting. Honestly, I think I would have lost my mind if I had to spend time in there."

Grace's lips pressed together with sympathy.

"I've never experienced a piece of art like that before. Usually, there's just information to read about the art and the artist. This one was more...alive and possessive." I shivered and Blake put his arm around me.

Grace stood and clasped her hands together. "Do you think someone else might be able to navigate their way around that painting?"

"You mean, you?" I asked. My insides steeled themselves against a potential slam.

"Anyone." She waved a half circle in the air.

"I don't see how. It's too disorienting," I said. "I think it's your turn now."

Grace gave a singular nod. "There's no easy way to tell this story, no best place to begin," she said, then stared at her shoe. A little tell that told me she'd rather be anywhere else than where she was at the moment.

She sippped her wine and cleared her throat. "This started years ago...when Otto received a painting that, when touched by the right person with the right set of gifts—would transport them through time."

Blake and I looked at each other, then back at Grace.

I thought about the Monet at Fowler's house, how my hand had gone right into the painting, and how its traction had drawn me into it. Indeed, it did seem like I could have traveled through its history.

"Who gave him this gift?" Blake asked.

"Carolena. Did she ever discuss this with you, Blake?" Grace asked, but appeared to already know the answer.

The room went still and I counted in the awkwardness. *One one-thousand, two one-thousand...*

Blake shook his head only once, and barely. The muscle in the side of his jaw flexed. "Not specifically, no."

"As the story was told to me by John, Carolena was the one who actually found the paintings and discovered their long-held secret. They had been stored and forgotten in a special section in the basement of the Metropolitan Museum of Art. She worked there at the time, and she found them by accident, I believe.

"There were six in all, and the smaller-sized paintings were models for the room-sized murals that he intended to paint. We don't know if he ever finished the room-sized murals. The six smaller pieces that exist are a set of water-colors painted by Arthur Wentworth after his wife and child died from the flu in the late 1890s. He painted these pieces as therapy to help him overcome his loss. As a result, his undying love for them, and his longing to be with them in happier days gone by, was imbued into the brushstrokes of the paintings.

"Each time his brush dipped into the paint and spread across the canvas, he meditated on his love for them, until finally the painting opened a portal to a time one year before their death. He traveled through that portal and, as you might imagine, he was able to prevent their deaths."

Grace reached across the top of the wide mantel and selected a small thin book from a collection of three.

"He documented his experience in his memoir." She handed the black book to me.

"Of course no one believed his fantastic story. His peers accused him of hiding his family and then disappearing with them for the sake of selling books and paintings. Everyone except for one friend, that is," Grace said.

"Monet," I said.

"Monet." Grace nodded. Her eyes were now bright and clear once again. "We think several of his paintings may be portals. Unfortunately, none of the ones I've had access to have been a direct link to John and Campbell. We've either landed too early in history or too late."

Lexie leaned forward in her chair and it creaked.

"You traveled through Monet's *L'Ile aux Orties*?" I asked.

"I haven't tried it. In fact, I didn't want to try it until I was sure that you were safely hidden away from Otto. Sometimes those experiments don't go as planned. From what you've told me, I think this one is too dangerous to try at all. There are many inherent threats with this type of travel," she said. "Though Wentworth's are easier than Monet's, they all have their risks."

"So, Dad and Grandad are where, exactly?" I asked.

"They originally landed in 1895."

"*La Belle Epoch*," Lexie said. Her green eyes glowed with romance.

Grace nodded. "Yes, and knowing that, they spent most of their time in Paris. They were searching for a Wentworth and there was far more art to choose from in Paris than New York. Now they're back in New York, and it's 1920."

"Why couldn't they come back?" I couldn't believe what I asked.

Grace's face grew stern. "Otto left them there. With no way to get back."

I shivered and goose flesh covered my arms.

Now it made sense to me why I felt they were alive and why I couldn't sense their whereabouts.

"The paintings are like doorways and have to be accessible on both ends of time. One of the last things that Otto told John and Campbell was that he would destroy his Wentworth so that no one could get through it from the other side. A closed door, if you will."

"Aren't there other Wentworths they could travel through?" I asked.

"Once Wentworth understood the power of his paintings, he moved them often and to secret locations. His memoir doesn't mention where he kept them." Grace pointed to the book on my lap. "Only that he moved them every few months to keep them from falling into the wrong hands."

"Aren't there at least five other Wentworths we could find?"

"Isabella and I have searched for them for twenty years with no luck."

"So if Otto still had his painting, he could bring them back," I said.

"Addie—" Blake said.

I put my hand up to stop him. "I'm just asking."

"Hard to know," Grace said. "Since he hasn't. Carolena was the one who really had the gift for finding her way from here to there. At one point she did anchor a red cord to mark the path from here to 1920 so that Otto and other members of our crowd could travel on our own if we wanted to. The twenties were a favorite time for Otto.

Blake ran his hand down his face. "She marked the path with a cord? Like breadcrumbs for travelers?"

"Otto was different then," Grace said. "No one could have predicted that he would— Anyway, *if* he still has the painting, and *if* the cord is still in place, then yes, I guess he could get them back."

Isabella uncrossed her legs and leaned forward. "What we do know is that he has no motivation to bring them back. I mean, why would he?"

"So, they're alive," Lexie said. "And why did you keep this from us all these years?"

"Because the two of you have been headstrong enough to try this on your own." Grace's voice caught in her throat. "And I couldn't run the risk to lose the both of you as well." She moved slowly, like her sadness was too heavy on the inside. "I never wanted to hurt either of you. But I'd do it again if it meant keeping you safe." Her expression softened toward Lexie and me. "I'm sorry."

Grace didn't apologize for much, but when she did she was genuine. Alexa and I read the other's mind and agreed with a glance. Then we nodded at Grace and Isabella with understanding.

Instead of answering or belaboring the point, Grace turned a slow circle and continued. "John and Campbell took trips with Otto and Carolena for the business. They were able to salvage artwork that would otherwise have been destroyed, stolen, or lost in time. Those random announcements that some masterpiece was discovered in someone's attic or behind another canvas? Those discoveries were actually made possible by the work of these men. And Carolena, of course." Grace gestured toward Blake. He shook his head and I knew he wished his mother hadn't been involved.

"Then, travel became a more casual thing, and we took trips all the time," she gestured toward Isabella. "I learned how to traverse the depths of the canvas and navigate my own way without a guide.

"We all traveled through Otto's Wentworth as easily as if we were going to the coast for the weekend. We found the 1920s, and we figured out how to go to Paris..." Grace twisted her long strand of pearls, a faraway look glimmered in her eye.

"Anyway, cousin Eva found out through John about our trips." Grace shook her head. "And then one day she disappeared. We think she might have lost her sense of direction. She always drank too much, so we think she might have been careless, maybe traveling tipsy. From that we learned it could...happen to anyone."

"I thought she was killed in a car accident," Lexie said.

Grace sipped her wine, her attention directed out the window. A gentle, even rain fell outside and the drops pattered against the slanted roof of the veranda.

"We had to come up with a story, sweetheart," Isabella said. "We don't know where she is, or even if she's alive." Isabella stroked Lexie's hair and gathered it behind her shoulders.

"You were gone for several years when Lexie and I were young," I said. "Does that have something to do with the Wentworth as well?"

Grace sighed. "Seems I've rather a lot to apologize for today." She sat down for the first time since our meeting began. "It wasn't an intentional absence. We got lost."

"We?" Alexa asked.

Grace paused.

"Fowler and I."

"Oh." Alexa's eyebrows climbed.

"Your grandfather and I were on the outs, and we hadn't gotten along for some time. He wanted to be in New York, I wanted to stay in Savannah. You know I never liked the city. Anyway, I had the bright idea to show Fowler the painting. I guess I was trying to impress him, and we took a wrong turn and got lost."

"Isabella told us you were traveling around the world with a friend." There was the faint ring of whine in Lexie's voice when she said it. Her mouth remained open in a pout and I couldn't tell if Lex was offended over being lied to or because she had been left out of such a grand adventure.

"Well, I guess I rather was." Grace stood again, wine glass in hand. "I didn't mean to. Just as in the Monet, Wentworth's emotions ran strong when he painted, and the currents inside the art were disorienting."

"And that's when you met the Fitzgeralds," I said with more enthusiasm than I meant to.

"Well, we didn't intend to meet them." Grace's words suggested another apology, but I felt excitement in her heart. There was also a spark of happiness in her eye I'd never seen before.

"You enjoyed the trip." I thought of her bright smile in the Fitzgerald photo. "How could you not?"

"You'll have to tell us about them," Blake said.

"I will. It was all very grand. But I hated being away from my young granddaughters who needed me," Grace said. "Also Wentworth moved his paintings before we could get back to them. We were stuck. He started moving them every so often once he discovered that they could be a link between his time and another. He was constantly afraid someone would use them for the wrong reasons. In fact, it was just a fluke that we managed to get back at all."

I felt her heart tangle in a morass of guilt over not being there for Lex and me.

"We survived," I said to comfort her. "And you did make it back."

Like the release of a balloon, I felt the old childhood anger of abandonment lift from my heart and drift away. Grace, the steel magnolia we depended on so heavily when we were children, hadn't left us to travel the world. At least not intentionally.

Alexa, Grace, and I met at the midpoint of the room. We hugged one another and the tears and forgiveness flowed freely.

"Promise me that you won't try this." Grace took both Lex and me by a shoulder and looked us in the eyes.

Alexa promised right away.

I thought about the currents that blew crossways

through the Monet, and how they tugged me in different directions and knocked me off balance. The last thing I wanted was to be lost in some other time, away from Blake, separated from my family.

I wanted to be strong enough, gifted enough to tell her that I couldn't make that promise. Much as I wanted to be the hero for my father and grandfather, I thought of what I'd faced in the Monet and didn't think I could.

"I promise," I said.

When I returned to the couch Blake squeezed my hand.

"The truth is that I don't know if we'll ever get to them," Grace said. "Though we'll never stop trying."

"The best thing you can do now is to leave. Get away from Otto and enjoy your life together," Isabella said with tears in her eyes.

"Isabella's right, Addie," Grace said. "We'll take care of Lexie. We'll keep her safe from Otto."

"I just wish there was something I could do," I said. "I feel so helpless."

Blake took my hand.

"We all do," Lexie said. "But they're right. You and Blake need to be out of Otto's reach."

"If Otto becomes unbearable we'll all take a trip. Somewhere," Grace said with a smile that was intended to comfort.

The idea that I might not see my family again was not comforting.

"There're no guarantees in life," Grace said. "No guarantees that you'll find the love of your life, or if you do, that you'll be able to spend the rest of your life with them."

My chest clenched hard. Her words echoed the fear I'd felt since Blake and I had found one another. And even before then.

## 34

F owler called. He said he had a hit on who was hosting Alexa and Todd's video footage. Grace, Isabella, and Lex left the room to take the call.

Blake stepped outside to call Carolena.

As much as I wanted to be a part of both conversations, there were two missing pieces of information that I needed: the reasons why Otto banished my relatives to another time, and how they and Grace and Isabella were able to correspond with one another.

I could have waited for Grace or Isabella to answer these questions when they returned, but I had doubts that Grace would ever completely come clean about her secrets. I had to reasonably suspect that she would always keep a few to herself. Which meant if I wanted to know the answers, as usual, I'd have to find them myself.

My grandfather's private office swirled with precious memories. Somewhere in there I'd find the right conduit to the answers I sought.

The distant scent of singed paper brought my attention to the blue binding on the F. Scott Fitzgerald book. Once again there was a tiny, glimmering light. A few seconds later there was another.

I removed the book from the shelf. A subtle current of electricity ran through my hand and up my arm. Another folded, yellowed letter slid from the inside and my heart flooded with delight.

DEAREST ISABELLA & Mama,

Dad has secured our access to the basement area. We'll spend the next few months cataloging and organizing the artwork down here. Though they have not yet allowed us access to the desired area. We are, we hope, closer to the Wentworth we seek.

Your devoted son,
Campbell

THIS TIME A PHOTO WAS INCLUDED.

The two men wore brown, vested suits, thin ties, and slender jackets. They sat next to one another on a park bench with an early version of The Metropolitan Museum of Art in the background. The slightly haunted, vacant expression that plagued all people in antique photos now reflected on their faces as well.

My heart ached. I traced their faces with my fingertips. It was my first visit with them in over twenty years.

There's something very special about connecting with someone who loved you when you were a child. They forever hold a tender, trustworthy place in your heart. The very roots of your identity can be traced to the way they used to see you.

My father's and grandfather's belief in me was like a

balloon that lifted me over almost any trouble I encountered. Except, perhaps, their absence. They were the basis for my hope for the future, and through their eyes I felt I could do anything.

For a moment I was back in their world, my tiny hand in the middle of theirs, and the world around me a safe and comfortable place.

When their 1920s world came into focus, I didn't feel the strength they used to share with me. Instead, it felt as though they were soldiers in a battle. They emanated a weighty hopelessness of being stuck, a despair over the loss of their family, and the fear of being only a memory, long before their death.

My once ever-positive father and grandfather appeared to be losing the very spirit that we all had relied on so heavily.

I picked up a pen and a new sheet of notepaper from my grandfather's desk, then stopped and wondered if a note from me might worry them even more. What if they had an agreement with Grace that Lexie and I wasn't to know where they were or how they got there? I wanted to ease their loneliness, not create new worries.

Then I ran upstairs, tiptoed past Lexie's closed door, where three of the Montgomery women held court about Lex's current predicament, and grabbed my purse from the floor of my room. Inside was a photo Grace had taken of Blake and me when we arrived.

*Dear Daddy & Grandaddy,*

*You just can't imagine how long I've waited to see your faces and to correspond with you both. Grace has told us everything. Reluctantly, and under duress. Please don't worry. We under-*

*stand how dangerous the path is and we won't try anything stupid.*

*All is well here. We pray for your safe return.*

*Enclosed is a photo of someone I hope to introduce you to very soon.*

*With all my love,*

*Addie*


I FOLDED the note around the picture, sealed it with a kiss.

Then I wondered. What if there was only a certain time when the letters could be transported? What if that's why I saw Grace retrieving the letters in the middle of the night? And if they were in New York, how did the letter get to Savannah?

Grace would kill me if I screwed something up .

I decided I'd ask Grace how it worked before I tried it. Surely, she wouldn't say no to a letter. Not now that so much was out in the open.

I left both letters and the photos on my grandfather's desk and sat in his leather chair. I rubbed my hands over the memories in the rich cherry wood of his desk, and found the one of our last meeting together. There I sat, the essence of childhood summer, cross-legged on the flat of his desk. Pig-tails, white eyelet halter top, rolled up jean shorts, and lightly skinned knees. There was a trace of chocolate ice cream at the corner of my mouth and a serious focus on the hand I'd been dealt.

"Go fish," my grandfather says.

"Argh!" I say and draw from the deck.

His eyes twinkle and he laughs. "You always were the serious one," he says. "That's a sign of intelligence, you know. Give me all your whales."

"Go fish. I'm not as smart as Lexie. She gets better test scores than I do," I say. "Give me all your lobsters."

My grandfather lays down two large cards with bright red lobsters on them. I snatch them up like I've found gold.

"Eh, smarts don't come in only one kind of package. Intelligence can't be measured in only one way. *You* are smart, my princess. What about your gifts?" he asks, and cradles my cheek in his palm. "That is a very special intelligence, yes?"

I lean into his comforting touch and place my hand over his. Two of my fingers touch his watch, and visions of Vermeer's *The Concert* materialize in my mind.

"Oh, Grandpa, you have new art," I say, and watch him and Otto carry the frameless pieces into a small, vacant room. "It's *so* beautiful. Isn't that Vermeer? Can I read it for you? How did you get a Vermeer?" I stare at him with innocent curiosity.

My grandfather pulls his hand away. I feel him wage war with a flood of anger, but it shoots through me anyway.

I jump off the desk and step away.

"I'm sorry," I say. "I'm sorry." I stand at the side of his office, afraid to move and wanting to run.

He stands and runs his hand across his face. "It's okay, Addie-belle. Let's forget about it, okay?" He walks over to me and hesitates before he put his arms around me. Through the uncomfortable distance that widens between us, I stare at his expression.

"You've...you've done something you weren't supposed to," I say while I feel the guilt beneath his anger. "This is the Vermeer, and the other paintings they talked about at school. Someone stole them from that museum in Boston. You stole these paintings," I say and step away from him.

He turns in a circle with his hand over his mouth, then he lunges toward me and grips the outside of my shoulders.

"Addie, I need you to pretend you didn't see this, okay? This is very important." He shakes my shoulders once, and too hard. "Otherwise, something very bad could happen to me. You wouldn't want that, would you? If anyone finds out, I would have to leave for a very long time. Do you want your grandfather taken away?"

I shake my head and lean away.

"I'm going to make sure the museum gets them back," he says. "I promise. Okay? I'll take care of it. Just forget that you ever saw this."

I lifted my hand from the desk.

"Reliving old memories?" Grace leaned against the open doorway.

## 35

U ncovering Carolena's secrets had become his most unwelcome chore in life.

She refused to reveal her secrets willingly, insisting instead that they were better left dead and buried.

Blake's warrior mind didn't see her quiet secrets as a favor. He knew they were threats that lay in wait.

"Nothing like having a near stranger tell you about a secret your mother has been hiding from you all of your life," Blake said.

"What are you talking about?" Carolena scolded.

"I'm talking about a gift that you gave Otto that he used —" He dropped the phone to his side. "I can't believe I'm saying this," he mumbled, then lifted the phone to his ear again.

"What gift?" Carolena asked.

"You gave Otto a painting that has a special ability…"

"What about *this painting*?" she snapped.

"Otto didn't kill John and Campbell. And he's not hiding them. He sent them back in time through this Wentworth you gave him," Blake said.

"Oh, no," she said breathlessly.

"So this is real?" Blake asked, even though he knew the answer. He wanted to hear her say it.

She didn't.

"I remember the stories you told me when I was a child —about how certain pieces of art could transport you to another place and time. I thought you were speaking metaphorically."

"I was. And yet, the Wentworths are more than that."

"This gift that you gave him wrecked Addie's family."

"Blake...I'm so sorry. Je suis désolé, mon amour..." she whispered.

"Why didn't you tell me?" he asked.

"How did you find out?"

"Grace," he said. "Addie said she found proof of John and Campbell's existence, and eventually, Grace had no choice but to tell us. Of all the people in the world who shouldn't have something like this." Blake flexed his fist. "Is it real?"

Carolena exhaled long and slow. Her breath brushed across the phone and sounded like static. "Yes. It's real."

"Then why didn't you tell me?"

"Because I was concerned you would try to change the past as it related to Otto or Addie. And it's very dangerous to meddle with the past. You could destroy your present or your future."

The gravel crunched under Blake's feet when he paced. He picked up one of the rocks, rolled it between his fingers.

"Still, I should have known," he said without much conviction. Because she might have been right. He didn't know if he would trust himself with access to such a painting. The temptation to go back in time and kill Otto would have been too sweet to resist. "Were you ever going to tell me?"

"Doubtful," she said. "I hoped that he had lost it. Destroyed it. Or maybe that someone had taken it from him."

"Did you know that Otto used the painting to send John and Campbell away?" Blake hated that he had to ask, but Carolena rarely answered an unasked question.

"Non," she said. "I wondered, but non."

Blake threw the rock at an oak at the far end of the drive. "Why did you give him such a thing?"

"It wasn't a gift, Blake."

"You gave it to him," Blake said.

"I—sort of. Why do you need to know this? What difference does it make now that I can't do anything about it?"

"Because I'd rather not be blindsided by any more of your secrets. You gave a painting to a criminal, who then used it as a weapon to destroy the family of the woman I love. Not to mention the damage that their disappearance has done to every woman in this family—especially Addie. If that woman ever fully trusts a man again in this lifetime it will be no small miracle!" Blake paced halfway around the circular drive and stared down the main thoroughfare.

"It's not enough that I have to protect her from my father, but my mother, and all of her secrets, too?" He felt a disconnect and checked his phone to make sure she hadn't yet hung up. He breathed the cold air deeply, and felt the burn in his lungs.

When she still didn't say anything, he knew he'd gone too far. He squeezed his eyes shut "I'm sorry, Maman."

There was no response. So he opened his eyes and waited.

"It wasn't a gift," she finally said.

"How did you get it?"

"Why do you need to know this?"

"Because Addie is hell-bent on her father's and grandfather's safe return. There are other paintings out there like the one that Otto has, and I need to do something to make this right for them."

"You can't go through the paintings, Blake. They are much too dangerous."

"Do you know where these paintings are?" he asked.

"I know enough about them to know that they do not offer a safe passage," she said. "Because—"

"Because why?"

"Because I taught Otto too much about this type of thing. If he wanted to make it difficult or even deadly for someone else who traveled behind him, he could. There are ways to manipulate the elements in the painting. You can create traps, someone could die."

"Carolena..."

"Blake, for that very reason you can't—"

"If there's another Wentworth out there, we will have to, Maman. I know Addie and she'll not give up on this, no matter what I say. Not to mention that Grace and Isabella will continue to try to help them."

"I see," she said. "Then we have to hope that Otto has lost access to the Wentworth he used to have, or that he forgot what I taught him about manipulating the paintings."

"Why would you teach him such a thing?" Traces of his fury bled into the air and he knew he'd regret it later.

"It was more of an experiment. I didn't know it was possible until I tried it. Plus, he was different then. *I* was different then." She sighed, sounding exhausted when she said it.

"Tell me how you got the painting," Blake said. "So we can try to find one of the others."

He heard the sound of wine being poured into a glass.

"When I worked at The Metropolitan Museum of Art, the Wentworth was one of the items he pushed me to steal." Her voice sagged. "I had access to all of the collections, including the ones in the basement. No one at the museum really knew what they had down there. They thought the Wentworths were just pretty watercolors from another talented, dead artist. The public doesn't know, but the Met only displays about ten-percent of its holdings. The other ninety-percent is hidden away in their many basements and storage areas. It's not unusual for pieces, even priceless pieces, to go missing. He wasn't that well known, his art was never publicly displayed, and no one missed them when they were gone."

"Does he have the others that are in the series?"

"No." She sounded relieved. "Just the one, as far as I know."

Blake dragged a hand through his thick hair.

"I don't think the Met has any of the others, but I don't know for certain. If I had to guess where the others were I'd say private ownership."

"Meaning, they traveled along the black market?"

"Maybe. Does Grace know where John and Campbell are? Exactly?"

"New York City, 1920. Same month and day as our time. She's found a way to communicate with them. Where did Otto keep the Wentworth?"

"Blake, no—"

"If he has the power to change the present or the future, he could destroy our lives all over again. Especially now that Addie has pushed him away altogether, he might go back in time and kidnap her or keep us from meeting. He could kill her grandfather and keep her from even being born. Someone has to stop him."

"I don't know that anyone ever will."

"If I can find out where the Wentworth is, I'll take that away from him."

"He used to keep it in his office, right on the wall. Only a few of us really knew what it was and what it was capable of. I don't know what happened to it after I left."

"It wasn't in his office when I was at the firm." Blake stood in front of the Montgomery mansion, the Southern winter wind swirled around him and chilled him. He had the unmistakeable feeling that Carolena was hiding more, which meant he wouldn't be able to protect her the way he wanted.

"I'll do whatever is in my power to make this right with Addie and her family," Carolena said.

"No, don't do anything. I'll fix it." Blake said.

"Je t'aime, Blake."

"Je t'aime, Maman."

## 36

"Grandpa did the Gardner heist with Otto?" My hand was frozen mid-air, I wasn't ready to touch anything else.

"Addie..." Grace walked toward me, then sat on the edge of my grandfather's desk. Her eyes drifted to the letter and picture I'd taken from the book. "It's a hard day when we grow up and realize those we love aren't entirely who we thought them to be."

I felt the truth tilt my world into a devastating kind of perfect sense.

Grace put her hand on the desk in front of me. "I'm sorry, sweetheart."

Tears of shock and release welled up. "My grandfather is an art thief."

Grace patted my hand three times. "It wasn't planned. Not really." she moved to the edge of one of the green upholstered chairs across from the desk. "It began as an innocent discussion between Otto and John about how museums didn't invest in the security they should, how easy it would be for someone to break in and steal priceless works of art. And get away with it. Then one night they just did it. Completely impromptu."

"Why?" I asked.

"I asked John the same question. After the fact. I didn't know he was going to pull such a stupid stunt." She stood, and dragged her fingertips across my grandfather's desk.

"Not that I could have stopped him. He said they had stolen the art to teach the museum a lesson on how important security was. They were supposed to leave clues as to where the police could find the art. Unharmed, of course. Then, as the plan went, the museum would invest in additional security. John and Otto would have done their good deed for the century," Grace said.

"Did you believe him?" I asked.

Grace's lips thinned into a frustrated flat line. "I've known John for a long time. And if I were going to be honest, I'd say that he wanted to own one of those masterpieces even if it were just for a short time. I think he did plan to return the pieces to the museum."

I agreed with a nod.

"But, once two people commit a crime together, everything changes. Otto wanted to hang on to the art. So he told John that it was too dangerous to return it, that the heist had become a media obsession and they might get caught if they tried.

"John was firm that the art needed to be returned to the museum. He tried to convince Otto that if they played it right, they could return the art and collect the five million in reward money. It wasn't long after that that John and Campbell disappeared."

"Did Dad have anything to do with—?"

"No. But Otto thought John and Campbell might expose

him. So he condemned him to the past." Grace stared out the window.

The energy from the corner of the desk grabbed at my attention, and I eyed the spot where I'd seen a part of my grandfather I hadn't wanted to see. "I was nine when they left, That was about the time—"

"That was the year you began trying *not* to see," Grace said. "And I've spent your entire life trying to talk you out of doing that. There was just no convincing you."

"I was afraid I would see something else I didn't want to see. Something that would incriminate someone I cared about," I said. "How is it that he's the one who did something wrong and I'm the one who felt guilty for seeing it?"

Grace clicked her tongue and sighed. "Love is a faulty process."

"All these years you've pushed me so hard to use my gifts—"

"I didn't want you to make seeing a fault. I guess I tried too hard, and I'm sorry. No one lets go of their fears just because they should."

My insight and her empathy gave wings to the years of fear and resistance within, and my heart grew wider, became lighter. Decades of guilt tumbled away with these realizations. I felt oddly free, like the secret was no longer mine to keep.

Bits of my past and present knitted comfortably into one, and finally, no longer fought one another for control.

Grace ran her hand along the outer lines of my face and looked at me like she always had—like I was the one she needed to work extra hard to help. I understood that now as a kindness, not a criticism.

"All this time, I thought you didn't have any faith in me."

Grace wiped the tears from my cheeks, then held me

close. Like she had when I was young. "My sweet girl. I pray that one day, you will know how much faith I have in you. Because it will lift your soul for the rest of your days."

She kissed me on the forehead, then blessed me with her triple pat.

When she walked to the other side of the room, I saw Blake standing in the entryway of my grandfather's office. His smile slowly widened.

"I have one more thing to show you," Grace said.

## 37

Grace opened one of the heavy, double wooden doors to her bedroom and it creaked. It was impressive. Not the canopied four poster bed with all of its textured upholstery, and not even the outright size of the room, with its grandeur overlooking the picturesque sound.

No, it was the sheer volume of framed photographs around the room. They covered the walls from waist to ceiling, while others were gathered on tables and atop the mantle. All of them black-and-white imprints of my father and grandfather.

"These are a few of my favorites from what they've sent me over the years. There are countless others I've placed in photo books."

"Unbelievable." I walked around the room and looked into the eyes of the men who were lost in time.

Blake inspected a different set of photos against the nearest wall and shook his head in disbelief.

"John or Campbell will send me a letter and a photo or two every few months. Sometimes more frequently. It just depends how often they can get to Savannah. I've seen snap-shots from most of their travels. They've met quite a few interesting people. Then again, so have I," she said. "Knowing where someone will be in advance always helps."

Most of the photos were taken in Paris and New York, though several were shot right in front of the Montgomery mansion. My grandfather and father stood next to a tall, slender man in a white suit with a shock of thick, dark hair.

"Is this—"

"This is your great-great-grandfather. Horace Camp-bell." Grace smiled like she'd just seen an old friend. Blake peeked over my shoulder at the print.

"He's the one who purchased this property," Grace said. "And the Fitzgerald books."

My mouth must have hung open because she smiled. "It has something to do with the fact that the books sit in the same place now as they did then. They're sentries to the passing of time."

"Did F. Scott Fitzgerald actually endorse that book to you?" I asked.

Grace smiled and nodded. "Such a gem of a fellow. Unless he's drinking." Her eyes widened with the pleasure of another story yet to tell.

"Did you say books? As in plural?" I asked.

Grace put the photo of our relative back on the shelf and adjusted it into its exact same spot.

"Yes, there are two more. One in New York, the other in Paris."

"In New York..." I repeated. "At the firm?"

"No." She walked past me, then bent at the waist and visited with a few more memories in print. I followed her. "At your grandfather's townhome. On the bookshelf in the library." Grace winked at me. "Now you know why I allowed you to stay there only after you agreed not to move any of his things."

"I never knew." My mouth fell open again.

She walked to a new set of photographs where her husband and son wore white surgical masks.

"Why are they wearing masks?" I asked.

"This was New York in 1918, beginning of the flu pandemic," she said. "20,000 people died in New York between September of that year and November of the following year. John and your father were on their way out of town for a while."

"Good thing they knew their history," Blake said.

"Mmm-hmmm. And Isabella and I have helped." She pointed to a new photograph.

"Is that The Plaza?" Blake asked.

I looked over his shoulder and saw my father and grandfather in front of The Plaza Hotel in New York.

"That's where they're staying," she said. "I don't know if they're still there. I think they were trying to purchase the condo."

"It looks exactly the same then as it does now," he said.

"Here they are in Cincinnati at the 1919 World Series," Grace said, and tsked her disapproval. "Do you keep up with baseball, Blake?"

"I do know about this World Series."

My father and grandfather stood side by side in the uncovered stadium, the end of a Coca-Cola sign in the background.

"The Black Sox Scandal," I said. "Wow, to see *that* firsthand."

"They've made a lot of money on sports gambling. It was illegal back then, but people still did it," Grace said.

"Here they are at game four of the series in Chicago."

She pointed to another photo where my father and grandfather stood with a third man, who wore a white fedora.

"Otto," I choked on his name. "That's Otto."

"No, honey. Otto's not in any of these photos," Grace said and she angled her head toward the photo I pointed to. "That's Gary. Some no-good scoundrel John met at a party just before they left New York.

"John found a couple of pieces for him to move—you know he's making money however he can. Not that he didn't already have a taste for the underworld." Grace squinted at the photo. "I think Gary found them a betting connection, too. Somehow he was tied into that Black Sox Scandal. Never liked him." She twisted her pearls and they clicked.

"That's...Otto. That's who he used to be. In—in that lifetime." My heart rate sped.

"Otto and Addie and I shared a difficult past life together in the twenties," Blake said. "Addie has seen that Otto and Gary are the same person."

Grace swallowed hard. "You're certain?"

"I have no doubt."

"I have to write a letter." Grace dashed out of the room.

## 38

Blake and I walked to the pier behind the house.

The young Civil War soldier in the gray uniform ran in front of us, cocked his rifle under his arm and took aim at some unseen enemy.

"Down!" he yelled to us.

We moved to the side and let him pass.

The soldier flopped on his belly and began shooting. His gun was surprisingly loud, and I placed my hands over my ears.

Blake wrapped his arm around me and we watched the soldier disappear. "Never a dull moment," he said with a warm smile.

I relaxed into the embrace of the only man who had ever fully understood me and loved me because of who I was. Not counting, of course, my father and grandfather.

Then I closed my eyes and braced myself for the crippling worry that came next. It was the follow-up act to my realization of Blake's abiding love, that I would be without him someday, that the abandonment was inevitable—as it was for every woman in my family.

The worry was, in part and as Blake had suggested, a past life hangover.

But then I remembered. My father and grandfather were alive.

I turned to Blake and I watched a new light thread between his heart and mine—it was the infinity symbol.

As if he'd seen it, too, Blake tipped my chin and he kissed me. He kissed me like forever was ours to enjoy, like now was all we had.

"This is not quite the visit I thought it would be," I said. The wind stirred the water into waves and turned the leaves bottom side up. A storm was coming.

"Me, either," Blake said.

Hand in hand, we walked to the large water oak and I sat in my childhood swing. Blake leaned against the tree trunk. I sat on the swing and coasted gently. It was a thick piece of birch that my father had lovingly sanded all those years ago.

The scene in front of me was.a familiar one—sparkled sunshine on choppy waters, and I felt eight again—ensconced in my perfect world, oblivious to the threats that once laid ahead.

I lifted my feet, tugged on the ropes, and swung forward into the breeze. "I thought by now I would be on my way to William's office with Grace and Isabella's blessing, about to find my father and grandfather again. As well as the Gardner art."

"With or without your red cape?" Blake said.

I raised an eyebrow and kept swinging. The toes of my black boots lifted over the horizon.

"I probably should have guessed that there was a catch since Otto was involved."

A pang of regret zinged through me. I'd thought I could right the wrong of my father's and grandfather's absence.

"I don't think either of us could have guessed what that catch was," he said.

"No. But, we can still try to help them. We know it's possible. We just have to find another Wentworth to get them here.

I watched the Civil War soldier sit on the grassy bank, several yards from Blake and me. My swing slowed and I dug my heels in the soft dirt. "We either have to hire someone to find Otto's Wentworth, or we have to find one of the other ones. They're the only way."

"Remember what Grace said, that even with a Wentworth, the trip wouldn't be without its dangers. Carolena said the same thing when I called her this morning."

"Couldn't Carolena get us through the painting? She's obviously done it before," I said.

Blake nodded slowly.

"Or maybe you don't want her to do that since Otto may still have one," I said. "I mean, could we run into him somewhere along the way if we were all traveling at the same time?"

"I have no idea. She did say that Otto could lay traps in the Wentworth to stop another traveller. Maybe even kill them. She also said that she wanted to do whatever she could to make this up to you and your family. She feels responsible for what happened to John and Campbell."

I shook my head. "I don't blame her for this. I blame Otto, but not her."

Blake nodded. The grimace on his face told me he blamed both his parents for what happened to my family.

"Did she say where the rest of the Wentworths might be?"

"She said she found the one in the basement of the Met. She doesn't know where the others are. Black market or private ownership, most likely. William could have some old files on stolen art that might offer some leads." Blake broke a small piece from a twig and pitched it to the ground. "And Otto isn't that young. The life he leads isn't conducive to old age, and the company he keeps is pretty shady, so maybe he'll be gone soon."

"One can only hope," I said. I tore my eyes away from the mesmerizing currents in the water. Blake rounded the swing and stood in front of me.

"Come on." He extended his hand to escort me and we strolled down to the water.

The water lapped against the edges of the wooden pier.

Blake and I encircled our arms around one another. Cold breezes tumbled over the warm when they reached the shore, a sign that change was afoot. An interloper on the status quo.

I turned and looked at the idyllic home that had taken care of our Montgomery clan for over a century. There seemed to be a yellow aura around the edge of it. "It still seems strong in spite of everything our family has been through."

Blake turned his sight toward our homestead, then kissed the top of my head.

"I know you'll miss it while we're gone," he said. "We'll return when it's safe."

I tried not to think about who else might not be here when we returned. "By then it could be...different."

"We'll be the constant amidst any change. And maybe our sojourn won't take as long as you think. This could all just work out better than we imagine." He stroked his thumb against the upper part of my back.

"You're right," I said. "In fact, that's the 'what if' I should ask every day. What if this all just works out?"

"Speaking of what-ifs, what were the chances that my grandfather and past-life Otto would meet? They must be infinitesimal. And what impact does that have on our present? They shouldn't have met then."

"Hopefully nothing," he said simply. "Hopefully he'll distance himself from Gary as soon as he reads Grace's letter."

Noisy, nit-picky doubts knocked at my brain. I chose not to tell Blake about them. Maybe he was right. Maybe this would all just work out. It could, after all.

## 39

I t was his fifth time to the once-bricked room.

Finally, the heavy metal end of the sledgehammer shot through the brick and the man with the black baseball hat was finally at his goal. He felt a smile spread across his face.

He swung the sledgehammer twice more to knock out a sizable entryway for himself. Not that he could walk through it at his height, but the opening was large enough for him to remove what he'd come for.

The room inside was not barren like the rest of the vacant space that surrounded it. Rather, it was arranged like a small living room, complete with a fireplace and mantel, an upholstered chair and couch, and a side table between them. A square frame with its edges jeweled in blue glass sat next to a lamp with a stained glass shade. He stared for a moment at the couple whose wedding day was captured on the imprint, and in a room that was very much like the one he was standing in.

Her veil cascaded past her feet—she was a true vision.

But the possessive gleam in the eyes of her groom ruined everything. It was a look he knew all too well. One he'd seen too many times to count.

He placed the frame back into perfect alignment with its dusty outline on the table then searched the room for the item he needed. He searched the walls for any sign that might reveal a hidden compartment and his shoes squeaked against the cement floor.

*Nothing.*

Then he cocked his head slightly when he noticed the framed mariner's scene that hung above the mantle.

He lifted the painting from its nail, and felt the wall behind it. It was not the false front he hoped it would be. He sat on the edge of the two-cushion couch and searched the room for anything he might have missed.

*Nothing.*

He inspected the couch beneath him. Bounced a couple of times on what he thought was the most uncomfortable piece of furniture he'd ever sat on. He stood and lifted the cushion.

There it was, in silver shining glory, with a black dial buried in the center. The safe. It wasn't very thick but it was plenty long enough to hold what he searched for.

He had long ago guessed the combination. It was the same code he'd seen used as a passcode on many security options: her birthdate. With each turn of the dial he felt a tiny, victorious click. On the final click, the latch on the door released.

The painting inside was an unframed oil on canvas. The artistic value alone was worth millions, but the Wentworth signature in the lower right hand corner made it priceless.

He took the painting and placed it on the mantel. He

was almost ready—he just needed to call a friend to help cover his tracks by hiding the painting after he left. Not that he ever cared about coming back—he'd dreamed for years of his escape. Now, before he left, he had one last thing he had to do.

## 40

B lake's pilot kept us flying above the sporadic storms that battered the eastern seaboard. Blake worked on his laptop while I stared out the window and thought about everything I'd learned over the past few days.

I had hope we could help my father and grandfather. Between the five of us I thought we could find at least one of the Wentworths.

When we went into the Wentworth, I would miss my family, especially Lex, who had chosen to stay in Savannah for a while longer. Thanks to Otto, and on Grace's advice, Lexie cancelled her long-awaited show. She couldn't be certain what Todd's sister knew of the footage, or even if she were in on Todd's scheme. The date of Alexa's show was rapidly approaching and Piper hadn't yet contacted Alexa about progress on her pieces or potential attendees, as was the custom before a show. There was only quiet disinterest.

Grace suggested Lexie leave New York altogether and move back home. Lex considered it. I encouraged it. She needed Grace's protection. No one needed to be that close to Otto.

I leaned onto Blake's shoulder and felt the muscles in his arm tense.

He glared at his laptop screen. "Our flight to Paris is postponed until tomorrow. Bad weather in Boston." He got up and walked to the cockpit.

Adrenaline chilled inside of my stomach.

"Can we turn around or land somewhere else?" I asked when Blake took his seat again.

"We're going to reroute to New York." The hollow sound of thunder drummed around the plane. "International flights are still running there." Blake gave me a smile that was intended to comfort, but his jaw muscles worked.

"I really don't want to be that close to Otto," I said.

"We'll never leave the airport, and we'll only be there a short while to change planes. He has no way of knowing that we'll be there."

I picked up a magazine and mindlessly flipped the pages until we landed in New York.

The pilot walked down the aisle, smiling a reticent friendly-sky smile. His hands stayed in his pockets. "The airport isn't allowing any flights to take off until morning. They're playing it safe with the weather. Your next flight is delayed."

"Any idea how long of a delay we're looking at?"

"They're saying five to six hours. But I don't think you'll take off before morning."

Blake nodded. The pilot did as well and disappeared into the cockpit.

"A short delay. We'll find a hotel and we'll stay out of sight," Blake said.

"We should stay somewhere close to the airport, and someplace Otto wouldn't think to check for us," I said.

When the plane began its descent, Blake took two dark

baseball caps from his bag and handed me one of them. "Put this on with your sunglasses. Tuck the length of your hair into your jacket."

"Won't wearing sunglasses at night make us look suspicious?" I twisted three lengths of my hair into a low, braided ponytail.

"The less people see of our faces, the better." He pulled the cap low on his forehead.

"Wait," I said. Fear traveled through my nervous system. I held onto Blake's arm.

"What's the matter?" he asked.

"No, just— Something's wrong." A sick, nauseated feeling crept to my throat. The kind of feeling that told me our perfect plan had jumped the tracks. I tried to calm myself and took a deep breath, but calm wouldn't come.

"Addie—"

I shook my head. "I just need to calm down." I felt like we were flying down white water rapids with no safe way to get off the boat.

Blake leaned close to me. "What do you see?"

"I don't know, specifically." I tried to make sense of everything my body knew but my brain didn't. "But something's not right."

Blake went to his laptop and sent a message to Carolena:

*Might be nothing. Or Otto might be on to us. Bad weather. Can't fly out tonight. Watch for my or Addie's call.*

Then he sent the same message to William.

"What's this?" I squinted at his laptop screen.

"I'm lining up support for one or the both of us in case you're right."

The thought of something happening to Blake, made me feel worse. Memories of Jack's death were thick and present. Like they were about to repeat.

Blake reached into his briefcase, tore off a small piece of paper, and wrote something on it.

"Here." He handed it to me. "These are Carolena's and William's phone numbers." He folded the scrap until it was the size of the head of a thumbtack. "Put this inside your sock. If you're caught they'll likely take away your phone and search your pockets, but they won't search inside your socks."

I took the paper. I slipped my foot out of my black boot, slipped the sock off, and stuck the miniature note between my big and second toe.

"What about you?" I put my sock and boot back on.

"I have the numbers memorized."

I felt inexplicably afraid, and I couldn't figure where it was coming from. Maybe it was the result of being in the same town as Otto again. Or maybe it was because we were so close to getting away. Or maybe I'd never feel completely unguarded and relaxed for as long as Otto hunted for us. It didn't matter.

"We need to call William. Something doesn't feel right, I can't shake it," I said.

## 41

We stepped into the bitter cold and a flood of tiny white flakes blew around us.

The airport lights shone bright. I flipped my coat collar up to further hide my face.

"William is sending two men to guard us at the hotel. They'll stay with us until our next flight leaves."

I sighed relief. "Thank you."

Blake took out his phone and dialed a number. "Thomas. We're here. We'll meet you on the side entrance."

"Thomas?" I asked.

"I'm shutting the gallery down while I'm gone. There are several papers to sign. I could do it electronically. But I don't want any trails to our new location." He searched the sparsely populated lobby of the private airport, and the ceiling lights reflected off of his sunglasses. I still wasn't sure if the glasses brought more attention to us, or less, as Blake had suggested.

Blake placed his hand on my back and urged me along. We walked at a hurried pace toward the side door of the airport.

Thomas stopped the limo next to the curb and popped the trunk. He and Blake tossed our bags inside and we sped off. The snow fell faster now, the tires spun on the ice, and I didn't think we would be up in the air a few hours from now. I looked behind us twice. We were no longer in public view, and no one was following us. I could relax now.

At least in theory.

My chest still held too much anxiety and the sight of Thomas did nothing to alleviate it.

I had never felt comfortable with Thomas. I placed my hand on the seat back in front of me to get a read on him. But there was too much cushion and divider and I couldn't get anything.

"Everything okay back there?" Thomas asked.

Blake turned to me, his features were hard and fierce.

"Yeah, Addie's—"

I shook my head no. "I'm just tired," I said. "Long day."

"Well, you'll rest as soon as I get you to the Four Seasons. Blake, the documents you needed are in that envelope back there," Thomas said.

"We're not going to the Four Seasons. Take us to that new hotel around the corner instead," Blake said.

"Not the Four Seasons?" he asked.

"No," I said in a tone that silenced Thomas. And to make sure he stayed that way, I reached across Blake's lap to the control panel on his armrest and pushed the button that raised the partition between us.

"I don't trust him," I whispered. "He's always unnerved me."

"Thomas?" Blake asked.

"Always," I said.

Doubt misted across Blake's face.

I couldn't put my finger on what bothered me. But what I felt was enough to make me question him.

"He's an old friend," Blake whispered. "He' stood by me for half of his life. He knows about Otto."

I shrugged.

Blake signed several pages from the stack that Thomas had left for him. One collection of stapled papers contained photos of two paintings by Canaletto. They had been left to Blake by a friend of his mother's and kept in a vault at his gallery.

"Where are those going?" I asked.

"Nowhere. Unless something happens to me. Then they go to you." Blake continued to scrawl across the signature line.

I focused on the drops of snow on the window to find some equilibrium. "I don't want the Canalettos," I said.

Heat poured from the vents. Blake put the pen down, smiled and wrapped his arms around me. His blue eyes glowed in the hue of an outside light and I realized that the car wasn't moving anymore. I looked out the darkened window and expected to see an illuminated hotel sign. Instead there was only the sparse lighting of the garage.

Thomas knocked on the divider and Blake lowered it.

"We're here," Thomas said without turning around.

We surveyed the garage with caution.

"Where are they?" I asked.

Blake texted and stared at his phone screen. "Inside," he finally said.

With a loud ding, the elevator door opened in the distance and a young couple exited. They walked toward a row of cars against the far wall.

I couldn't decide if I would have felt more comfortable entering the hotel through the bustling lobby. We would have run the risk of being seen, but the near-empty garage left me feeling exposed.

I ducked under the long strap of my cross-body bag and adjusted it on my shoulder.

Blake stepped out first, searched the surroundings again, then gestured for me to get out of the car.

The chill in the garage was sharp in contrast to the warmth of the car and Blake's embrace. Thomas lifted our bags from the trunk and raised the handles for us. He grabbed a gun from the front seat, cocked open the chamber, showed Blake it was loaded, and handed it to him.

"I'll be in touch," Blake said in a low voice. He tucked the weapon into his waistband and we moved toward the elevator.

WE TRAVELED through the hotel passageways like spies, never once taking for granted the apparent emptiness of a hallway or elevator lobby. When we arrived in our room Blake made me wait at the open door with one FBI agent, while he and the other agent checked for unwelcome visitors. Then they traced lampshades and picked up vases and searched for listening devices.

When everyone was convinced we were alone in the room, the agents took their posts outside our door. Blake shut and locked the door behind us, and placed his gun on the bedside table. I stood in the shallow foyer with the suitcases, a strange mix of angst and excitement coursing through me. How did you live a life under constant threat? Would our every entry into a new place begin the same way?

He lugged and organized our suitcases, checked the flight schedule with the pilot, then sent a text to William.

Like most men he was his most confident when he was fully in control. I realized that not only did he need to be in the lead to protect us, but that it served him somehow. Fed him. Like not doing it was unfulfilling, weakening.

The presence of the two agents made me feel safe, though I knew we had no guarantees. Today was all we had. Grace and Isabella had been right about that.

Suddenly I could relate to every ghost I'd ever met. If I resented the past and was afraid of the future, then I was a ghost myself. Suffering in a state of neither fully here nor there.

## 42

E xhausted, we settled onto the bed, Blake's arm cradled me behind the neck and I examined his hand. His nail beds were nearly the exact same shape as I remembered my father's. I ran my finger against the edges of their short, clipped length, then kissed them.

Though the heater was on in the room, it rattled and struggled to fully warm the room. I curled against Blake's chest. His heart beat was regular and strong against my cheek.

"Not exactly what we're used to." Blake studied the room that had clearly been designed for guests with long layovers, cancelled flights or extramarital interests. From his vantage point on the bed he could see everything but the door, a flaw I knew he hated.

The hotel wasn't that old but desperation from previous guests had already seeped into the walls. I hoped we could leave soon The snow had stopped. Hopefully de-icing had begun.

The text alarm on Blake's phone beeped and he glanced at the screen.

"Flights resume at 8 a.m." He said it casually. Factually. Though I caught his slight grimace.

"That's later than we'd like, isn't it?"

"Yeah." He put the phone down and rolled toward me, his head rested against his fist.

His mouth touched mine, his tongue gently seeking. He tasted of his own piquant flavor that reminded me of honey and red wine.

He jerked away and stilled.

"What—"

He shook his head, shushed me, and reached for his gun.

I sent my awareness into the hallway, expected to find the two FBI agents who were outside our door, but instead I felt the absence of them.

The door lock clicked.

Blake pushed me off the far side of the bed. I hit the floor.

The door bounced off of the wall with a bang.

Several shots rang out and someone fell to the floor.

"We meet again," a voice said, cold and vapid. "Put the gun down."

"I don't think so," Blake said.

"My orders were to take you alive. I don't have to. The only one I have to take alive is her."

I peeked over the edge of the bed and saw Blake, belly down on the bed with his gun aimed into the small, dark hallway that led to the door. I hunched behind the bed and tried to think of the right next move.

I felt Blake push the hidden gunman energetically.

Three more shots rang out.

"Argh," Blake grunted.

Then a thud.

I stood halfway.

Blake scrambled toward the floor and the man pointed his gun at him. "Leave it."

The man shot his eyes toward me. His lips spread into a wicked smile.

The man shifted his eyes to Blake.

"Back away." His voice was flat.

Blake lifted himself fully onto the bed. He held his left arm and blood drained through his fingers. I rushed toward him and the man pointed his gun at me.

"Easy," he warned. The man kicked Blake's gun toward the far wall with his scuff-marked shoes. Then he picked it up, and put it in the waistband of his jeans.

"I'm just going to help him." My hands shook in the air.

The gunman's head shook back and forth. He moved slowly.

"No—"

"You want her to help me." Blake pushed the gunman.

The air in the room shifted and the gunman's resistance relaxed. He seemed none the wiser about his sudden cooperativeness, but I moved cautiously, just in case.

"What a pretty sight," the man said to me.

I recognized him as the dark-haired half of Otto's pair who confronted us in Blake's gallery.

Blake backed in my direction. He stood between me and the gunman and I peeled his hand away so I could examine his arm. Bright red liquid slid down the front and back of his arm and down his torso. The scent of his blood, the burnt air of gunshot, and the stale molded odor of the hotel room filled my nose.

"There's an exit wound," I whispered to Blake. "I think the bullet is out."

He lifted his arm and inspected the hole in the back of it.

He steadied himself on the bed with his other arm. Dizziness, I expected.

I forced him to sit while I ripped at the white sheets and managed several long strips.

The gunman's high cheekbones rose up with his grin and his dark eyes brimmed with malice.

"Hurry up." He waved the gun at me.

"I don't know what I'm doing," I said softly to Blake, and wrapped the lengths of white fabric around him.

"Right now we just want to stop the bleeding. Wrap it tighter."

He groaned when I did. His breath was faster than normal, and I tried to remember the signs of shock.

"What about infection?" I kept my voice low, and lightly caressed the fabric that attempted to hold his skin together.

Blake didn't answer. There was no answer. Wherever we were about to go I was sure it wasn't the emergency room. His blood oozed through the torn sheets, and I felt our life together slipping away.

"Blake, it's not working." My eyes welled up.

"Wrap it again," he said. I redressed Blake's wounds with white washcloths over the entry and the exit sites this time. Blake pushed the gunman several times to leave, to no avail. The normal bronze left Blake's face and left an ashen paste. I searched the room for anything I could use for a weapon.

I lowered myself to Blake's eye level. "Just focus," I said. "You can do this."

Blake took a long inhale then focused on the gunman. "You need to put the gun down and go back to your car. Hurry."

The gunman cocked his head a fraction of an inch and lowered his gun, then walked rote and zombie-like toward the door. He stepped over the body on the floor and left the room.

"You're amazing," I said, breathless.

I found our black caps and sunglasses and we put them on. We stepped over the gunman's blond partner, who lay in the hallway with a dark red blotch on the chest of his gray sweater. His spirit stood next to his body, attached by an etheric cord. I guessed his body must have been slightly alive.

Blake opened the door an inch, then another, and searched the hallway. The two FBI agents sat outside our room, slumped to the side in their chairs, matching bullet holes in their heads.

Blake held my hand and stepped to the right.

I stopped. "There's someone down that hallway."

I searched the stairway and decided it was empty.

"The stairway." I nodded in its direction.

Each down the stairs, I kept hearing the word —how. *How?*

How had the gunmen gotten the door unlocked? How had they gotten a keycard? Why was our room positioned on an empty hallway? Someone had known to set it up this way.

Blood seeped through the bandages I'd wrapped around Blake's arm.

"You're still bleeding." A faint, sickly sweet stench filled the air.

Blake eyed his arm and winced. "I'll be fine."

He lied to keep me calm. Hero of my life he was. Superman and bulletproof, he wasn't.

"Lobby level," I said and pointed to the sign above the doorway. "Cab or ambulance to the hospital. I'm screaming for help when we get to the other side of that door."

Blake nodded. Little beads of sweat bloomed on his forehead.

We edged through the doorway into a vacant hallway that was flanked with ice and snack machine rooms. The ice machine rumbled and a load of ice dumped into its bay.

"Help! Please!" I yelled.

A bald, oversized man with a light-colored mustache and chin beard rounded the corner cautiously. He saw Blake and ran toward us. "I'm security, what's happened?" he asked.

"He's been shot—we need an ambulance."

The man tapped his earpiece and took ahold of Blake's other arm. "Uh, yeah, we have what appears to be a shooting victim here, and we need an ambulance. Roger that."

"It's going to be okay, Blake. We're getting help," I said.

"Ambulance will arrive out back." The man looked behind him. No one else was coming. "Let's stay out of the way of the other guests."

"Two FBI agents were shot outside of room 325," Blake said breathlessly.

"Heckuva first week on the job." He shook his head and tapped his earpiece again. "The shooting took place at room 325 and it sounds like a couple of others may have been shot. We need the police out here right away."

"It's going to be okay," Blake said to me.

The security guard escorted us into the stairwell we'd just exited. We walked into the same level of the garage we'd left several hours earlier. I stopped cold when I saw that the town car Thomas had driven was still parked off to the side of the building. There was no ambulance in sight.

There were two black town cars that ran idle, one behind the other.

The bald security guard grabbed Blake under the good arm and jerked him toward one of the cars.

"No!" I yelled and lunged for him. "Blake!"

"Shut it." A man appeared from behind me. He grabbed me around the neck and shoved what felt like a gun into my back. He dragged me toward the other car. Two drivers emerged wearing dark glasses, one from each car.

When we passed beside Thomas' car, I saw him in a heap between the open door and the car. His head was twisted awkwardly to the side. His spirit hovered while still connected to his body and he watched Blake and me as we passed by.

"I'm sorry," he said. "They gave me no choice. They were going to kill me if I didn't tell them where you were." He ran his hands over his short hair and oversaw the irreparable damage to his body.

"You're a fool," I said.

Blake stared at Thomas' body and struggled against his captor.

A second man with a gun appeared and Blake stopped. The men handcuffed Blake, shoved him into the backseat, and slammed the door.

"No!" I screamed.

The man squeezed the upper part of my arm with an iron grip. He dragged me toward the car and my arm felt an inch within broken. He opened the back door of the town car and I saw Otto.

"Come in," Otto said with a Cheshire cat smile, and patted the leather of the empty seat next to him. "Let's have a chat."

I turned to stone.

Like the turning of a page in a story that began too long ago, the inevitable happened.

My lips went numb, along with the rest of my body. I could neither form a word nor command my body to move. We were dead, Blake and me. Just as the last time.

He was going to kill Blake, kidnap me, and force me to live the rest of my days in service to him.

The gunman shoved me into the car, then slammed the door.

I shifted uncomfortably in my seat.

"Wine?" Otto asked, and offered a glass in my direction.

I shook my head.

"I was disappointed you left so suddenly at our last meeting," Otto said. "I'm sure you didn't mean it as such, but it seemed you might not come back."

I stared at the aristocratic lines of Otto's face and his tan skin. Even in the middle of winter he managed a gentle, even tan. Like he'd just vacationed in the south of France. Every inch of his image was perfect. Perfect forgery.

In spite of the damage the trial must have done to his reputation, most would still see Otto for the image he presented, and that perfection allowed him mobility in the world. The closing of the firm must have shown at least some culpability. Only those in legitimate circles would have been concerned about that.

"Where did you go?" Otto's jaw muscle worked.

I turned away from him and caught sight of Thomas' black shoes that peeked out from behind a pair of tires.

"I see," he said in response to my silence. His wedding ring tapped against his wine glass three times in rapid fire. I shuddered at the sound.

"Addie, I think you'll soon come to see me as the hero in your life. The one who has rescued you from a life on the run and offered you the opportunity of a lifetime."

My head swiveled toward him and I scoffed.

Otto raised his wine glass in a toast. "I have to take care of a little something first. I'll be back. And then we'll begin."

He placed his wine glass in the holder and turned toward the door.

"No!" I yelled, assuming that his "little something" was killing Blake.

Otto turned back to me, darkness brewing behind his eyes.

"If you don't get him the help he needs, if you kill him, I'll never help you." I felt the light within me vanish.

Blake and Grace had been right. Bargaining with Otto was a dance with the devil. No matter how important the reward, even when it was someone else's life, there would be a high price to pay for it.

Otto moved toward me with all the slowness and surety of planned evil.

"You'll help me, Addie," he placed his hand on my knee. His thumb rubbed the outside of my leg in a slow stroke, like he appraised the form of an object.

I moved my leg just out of his reach.

"Or I *will* kill him," he said.

## 43

I t was a silent trip across town.

Then Blake and Otto arrived at the office. Otto's son, Nicholas, parked the car at the rear entrance of the firm.

"This is going to be an interesting day for you," Otto said. "This may be the best idea I've had in years. It's definitely the best solution when you need someone out of your life once and for all."

Otto's tone was grim and Blake had a vision of him bleeding out in the basement of the firm. He struggled quietly in the handcuffs, only to send the pain of a hundred knives into his arm.

Otto's other son, Philippe, walked beside Blake when they entered the firm and kept the end of the gun flush against Blake's ribs. He jabbed the gun against Blake's side whenever he thought Blake wasn't moving fast enough.

The four of them walked down the sloping walkway to the service elevators, the air inside nearly as chilled as the wind outside. Blake thought about the uncomfortable connection between the four men.

Three brothers with their patriarch leading the way, three of the four completely unaware of the fact that Blake was family.

Blake could have told Otto that he was his son, but Otto wouldn't have valued his life any more. He would see that information only as a link to finding Carolena. And Blake wasn't going to sell her out.

There had to be another way. He scanned the hallways for something—anything—he could use to turn things in his favor.

When they finally entered the vault area, Otto headed down the long hallway to the one vault in the back that had been sealed for as long as Blake had interacted with the firm.

Otto twisted the dial but the combination didn't open the door. He pressed his lips together and headed back the way they'd just come. "Bring him this way," he said. "I have to make a stop by the safe in my office."

They passed the nondescript door at the end of the hallway and Otto stopped abruptly, rage building just beneath his polished surface. "What's this doing open?"

They entered the warehouse area just as a delivery truck rumbled by and rattled the darkened windows at the top of the room. A faint scent of exhaust traveled through the air. Otto stalked alongside the brick wall that cornered off one quarter of the room. He came to a hole in the far side of it.

"What—?" Otto exclaimed. He bent to enter the small room, and went straight for the couch. The three brothers followed and watched Otto lift both cushions to reveal the top side of a safe. One twist to the right, one to the left, two more to the right, and the lock released. Otto lifted the heavy door and sighed his relief at the sight of it.

He took the painting from its crypt and ceremoniously propped it against the fireplace.

"Well, at least they didn't get this," he said and admired the painting.

Blake eyed the artist's signature and his realization of what was about to happen drained his strength.

Otto leaned forward and touched an edge of the painting gently. His finger sank into it like he'd stuck it in a bowl of pudding. A swirl of scenery stayed attached to his finger when he took it away, then it returned to the canvas.

Without straightening, Otto eyed Blake.

"I'm going to take you on a little trip," Otto said.

Blake thought of John, Campbell, Frank, and how they all lost their lives at Otto's hand in one way or another. He sat in the nearest chair and felt blood trickle through the makeshift bandage and down his arm.

He watched Otto take two hanging suits from the closet at the back of the room. He laid one over his arm and placed the other one on the chair in front of Blake.

"Nicholas is going to take your handcuffs so you can put this suit on." Otto dropped a pair of shoes in front of the suit with a clatter. "Both boys will have guns on you, so you won't get any ideas." Otto scowled at Blake's arm. "Put a fresh bandage on there, Nicholas. I can't drag him around town with blood running everywhere."

"Me? I'm not touching that." Nicholas sneered at Blake's wound.

"Philippe." Otto gestured to Blake's arm and Philippe left the room.

"You should remember that we don't actually need you alive. Not now that I have Addie," Otto said. He headed toward the bathroom with his suit over his arm.

"Why don't we just shoot him?" Nicholas asked.

"Well, he has already been shot once today," Otto said like he ticked items off a to-do list. "And I rather like the idea of him having to live with the loss of someone he loves."

When Otto returned to the main room he looked all the rage in his gray vested suit, starched white shirt, and slender tie. He carried a matching gray hat and umbrella.

"Wouldn't want to travel without this, remember, boys?" Otto waved the umbrella.

They nodded in return and Nicholas grinned at an apparent memory.

Philippe finished bandaging Blake's arm with fresh gauze from the firm's first-aid kit and torn strips of white fabric that were once part of a shirt. When he turned away Blake fished several packets of ibuprofen out of the kit and hid them in his pocket. Then Philippe buttoned Blake's shirt and knotted his tie. Blake examined his image in the full-length mirror. The dark gray suit had a close fit, as was the style in the early 1920s. He didn't want to know how it was that Otto got the sizing right. He assumed Thomas had given Otto or his sons the information they needed.

*Thomas.* Blake shook his head.

Otto opened the lid on the mahogany roll top desk and lifted a small cash box from the middle compartment. Blake watched in the mirror while Otto took out a stack of bills and transferred half of the money to a different wallet. Then he placed the other half in front of Blake.

Blake noticed with that his and Otto's build appeared nearly identical in their suits. A wave of regret poured through him.

He eyed the antique wedding photo of his mother and father, then he picked up the bills that were made with blue ink, and put them in his wallet.

Otto gestured for Nicholas to reattach the handcuffs.

When they were on again, Otto looped his arm around Blake's good arm.

"You should know that they are under strict orders to kill Addie if I don't come back alive." Otto searched Blake's face for reaction. "If you try anything while we're in there, I'll drop you. You don't know what that means, yet. But suffice to say you wouldn't like it.

"Shoot. I don't think you would survive it."

Blake thought of how the Monet tried to take possession of Addie. "I'll take your word for it."

Otto reached into the painting, searching like he fumbled for something. The pale impressionist colors climbed Otto's arm and Blake watched in horror. There was no avoiding this, no way out, and no guarantee that he would make it back to Addie, much less survive the trip.

"Aha," Otto said. He turned to Blake, "Hang on."

Blake reluctantly grabbed ahold of Otto's coattails just before paint colors coated them completely. His arm ached and he groaned in agony when the painting took control of him, adding him to its world. When they were completely inside, Blake scanned the area behind them. Oddly, he could see the room they had just left. Philippe and Nicholas stood and watched them.

Otto walked carefully forward, step by step, hanging on to a thick, red cord which seemed to be tied both to where they had been, as well as where they were going.

Blake squinted against the windy emotional currents, which burned his eyes and left him feeling half-mad. It was impossible to tell which feelings were the artist's emotion that was embedded into the painting, and which were his own. What he could see of his surroundings showed exactly like the painting. Anything he focused on offered a path in that direction.

Otto headed straight toward a gathering along the river and toward one man, in particular. The red cord was tied to a post next to where the man stood. Otto stopped at the post and appeared to focus, like he braced himself for whatever was next.

The pain of Wentworth's loss seared through Blake, brought him back to his childhood when he learned that fathers weren't always the protectors and the defenders that they were supposed to be. Sometimes, no matter how much you loved and needed someone, they couldn't have a place in your life.

Otto placed hand over hand on the cord, moving both of them forward.

The scenery morphed from an outdoor gathering by the river to a quiet dirt road through the forest. Blake couldn't rise above the sadness and loss that surrounded him, owned him. Several times he stumbled and fell out of sheer emotional exhaustion, and lay in the fetal position on the dirt path. Each time Otto yanked him up and laughed at him. Finally, he closed his eyes, followed Otto's steps, and prayed for an end.

Otto took Blake's arm and wrapped it around a small tree, then Otto left. Blake watched while Otto took the last twenty feet or so of the red cord and tied it off in the bushes. It was now unseen from the path. When Otto finished, Blake turned away and closed his eyes again. He knew Otto wouldn't want anyone to know what he did.

Otto guided Blake several steps in what felt like a half circle. "Open your eyes!" Otto barked.

Blake did so slowly and admired the painter's atelier laid out before him. There were burgundy walls with wainscoting, easels with half-finished portraits, and bright sunshine that highlighted blotches of paint on the faded wooden floors. He saw the room just as he had seen the room they had left—like it was on the other side of a foggy window. The closer they came to it, the clearer the room came into focus.

Otto dragged Blake to the near the edge, untied the end of the red cord, and disappeared. When he returned, Otto pressed close to the surface and scanned the room.

Holding tight to Blake, Otto reached through the filmy screen and they poured out of the painting and tumbled onto the artist's cold floor.

Blake lay on the floor, still in handcuffs. He groaned. Nausea, dizziness, and extreme weakness made it impossible to move. He watched from the ground while Otto rolled to all fours, crawled to the slightly open window, and took in deep breaths of cold air. He dabbed his forehead with a white handkerchief.

Their coats, hats and umbrellas lay on the floor, like they'd been tossed without care. Blake imagined what he and Otto must have looked like when the painting birthed them into this world. The painting in question hung among a wall full of other paintings by the same artist. It appeared as it did in the small room outside of Otto's firm. Innocent. Unassuming.

"Not something you can describe, is it?" Otto pointed toward the window. "See for yourself."

Blake tried to stand, but stumbled like he was drunk. He fell to the floor. His cheek lay against the hard wood, the scent of oil-based paint filled his nostrils.

Otto laughed.

Blake crawled toward the window and lifted himself up to the view. What little strength he had, returned. But slowly.

Brick chimneys sat on slanted rooftops across the street,

and below them were fairly quiet streets with the occasional Model T that rumbled by. Women in black coats and black hats pushed black prams with large tires. Men wore narrow-brimmed hats and their coattails flew behind them.

Blake skin felt clammy. His arm and hand throbbed to the beat of his pulse.

Once again he was as far from Addie as he had been before they'd met. He slipped from the edge of the window to the floor. "I need a doctor."

Otto laughed, smug and hardy. "You can find that on your own when I'm gone."

## 44

Fresh air helped. As did moving about.

What didn't help was half the bar yelling, "Otto!" when they walked in.

He was a celebrity in this New York neighborhood.

"My friend has had a long journey and needs a good meal. What can you get him, Harvey?"

The bartender eyed Blake suspiciously. "You sick?"

"No, he's not sick. Just tired. He needs to eat. What does Rose have back there today?" Otto slapped Blake on the back and gave his shoulder a shake.

Blake stifled a groan. He waited until Harvey disappeared into the kitchen then he brushed Otto's hand from his shoulder. He arm swelled against the bandages. He headed for the door—he needed to find a doctor or a hospital.

"Where are you headed there, Blake?"

Blake kept walking until Otto stepped between him and the door.

"To the doctor," Blake said.

"Ah. Yes. The arm. Pity that had to happen. You need

food, though. Everyone does after they make the trip. The doctor, of course, wouldn't know that. He might even keep you from food based upon your wound."

Blake relaxed his resistance. Reluctantly. He couldn't tell if Otto was telling him the truth or not, but he was too weak to fight.

"You okay, Mr. Albrecht?" A clean-cut young man in a navy sailor's uniform stepped up with his chest puffed and arms slightly back. A scent of bleach and detergent and beer filled the air.

"Dickie! So good to see you. How's your mother?" Otto patted Dickie on the shoulder and kept his body in Blake's path.

"She's fine, now, Mr. Albrecht. Thanks to you. I don't know what we would have done if you — well, if you hadn't helped us after my Dad left." Dickie pumped Otto's hand, then leered at Blake with a slight lip curl. "Do you need any help with this?"

"No, thank you, son. We were just about to take a seat. Weren't we, Blake?" Otto slapped Blake on the shoulder.

Blake nodded, the searing pain in his arm forced a bead of sweat down his cheek.

"He doesn't look so good."

"He just needs a good meal, that's all." Otto looked over Blake as a caring father would, and kept his arm wrapped around Blake's shoulder.

Blake's hatred of Otto boiled and burned inside of him.

"You're always helping someone aren't you, Mr. Albrecht?"

"Just trying to do my part," Otto said with a proud smile. "Help me, if you would please?"

Dickie guided Blake to a nearby booth and Blake

dropped to the seat. Dickie walked back to his stool at the counter but maintained a stare at Blake.

Blake thought Dickie might be jealous of the attention Blake received from Otto.

"You'll feel better after you eat, even with that hole in your arm. There's a doctor's office a few blocks from here. You can go see him after we're done. In fact, it's not far, so I'll walk you half-way. You still have the money I gave you?"

"You're helping me, now?" Blake asked. "I thought you wanted me dead."

Otto leaned toward Blake's ear and whispered, "I said I wanted you to suffer, not die. There's a difference. I'm going to leave you here in fairly good health so you'll be fully aware of what you don't have. And what I do have." Otto leaned away when Harvey returned with two plates of salty ham and mashed potatoes.

Blake mistakenly reached for his fork with his right hand and he winced. Harvey's lip plumped out in an overtly skeptical manner. A dish shattered in the kitchen and Harvey left the table in a rush.

Blake took the fork in his left hand and ate small bites at first, unsure how it would affect him. He didn't much feel like eating, but he quickly found that the food strengthened him. It was partially what he needed, at least.

Otto didn't want him to die.

At least not physically.

Otto paid the bill with two small coins and they stepped into the cold winter sun. "I know you don't think it right now, but I've done you a favor by bringing you here. No better time to be alive."

Otto stopped next to a young boy calling out the day's headlines in his prepubescent voice. He bought a paper from him, then folded it to highlight the date and handed it to Blake.

"Just in case you were wondering," he said.

*January 5th, 1920*

Blake nearly lost his footing.

Otto said, "You tried to take something valuable from me, so I've taken something valuable from you. It's very simple."

Otto's voice wasn't threatening. It wasn't even intimidating. He didn't have to be. He'd won. He was taking a trot around the winner's circle.

"Your arm is getting a little worse for wear there, sport."

Blake studied the widening red spot on his arm. The splotch doubled in his vision and he tried to blink it back to just one.

"Oh—and you'll have to get a job to support yourself," Otto nodded Blake's pocket where the money was kept. "If you remember your history lessons well enough you can make a fortune here. Hopefully you paid attention in school since there's no internet for research." Otto winked at him.

Blake ignored Otto's comment and thought only of ways to get home to Addie.

The only option he could think of wasn't an easy one, and not just because he only had one good arm. He'd have to find a way to take Otto out, then go back to the painting and find his way home. Assuming he could find that red cord that Otto had buried. Assuming Wentworth's emotions didn't took him over.

Still, what if he got back to the painting and couldn't find the cord? What if the painting didn't work for him the way it worked for Carolena, Grace, and Otto? What if he ended up lost in time like Grace's cousin?

He'd never find Addie again.

Blake thought about the date—it was the same month and day as it was at home. John and Campbell had verified that. That meant that John and Campbell were here as well.

After several blocks of walking against the wind, Blake had completely lost his strength, and he had a chill he couldn't shake.

Otto led them into Keramic Supply Company, an artists' supply shop. Camel's hair brushes, palate knives, and a seemingly endless supply of paint.

Blake sat in an empty chair at the end of an aisle and held his arm close. His surroundings blurred and swayed. He gazed out the window and tried to figure where, exactly, they were in New York, and where a hospital might be. His line of sight drifted to the bright copper cash register that shown like a new penny. The cashier squinted at him with lips pursed and studied Blake too closely for his comfort.

He was a stranger in a strange land. He realized there was no one to vouch for him if he got into trouble. He managed a smile to the woman and swiveled toward Otto who was lost in his own world.

"Now you know why many of my forgeries go unquestioned," Otto said, oblivious to Blake's suffering. "The composition of the paint is authentic to the time, and of course I've perfected the aging process."

Otto picked up several bottles of each color. "Claude Monet is probably using this same paint, right now." He took his items to the front desk and laid down a coin for his purchase.

"Thank you, Madam." Otto tipped his hat.

The saleswoman smiled at Otto.

Though the smile fell off key when her eyes fell to Blake.

"Imagine the stir I'll cause if I can find my way back to the 1600s. There will be all sorts of new discoveries from the masters," Otto whispered. He tugged Blake's good arm and they re-entered the main and crowded thoroughfare.

Otto was going to flood the market with forgeries that would fool the most skillful experts.

"Enjoy your new life, Blake," Otto said. "You'll have everything anyone could dream of having. Except for the one thing you really want, of course."

Otto clutched his bag of authentic early 1900s paint. "You see I've lived that life. I've had everything anyone could ever want. Except for the one who left me, my one great love, the one I needed most in the world. I know firsthand the pain you're going to suffer." He backed away. "Don't worry. Addie will be safe with me."

Blake's fury surged and he grabbed Otto by his collar. "You leave Addie alone," he said through clenched teeth.

"Careful, Blake," Otto sang. "You don't have any identification, no one to vouch for you. All that money in your pocket, a bullet hole in your arm, and no way to prove who you are, the police are going to think you've stolen it. So they'll take it away from you and leave you with nothing. You'll die in jail."

Strangers stared and whispered at them. Blake loosened his grip.

"That's better." Otto smoothed his coat. "Doctor's office is one-half block that way."

He nodded up the street, bowed slightly, turned, and left.

Blake stood alone in the crowd and watched Otto stroll in the direction of Wentworth's atelier. The steel tip of his umbrella marked off every other step.

Blake clenched his fists hard.

He read the street signs on each corner, got his bearings, and walked in the opposite direction of Otto.

He knew what he had to do.

## 45

Philippe walked me into my own home.

He turned and locked the new key-only dead-bolts on the door and dropped the key into his front pocket.

He took away my purse and phone.

He opened the cabinets and drawers in the kitchen and showed me that all the glasses, knives, and silverware were gone.

The drapes were closed, but when I stood in the salon I felt the thick, snowy stillness outside. It was too late, cold, and icy for runners or other pedestrian traffic. There were no passersby for me to signal.

"We had the trim painted while you were away. So, in case you were thinking of opening the windows to signal someone, the windows are painted shut," he said.

There were no escape routes, and no weapons. Otto had been planning this for a very long time.

Philip paced in the kitchen, arguing with his brother Nicholas on the phone.

I read the dynamics of their relationship and saw that

the two of them were in an age-old sibling rivalry. Nicholas had his father's approval, Philippe did not.

I didn't think Philippe had missed out on anything, but childhood wounds rarely listened to logic.

I closed my eyes and raised my hands, palms turned outward. There was nothing to touch, nothing I could read, but I reached anyway and hoped I could sense where Blake was, and if he was okay.

My mind was full of what-ifs that explored the worst possible scenarios. I wished I had Grace's or Alexa's gifts. Just a small piece of them such that I could see how he was, where he was, and how I could work this out.

But...nothing. I couldn't sense my way out of a wet paper bag right now.

I started pacing, my well-worn habit. First through the library, then through the salon and back again. The routine that had so often given me peace now gave me nothing but annoyance.

I sat on the edge of the suede couch in the library and I felt my strength disappear.

Every man I'd ever loved had been taken away from me. By Otto.

Last life, this life, the timing didn't matter.

There had to be some way to make it stop.

IN A HOME as old as mine, there was always a draft.

A breath of fresh air.

Now it felt like a coffin.

I mentally searched the house for something to help me out of this mess.

Did I have tucked an old phone away somewhere? No,

each time I got a new phone I donated the old one to the women's shelter.

Did I have a weapon? A knife? A letter opener?

No, no, no.

A familiar darkness descended into the next room and I slid off the couch and hid in the corner. I drew my knees close to my chin and watched the opening to the library.

A man peeked around the corner. His alarmingly dark eyes betrayed his grandfatherly appearance. I disliked him immediately. His blue-and white-striped button-down shirt was rumpled and littered with vomit.

He found me.

"Do you know where she is?" He pointed a bony finger at me.

"No." I stifled my gag reflex. He reeked of sick and death.

"I'll bet you know her. You even favor her." He squinted and glided toward me. "I think she put something in my oatmeal."

He must have been wealthy and married a gold digger.

Before Blake, I was haunted by ghosts all day long and half the night. When Blake came along, his protectiveness kept them at bay. For the first time in my life I didn't have to deal with them.

After Blake, they were back.

I ran my hand across my forehead and over my left eye, and the pressure that built there. A migraine.

"Have you tried the hospital?" I held my hand out to stop him. "She might be there."

He considered it. "Jenny?" He walked into the salon.

I lowered my forehead into my hand.

The old man would be back, and I wondered how many more ghosts would find their way to my hermitically sealed nightmare.

I wiggled my toes against the tiny paper between them. Those phone numbers wouldn't do me much good without a phone.

The air pressure shifted and Frank strutted into the room. He sat in the chair across from me. "Missing your boyfriend?"

"Do you know where he is?"

Frank gave a slow nod. Then he crossed his legs in a way that was oddly reminiscent of Otto when he sat in the same seat.

"If you want to get back at Otto, helping me would be a good way to do that," I said. "And need I remind you that if Carolena finds out that you've harassed me, you'll regret—"

Suddenly he was behind me, his hands around my throat.

"I'll do as I like." Even Frank behaved like his pre-Blake self.

He grabbed a fistful of my hair and jerked my head to the side. I felt cold steel, a nick, then a warm trickle. I gasped and touched the wetness that traveled past my collarbone. I examined my fingertips. Bright red blood.

"I understand," I said, uncertain how much damage he could do. "Think of your mother, Frank. She misses you. Maybe you'd like to see her again? Maybe there's a way to work that out..."

His grip on my hair relaxed an inch.

"Have you seen Jenny?" The old man appeared in the doorway and started when he saw us.

"Who are you?" Frank stormed after him with the knife in play.

With both ghosts gone I grabbed a tissue from the side table, pressed it to my neck, and stared forward. That's when I saw it. The old key that Otto placed on my coffee table was still there. With the tissue stuck to my neck, I lunged for the key.

I might not read situations like my relatives did, but I could read objects.

I sent my second sight out and around the townhome to make sure I was alone. I didn't want to delve into the key if I was going to be surprised by Philippe. Or worse, Otto.

*No one.*

I placed the key in the palm of my left hand and squeezed my fingertips against it. I was sure that Otto already knew what he planned to do with Blake when he found me on the couch that morning. Since he had the key in his possession then, maybe the key would know where Blake was.

"Show me your history, sweetheart," I said to the key. "Show me everything you picked up."

I prepared myself to be flooded with the evil of Otto. Instead, I was drawn to the kitchen where a key holder in the shape of an old-fashioned iron key was nailed to the wall. Not exactly where I thought I'd go, but I went with it.

The evening sun floats in on a warm breeze through partially open windows in the library. Dressed in a sleeveless, silver-beaded, light pink 1920s gown, Ellen sways gently in my grandfather's arms to Bessie Smith's *I Need a Little Sugar in My Bowl*. She takes a sip from her wine glass and slows her dance. My grandfather kisses her red-stained lips.

"You two should leave a little to the imagination." Otto swaggers by. A glowing Carolena floats effortlessly in his arms, the jeweled bracelet adorns her wrist. He twirls her while Bessie hits her high notes with gusto, then he lowers Carolena in for a stylish dip.

Ellen and John "ahhh" and applaud Otto's and Carolena's snazzy dance moves, and the small, retro-dressed gathering rides high on illicit love.

My grandfather walks across the room. His face is smooth, and handsome. He takes the key from the rack and hands it to Otto. "Just until her apartment remodel is complete," he warns, and holds the key out of Otto's reach.

"No more than a month," Otto says. "Two tops."

My grandfather pauses, then hands Otto the key, who then hands it to Carolena.

"Thanks, old man." Otto slaps my grandfather on the back.

"Thank you, John," Carolena says. "Please, come and enjoy yourselves any time you need to. Tristan and I don't take up much space." Carolena peeks to the corner where a young, dark-haired boy sits in the ray of the sun and pushes tiny trucks around him.

My heart thumps hard at the sight of him. Tristan. Of course Blake wouldn't use his real name.

"We can meet at my place," Ellen whispers to John. They dance with one another, hip to hip. "I'll have my mother take Nate to the park." Ellen and my grandfather look at a young, blond-curled boy in brown cotton pants and he tugs on my grandfather's jacket.

"Up, Dada, up," he says in a tiny voice.

"That's my good boy," my grandfather says and picks him up, then kisses the boy's apple cheeks. The three of them dance together until the shrill ring of a phone interrupts them, and my grandfather answers the black landline that sits on a shelf beneath the bookcase.

I popped out of the reading with a jolt, the key's memory of the party vanished. Taking two and three steps at a time, I dashed toward the spare room. It was a small space with an angled ceiling, room enough for a modest study or apparently, a nursery. On the side wall, and behind an old armchair, was a small, square-cut door that led to the attic space. I pushed hard on the door and found a cardboard box inside.

I dragged it out and found all the odds and ends I'd stuffed in there when I moved in. Grace had forbidden me to remove any of my grandfather's things. I hadn't, really.

One of the items I'd taken from the library was an old black landline. The exact one I'd just seen my grandfather talking on.

I unwrapped the long wire that was still attached to the back of the phone and plugged it into the outlet across the room. I wasn't breathing when I lifted the receiver, but when I heard the dial tone I exhaled in a *whoosh*.

The small paper where Blake had written Carolena's and William's phone numbers was right where I left it.

"Yes," William answered.

"It's Addie," I said breathlessly. "Otto's kidnapped Blake, you have to find him."

"What? Where are you?" William asked.

"He's holding me captive in my town home. He's going to take me to the Gardner art."

"Why is he taking you to the art?"

"He wants me to help him. I—I don't have time to explain," I said, and knew there would never be a time when I could. "Today, I think. Maybe you could follow us. He could be back any minute. I don't know how much time I have. I think I overheard them say he's got the art in a warehouse somewhere by a river. You'll find Blake?" I said it all so quickly that my words ran together.

"This doesn't make any sense," he said. "You don't—"

"Please, please—" I realized that I couldn't give William anything solid that would allow him to help Blake. "Nevermind. Don't call me back on this line. They don't know I have a phone and I can't have it ringing."

"Addie, wait," he said.

I hung up and dialed the next person. No one answered, and I wasn't surprised.

The voicemail clicked on without a greeting, and I told Carolena everything I'd told William and then some. "I don't know where Otto's taken him. He's holding him until he's sure I'll help him with the Gardner art. I don't know how to get out of this."

I put the receiver back in the cradle and prepared to call Grace. But the front door slammed and I jumped beyond my skin.

I restocked the phone to the box, pushed the box to its hiding spot, and moved the chair to cover the outline of the opening. There's no way I would have time to get back downstairs before they found me.

## 46

There were no audible footsteps but Otto's presence was palpable and it spread through my home. I held my breath on the exhale then inhaled slowly through my nose to try and calm myself.

I felt his fiery gaze on the side of my face while I stared out the small window. I didn't move.

"What are you doing?" The energy that rode on his words hit me like a curse.

I waited a beat and gathered what calm I could before I answered. "Wishing I was outside."

Otto's perennial tan had disappeared. In its place was a fatigued shade of lime. Like he'd eaten something that didn't agree with him.

"Philippe is at the front door. With a gun. Go downstairs."

I did.

He dashed past me and I heard him jiggling windows. I prayed that God would direct him away from my hidden lifeline.

When he came down the stairs and he pushed me for

answers before he even opened his mouth. Carolena had been right when she said he was the best and the most dangerously gifted man she'd ever known.

A lifetime with Lexie, who pushed me for anything and everything, left me at least somewhat prepared. I stared out the framed round window that overlooked the park. I bolstered myself energetically against Otto. Awareness was the best protection.

Otto pushed hard for the truth. "What were you doing upstairs?"

My awareness felt like a cardboard shield against the fiery breath of a dragon. "I'm just looking out the window," I said. "Better than staring at a wall."

Otto pushed so hard my internal organs leaned away from him. "You want to tell me what you were doing upstairs."

I waited until the desire to tell the truth passed. It felt like a lifetime. "Nothing."

Otto brought Philippe in from the hallway. "Watch her and don't let her wander around. I don't think she could get out one of those windows upstairs, but I don't want her testing it."

He walked to the half bath and shut the door with a loud *ka-chunk*. A metal click followed when he turned the lock.

I hoped he was sick. Deathly ill. Or having a heart attack.

Philippe stood in the foyer, placed his hands on his hips.

I saw the gun in his front waistband.

I walked back to the library. A little girl stood quietly next to the right side of the bookshelf. She wore black tights and a crisp red dress that had a peter pan collar and four pearl-colored buttons just beneath it.

"I'm sorry," she said. Her blue eyes were filled with

worry. "I need to find my brothers. I was caring for them and now they're gone. I wrote this letter for them." She held a piece of folded stationery and clutched it to her chest.

"Do you want me to give it to them?" I offered my hand to take the letter but she walked toward the kitchen.

"I'll give it to them," she said.

*The letter.*

I gave a cautious glance behind me to make sure Philippe or Otto weren't stalking me too closely, then scanned the bookshelves for the F. Scott Fitzgerald book that Grace said was in the house at one time.

It would probably look the same as the navy Fitzgerald book I'd seen in Grace's house. My fingers flew over the antique spines.

I smelled something. It stopped me.

Singed paper.

I followed the scent to the right side of the bookcase and saw a tiny white sparkle illuminated briefly over one particular book. I took it from the shelf.

The gold lettering on the spine had faded beyond recognition, but the front cover showed the title clearly: *This Side of Paradise.*

I tried to appear casual.

In case I was watched.

I opened the cover and it crackled. Several letters slipped from the pages. My heart fluttered with a mix of anxiety and hope.

*My Dearest Ellen*, the first letter began. *Please do send more pictures of Nathan, and especially from graduation. I can hardly believe this handsome man is the same precious child who slept in my arms so many years ago.*

One by one, I opened the letters and read the first few

lines of each. They all began in the same way: *My Dearest Ellen.*

Philippe cleared his throat and I hastily peeked at the last three letters. Until I got to the final letter.

*We've had the most peculiar visitor. I thank you for warning me that Otto might send someone our way. He stumbled into our townhouse, shot through the arm of all things, and suffering with shock and a fever. We've taken him to the hospital and they're caring for him. The wound sites are quite infected, and unfortunately, these are the days before antibiotics. The doctors are using serum therapy and comfrey poultices to heal the infection, though they are doubtful. Pray for him. It appears he is quite fond of our dear Addie.*

My heart tumbled.

I turned in all four directions. Now I knew that no matter where I searched for him on this earth, I wouldn't find him. He was gone.

Shock and grief hit me hard, and I leaned on the bookshelf to hold myself up.

The bathroom door opened, and with a jolt I folded the letter and pushed it into my bra.

"Go get her," I heard Otto say to Philippe.

## 47

The winter air in the back of the van left me chilled to the core and visibly shaking.

Under the black hood, the warmth was smothering.

The handcuffs stayed cold on my skin. They were so tight I thought my wrists might snap.

"They're too tight," I'd said when Nicholas put them on.

"I don't care," he'd said.

The van turned a corner and I fell to my side.

I knew Philippe was nearby but he did nothing to help me.

I laid there, my head banging against the metal floor whenever the van hit a pothole.

"I'm going to be sick," I said through the hood.

Even as a child I hated having any sort of cover placed on my face and I would pull shirts over my head as quickly as possible.

The van slowed to a stop, the brakes let out a languid, metal squeak. The van lurched and we moved again, albeit slowly. When we finally stopped, the back doors to the van opened and Philippe jerked me off the floor and onto the pavement outside.

Wherever we were it was vacant. The traffic sounds of the city had faded into the distance. The sound of water lapped against a hard surface. The occasional seagull cried out like they had seen me and thought I was headed for an execution.

I knew Otto wouldn't do away with me, yet. He still needed me.

A heavy metal door rattled when it slid open on rails, and Philippe ushered me inside. I'd come to recognize his clean soap smell, which differed from Nicholas' too-heavy cologne.

Our shoed clicked against the bare cement floor until the sound of Otto's shoes echoed ahead of us. There were six beeps, like someone punched the buttons on a keypad. Then the pressure release of a sealed door being opened. Philippe moved me forward.

"Pleasure to see you again, *Ad-die*," Frank said mockingly while I was still under cover. I leaned away when the liquor on his breath permeated the cotton hood. Philippe pushed me upright again and yanked off the hood.

I gasped.

The small room had gray walls, wooden floors, and gallery lighting. It looked like a miniature museum. Mostly frameless canvases of Gardner theft art were propped against all four walls. It was disturbing to see several exact images of the same paintings in one room. There was only one reason such a scenario would happen.

"Just like when you were little, Addie," Otto began. "We're going to play a game." Otto placed his hands on my shoulders and gestured across the room. I shrugged his hands off my body.

His sigh was tense.

"You touch each one, then tell me which one is real and which are forgeries."

It suddenly occurred to me that when my job was done, he'd have no more use for me. "This might take some time," I said.

Otto walked around the room with his hands clasped behind his back and surveyed several pieces from his one-of-a-kind, world-famous collection. "I doubt that. I watched you do this as a child, and it took you less than a minute to do ten or so."

"It's just that—you have a lot of pieces here and—"

"I've seen you work, Addie," he said. "You're almost as fast as Carole—" He stopped himself, the memory of rejection evident in his eyes.

I swallowed hard. There was something evil in the air when Otto had Carolena's name on his lips. The anger he felt over her departure still lived strong in his heart.

"You're fast. You're quite good. Better than I anticipated, actually," he said. "The more you do, the better you'll get. That's the way it was with someone I once knew. Practice makes perfect and that sort of thing. If you do a good job with these items there's no end to the work we can do together." He dragged the backside of his knuckles down my cheek and gazed at me like he saw someone else.

I tried to swallow the fury that rose up.. "I'll tell you what." I moved out of his reach. "I'll tell you which of these pieces are original, and I'll even work with you on other pieces. *When* you bring Blake back. Healthy and unharmed."

His fist hit my jaw so hard I fell to the floor. Pain rang through my head. I never saw it coming.

"Now you're gettin' a taste of him," Frank said.

I pushed off of the floor. Drops slid from my face in bright red circles on the polished hardwoods. My head spun.

Otto knelt on one knee and shook a white handkerchief in front of me.

"Look at me," he said, like someone else had just hit me. He lifted my chin with his hand and dabbed the blood from my face.

Hatred poured from every thread of my being.

"After all I've gone through to bring you here. To give you this special work..." Otto gestured to the Gardner pieces around the room. His tone was cold and masked in sweet. "...and this is how you act."

He grabbed my upper arm too hard and yanked me to my feet. The pain in my head screamed.

He sighed with disgust and paced across the small room. "No one else in the world—at any point in time—has ever had the opportunity that you have right now. No one!"

When he stood in front of me again, he placed both hands on my shoulders and shook me like he tried to arouse me from unconsciousness.

My vision blurred and my stomach felt sick.

"Blake's gone now. Do you understand that? You and I are partners now—a brilliant team. Just as it once was." His eyes were distant.

He shook me once more and I nodded.

"Okay, then," he said. "Get to work."

Otto motioned to Philippe. He opened a small cabinet, and handed me a pair of white gloves.

There was no sound in the room. Just dark silence. It was heavy, weighing on me and winning.

I wiped the last of the blood from my face, pocketed Otto's handkerchief, then put the gloves on. "Where do you want me to start?"

## 48

Three images of Rembrandt's *Christ in the Storm on the Sea of Galilee* leaned against the wall. All three were the same size and each one appeared exactly the same as the next.

Though only one could be genuine.

To touch a real Rembrandt had been a childhood dream. To know firsthand what he thought and felt when he painted these masterpieces was a secret very few people would ever have the ability to know.

I was one of them.

But I was aware that this dream come true was surrounded by a nightmare.

I reached out to the side of the canvas.

"Oh, and Addie." Otto stood next to me. "If you should get this wrong—or if you're thinking of giving me false information—your new career with me will be cut vastly short."

I held my hand steady, but my insides fell apart.

The pain in my head throbbed. I had to keep blinking to focus. I probably had a concussion.

I leaned forward, and touched my left hand to the painting. The images poured through clear and steady. Otto at the easel, his intent to defraud, to deceive, to punish was clear. As was his undying need to set people up, to watch them fail.

I removed my hand and said nothing.

The next Rembrandt was the same, and I became increasingly aware of how intent Otto was to make people think that he had made their dreams come true, then to laugh at them for playing the fool. I, too, had been one of his pawns.

I crawled to the third Rembrandt and felt more frightened than when I'd touched the other two. What if this was the real one? What if it wasn't? Would Otto kill me if he didn't like my answers?

I rested the third finger of my left hand on the last Rembrandt.

Painting this one gave the artist little pleasure. It was the topic, he decided. Perhaps it was the water. He didn't know, but it was uninspiring. Out of his boredom he painted himself into the painting, and staring right at the viewer, no less. Though it was every bit as good as Rubens, which was his goal. Maybe even better. Maybe he'd keep this one for his own burgeoning art collection.

I opened my eyes to see what he had shown me. And there the artist was, peering at me from the past.

I stood and faced Otto. "It's this one," I pointed at the third canvas. "The other two are yours."

Otto walked to the canvas and ran his hand across the top.

"Very good," he said. "Now these."

*Very good? Did he already know the answers before I gave them? Was this a test?*

Otto pointed at four canvases reflecting Manet's *Chez Tortoni*. An ornate gold frame sat to the side. From what I'd read about the Gardner heist, I knew that *Chez Tortoni* left the museum in its frame, unlike most of the other pieces, which had been cut. I inspected the canvases first, each one holding subtle markings that said they had all spent time in a frame. *Smart.*

Then I touched the first canvas just next to the image of the black top hat. It didn't take long for the information to jump forth.

*Otto. Special. He considered himself and his ability to be so special.*

I dropped my hands into my lap. I hated to admit it, but his talent was extraordinary. "Yours," I said to him.

I sped through the next two and struggled over the final Monet. They were all Otto's. My body gave a convulsive shiver. Was this a trick? A test? Or had one of his sons sold a piece out from under him? He'd warned me before I started that he held my future in his hands.

"They're all yours." I braced myself to be hit again. This couldn't be the answer he wanted.

Otto inhaled deep and slow, his nostrils slightly flared, his face stoic. "Did you sell any of these paintings?" Otto pushed Philippe, but his energy didn't respond with any compliance.

"No," Philippe said.

"Did you?" Otto pushed harder, his face close to Philippe's.

"No!" Philippe yelled.

Otto walked away then spun around and punched Philippe across the jaw with a closed fist. Philippe took it without a response and I had the feeling that wasn't the first time.

"Did you remove any of the paintings from this vault?" Otto pushed Philippe hard enough that I felt my own insides start to crumble.

Philippe shook his head. "No," he groaned.

Otto shifted his attention to Nicholas with a push and Nicholas shook his head. Otto rubbed his knuckles. "One of you did. Unless...unless it was John," he muttered under his breath.

My ears perked at the sound of my grandfather's name.

"Do those next." Otto pointed to a side table in the corner with four tiny images. They were Rembrandt's self portrait. Each sketch was no bigger than a postage stamp.

They were easy to read. "They're all yours," I said. I hid my joy that someone had gotten away with something Otto valued.

Next was Edgar Degas' watercolor series, *La sortie du pesage*. There were five in the series—all three of the first one were Otto's. The rest were authentic, and I told Otto as much.

He pushed me through the rest of the pieces, all of which had an original in the room.

"Philippe, you know what to do with her." Otto gestured toward me. "Nicholas, package up these paintings." He pointed to the originals that he'd set aside.

I exhaled nervously, removed the white gloves, and placed them in my pocket. The energy from Otto's handkerchief told my sensitive fingertips what I'd already guessed. That he never had any intent to bring Blake back.

I was his prisoner, his replacement for Carolena, and he'd use me as such until I was dead. Or, I thought, until he was dead.

## 49

Philippe returned the handcuffs to my wrists and left my hands in front of me this time. He also put the black hood over my head again.

We descended from the crypt of priceless art, and Philippe's gun nudged me in the back of my ribs to hurry. My shoes clanked on the metal steps.

There was a muffled sound of an external door opening. Philippe stopped. He jerked me to the side and I stumbled. He dragged me along a crooked route toward what I thought must be the outer door. He grabbed the hood from my head and laid a finger across my lips in a shh sign, then nudged me with his gun.

The warehouse was quiet again, but I had the feeling that someone was nearby. Maybe several someones. I weighed the risks of yelling, but the gun in my side talked me out of it.

Philippe lifted me by the arm and hoisted me into the back of the van.

"FBI! Freeze!" I heard a man yell from inside.

*Pop, pop, pop!* Gunshots fired inside the warehouse followed by the deadly sound of silence.

Philippe slammed the van door, jumped into the driver's seat, and we sped out of the storage park through a back exit.

I'd missed my chance.

I shivered from cold and nerves and hoped that William had followed us.

Philippe drove past the highway exit that led to my home, and fear slammed into me. I didn't know where he was taking me next.

"Do you remember how our families used to be so close?" I asked.

Philippe quickly glanced at me in the rearview mirror, then his eyes returned to the road.

"I remember playing at the firm when we were about nine, Nicholas put on Ellen's long black coat. It was supposed to be a minister's robe. He married us. Lexie was jealous. I think she wanted you all to herself."

I waited a beat, but still no response. "Do you remember?" I asked timidly. "We all used to be such good friends."

"I remember," he said and searched the side view mirrors carefully.

"Philippe, I don't know where you're taking me. But you could just let me go." The van was silent except for the engine and the recycled heat that was forced through the vents. "We have money. My family would pay you for my life. You could use that money to get away, have your own life. Away from Otto and your brother."

"You don't need to worry about that. This will all be over soon."

Cold dread covered me inside and out. "You were always

the kind one, Philippe. Not like Nicholas. I need you to remember that now."

Philippe's phone rang, and he parked on a side street. Then he stepped back and put the black hood over my head again.

"Yeah. Yeah, we're on our way," he said.

He drove the van again.

Since my hands were cuffed in front, I removed the hood. If he wanted to kill me, he would have to look me in the eye while he did it.

After a long drive Philippe cut the engine. We were at the firm, in the back parking lot.

He swiveled in his seat to face me.

"Why are we here?" I asked.

THE LOWER LEVEL of the firm was empty. What life the firm had had was dead.

"Where are we going?" I asked.

Philippe walked silently ahead, solemn and resolute.

"Please," I said and grabbed ahold of his wrist. The vision hit me at once. He was young, bruised and beaten, humiliated by his father.

"Oh, Philippe," I said.

He paused while I held on to him. I felt the ridges of the scar and turned his wrist to see it. "When? I asked.

"A long time ago." He turned his head and pulled his arm away. He nudged me ahead of him.

Philippe's phone vibrated. "Hey," he answered. "Yeah, that's perfect, we're already here. No, he's not."

"Come on." He hung up his phone. "We have to hurry.

Or we may both be dead soon. This won't make any sense when I tell you, I need for you to just listen first."

I nodded quietly. I understood now.

Philippe was running from Otto just as much as I was.

"When Nicholas and I were kids, Mother was always arguing with Otto, telling him that he needed to spend more time with us. At the time we didn't know why he was gone so much, but we figured it out later.

"Anyway, Otto finally agreed to spend time with us, but on his terms. We came to his office where he kept a painting. Eventually he built this room where he kept the painting inside of a safe. It was a painting you could walk through. Or at least Otto's friend could walk through it."

"Carolena," I whispered.

Philippe said, "How did you know?"

I shook my head. "Small world story, and not enough time for the details."

He nodded. "So, he had her take us, as if we were a family."

"Where?" I asked.

Philippe watched me pensively, directly. "She took us back in time."

I nodded.

"I realize how this must sound," he said. "But it's true. The painting is a Wentworth and—"

I ran my hand over his arm, to give comfort and reassurance. He was no longer my captor. "I've seen this kind of thing, though only recently. He took Blake," I said quickly. "I've got to bring him back. He's been shot."

"How did you—" The realization slowly donned on Philippe that somehow we weren't so far apart in understanding, that his job was going to be a lot easier than he expected.

"Otto has talked about his plan since he was arrested over the summer—to throw Blake into the past, so he could force you to work the black market with him. I didn't take him seriously until he wasn't convicted. Then I knew I had to find his Wentworth. I was going to leave, but I couldn't let him do this to you.

"For a while I thought Carolena might have a Wentworth. I even bribed her to give me one. She says she doesn't have one. I also have a friend at the Met who has searched their hidden collections for me. Right now this is our only option. He'll never bring—"

"He'll never bring Blake back," I said. "I know, that's why I've got to get to him myself. When I said it I felt like I'd just agreed to land a hijacked airplane. It was something I had no idea how to do, and yet lives were at stake and depending upon me to figure it out. "Please tell me you know how to do this..."

Philippe nodded. "I've traveled through time a few times, though not entirely on my own. Carolena has coached me. So, I'm going to take you to where he is."

"Oh, Philippe." I threw my arms around his neck and hugged him hard. "Thank you."

Philippe grabbed my arms. He stared at me with intent. "I can get you there. But the two of you are going to have to get home on your own."

"Why?" The thought of navigating the painting on my own left me deflated.

"Because I'm not coming back. There's nothing left for me here." Philippe's expression was resolute.

"That's—are you sure?"

"There's no life for me for as long as Otto is alive. The past is the only place I can go where I can be my own person. And there's someone there who I care about."

"Won't he be able to find you there as well?" I asked.

"We're going to fix it so that he can't," Philippe said. "I'm going to need your help. For the last twenty or so years, he's used a rope to go from this time to the next. A red cord that Carolena left in place from her travels. It's sort of like a trail of breadcrumbs so someone can find their way from here to there. To keep John and Campbell from accessing it, he ties off the rope before he gets to the end of the painting. So that whomever accesses the painting from the end point won't have any guidance to get home. It's a dangerous path to go it alone."

"I've seen that." I told Philippe about the Monet I accidentally stepped into. "The emotional currents were overpowering and the number of paths available was overwhelming."

Philippe guided me through the small doorway that led into the bricked room.

"Why did he do this?" I asked, and gestured to the bricks.

"This started as just a separate room with a door and locks. It looked like a storage area. Then he added an alarm system. When he got suspicious of Blake, he bricked it up altogether. Just in case he found this area."

"Didn't the FBI search this space? Seems like they would have wanted to see inside."

Philippe shook his head. "This space is an entirely different property from the firm. It's privately owned under a separate company that's in Nicholas' and my names." Philippe grabbed the couch cushions, tossed them onto the floor with a muted thump. Then he set about twisting the combination.

I lifted the framed wedding photo of Carolena and Otto. "I guess we can add bigamy to his list of offenses."

Carolena's genuine youth and happiness glowed through the black-and-white photo. She sat on a brown tufted chair, and Otto sat on the arm of the chair and held her hand. The gold jeweled bracelet shone from her wrist and she held her cascading bouquet of white roses to the side.

"This chair." I inspected the photograph more closely and patted the chair in front of me. "Is it *this* chair?"

"The entire room is a replica of the living room from their house in 1920. He had it built after she left for the last time."

*For the last time,* I heard him say. *She must have left more than once.* I placed the frame on the table.

Philippe lifted the silver handle, but it didn't budge. He untucked a piece of paper from his pocket. He checked the numbers he'd written on the paper, then turned the combination again.

When he got to the last number he turned the dial carefully, slowly. When he twisted the lever he got the same result.

"What's the matter?" I asked.

"He must have had someone change the combination. I can't get to the Wentworth."

"THEY'RE NOT HERE," Nicholas said to Otto when he walked into Addie's townhome.

Otto slammed his fist on the counter. "What?"

Then his eyes burned with fury. "Philippe," he growled.

## 50

P hilippe paced around the faux apartment.

He was a toxic mix of fear and he did nothing to build my confidence.

"Hard to predict exactly," he said to someone on the other end of the line. "FBI showed up at the warehouse. I don't know if they got to them. Addie and I are here in the room next to the firm and, if Otto and Nicholas escaped, then I think we have at least an hour or so before they figure out we didn't go back to her townhouse.

"I tried that combination," Philippe said a. "I tried that one, too. And I did write it down. Exactly as he dialed it the first time. I knew he saw me watching him. He must have had one of the Pulizzi clan come in and change it.

Philippe ran his hand over his beard "No, I don't want you to do that. Alright. Bye."

He sighed and then he realized I was staring at him.

"I've got this," he said. "I do."

"Who were you talking to?"

"Carolena. I thought she might have a suggestion on the new combination."

Philippe's text alarm went off. "She's here. I'll be right back. Don't move."

"Who's here?"

Philippe ran out.

I left the small apartment and stood alone in the empty warehouse-like building. The air was frigid. I studied Otto's shrine to Carolena. His memory vault.

What a psychopath.

"These were near the others. They're not exactly the ones you asked for, but they're similar in style. Same era."

It was a familiar voice. Though just enough out of context that I couldn't place it. Like two entirely different worlds collided in the same place.

I watched the door.

"Elizabeth!" I was at once relieved to see her and simultaneously panicked that she was caught up in Otto's underworld.

"Addie!" She handed Phillipe two large portfolio cases and wrapped me in a tight hug.

"What are you doing here?"

Philippe rested the cases against the wall.

Elizabeth opened her mouth and shook her head, her dark hair flipping up at the ends and dancing along her shoulders. "I can't believe you're here! Are you okay? I haven't seen you in so long!"

"I'm fine. I'm good," I lied. "I guess I was just trying to keep you out of a...mess I've gotten myself into."

"What kind of mess?" Elizabeth asked.

I waved her off. "I'll work it out. What did you bring?"

Philippe was rapidly combing through the paintings inside each portfolio, each one was separated by sheets of glassine paper and dividers.

"Well, I was moved to the dungeon in the Met. Which

was fine, because I'm not useful to Otto there. And I really just care about the art and the museum, anyway...sorry," Elizabeth said. "I rattle on these days. Too much time alone in the MMA basement. Sort of like being the Chief Curator of the Land of the Misfit Toys."

Philippe gently lifted a large canvas from its carrier, unwrapped the glassine paper, and examined the art.

"Anyway, Philippe here called and asked if we had any 1920 Wentworths down there."

"Addie." Philippe turned the canvas around so that I could see it. Vibrant oils depicted a carefree picnic lunch for several couples by the lake. Two of them were in a state of undress. "It's a Wentworth."

I rushed to where he stood and placed my fingertips on the canvas. Just as had happened with the Monet at Fowler's house, the paint drew my fingers into its landscape and the world around me began to fall away.

With only a glance in their direction each character stretched toward me, begged me to experience their story. There was a tug on my upper arm and I saw a masculine hand and a bit of wrist.

"Not yet," I heard Philippe say.

I relaxed my focus on the elements of Wentworth's painting and directed my attention toward Philippe's voice. Within a few seconds I was back in the nearly empty room with Philippe and Elizabeth. The transition left me feeling dizzy, and I held on to Philippe's arm to steady myself.

"We need to get ready first," he said. "I'm going to get a few things from my trunk. I'll be right back."

I was absolutely ecstatic. We had a Wentworth. We were going to find Blake, and get him the help he needed. We were going to get my father and grandfather, and bring them all back. I turned to Elizabeth. She stood with her mouth slightly agape.

Under normal circumstances, I would have been overwhelmingly self-conscious and worried about what she had seen. Though, as I had become accustomed, normal was simply not my life, and no longer my masquerade.

"I would explain, but, I don't know that I could. Or even that it would make that much sense."

Elizabeth walked toward the painting and lightly ran her fingers over the canvas. Hers didn't sink into the world of Wentworth as mine had. "Philippe has told me the most fantastic stories over the years, about how a Wentworth can transport you to another time. I thought he was referring to the beauty of the art and the talent of the artist. You know, in terms of how all good art can carry you into other worlds. I didn't realize—" She stopped and shook her head in disbelief. "How did you do that?"

"It's the art more than me, I think."

Elizabeth pressed her fingers against the canvas several times, as if she were testing the dryness of the paint. "I don't know about that." She inspected the art closely. "Of course after what I've seen in the Met's basement, nothing would surprise me."

The door that lead to the firm swung open and Elizabeth and I bolted upright.

"Sorry," Philippe said when he saw that he had startled us. "Here."

He gave me the handle to one of the medium-sized, wheeled travel bags he brought in. I laid it down, unzipped it, and marveled at the contents: a bronzed sheath dress with beaded detail down the front, shoes, stockings, and a coat. All according to the style of 1920.

Philippe picked up a small purse that was tucked into

the corner and opened it. There were several stacks of blue-inked bills in an envelope, and a coin purse filled with change. "These are all authentic to the time," he said. "You'll have enough to last you several years. Not that you'll need that much..."

I nodded. There was no need to explain.

Philippe pushed his sleeve and checked the time. "We'd better hurry. You can change in the bathroom in there." He pointed toward the brick room.

Elizabeth picked up the suitcase and started toward the brick room. "I'll help you."

I KNEW Elizabeth was going to use my dressing time as an opportunity to ask questions. She was ever gracious, and perhaps, still not quite believing. So she kept her questions fairly indirect and open-ended.

"I have to help Blake. He's hurt," I told her. "And this is the best way to do it."

She agreed with a nod. There was no other response she could have given, really.

Elizabeth and I stooped through the hole in the brick wall and I began to dress.

"Philippe," I called. "It's a different painting from the one Otto used. How are we going to get there without the guidance of Otto's red cord?" I pointed at the Wentworth that was leaning against the wall.

Philippe brought the painting in. "This is one of a series of six that Wentworth painted," He squeezed my hand. "He worked on all six of them at the same time, like a mural." Philippe took his phone from his pocket and opened his browser to a saved page.

"Here's a wide shot of all six of them from Wentworth's atelier in 1920. They were never meant to be sold or even separated, see?" Philippe moved his finger along the series that hung around Wentworth's atelier. Each painting was in a different stage of development and depicted a separate scene from the gathering at the estate.

"The one we have now is this end piece, the picnic at the lake scene. Otto has this center piece. The location of the other four are unknown."

"Why weren't they supposed to be sold?" I adjusted the strap of the slip which had fallen down my arm. It felt strange that someone I had known since childhood had just bought me lingerie.

"These were done as models for his room-sized murals. See, they're all connected. It's the same scene, painted by the same artist at the same time. Years ago, when we entered the center picture, I could turn left or right and see the rest of the scene on either side of me. So, I think we could still get to where we want to go, but going in a different way. Once we're into this painting, we just have to go right, across the side yard of the estate. We ought to find the red cord that he had there." Philippe pointed to the left side of the center picture that he had enlarged on his phone.

"Okay," I said, though I wasn't entirely convinced. "What happens if we don't find it?"

"Then we won't make it."

I blinked twice. The suggestion that I might never find Blake took my hope and strength. Philippe's phone rang and my heart stopped on the downbeat when I saw Nicholas' name on the screen.

"What?" Philippe answered brusquely.

"Where are you, Philippe? What have you done with her?" I heard Nicholas bellow.

"We're right here. What are you talking about?" Philippe motioned for me to put on my shoes and grab the money-filled purse that were still in the bag.

"You're not going to survive this," Nicholas said.

Philippe hung up the phone. "They've figured out where we are." He picked up his gun and placed it in his waistband.

I threw on the dress and Elizabeth helped me fasten the stiff leather straps on the shoes. Then I hurried over to the painting and Philippe.

"Do you have a key to my place?" I asked Philippe.

"Why?"

"Give it to Elizabeth. Hurry!"

Philippe dug into his pocket then handed Elizabeth two silver keys. "The keypad code is 3478#," he said.

"You'll want to change the code and the locks because Otto has access," I said. "Go into the library and flip through *This Side of Paradise*. Every day. Watch for messages from us."

"What?" Philippe's head spun toward us.

I kept my eyes on Elizabeth, whose brown eyes were wide.

"Just do it. And don't—do not—tell anyone about this. Do you understand? Or you could kill us all."

"After we're gone, take the painting and return it to the basement of the Met. Hide it. Don't seal it up in any way. And above all, don't let Otto or Nicholas near it," Philippe said.

"We should go," I said, not even remotely understanding where I was going or how we were getting there. Not at all.

Philippe blew out a deep breath. "It's easier if you go first. Once you're in just stand still, and I'll be right there to lead the way."

I stood in front of the painting, then turned my head to Elizabeth. "Thank you," I said.

She nodded.

I placed my fingertips on the painting and varied hues of ink crawled up my skin. "Hurry," I heard Philippe whisper.

I leaned into the scenery just as a distant crash sounded. I spotted the picnic scene immediately, straight ahead and slightly to the left. Just in front of a light blue pond whose sun sparkles were so bright I had to squint.

Still on my belly, and half inside of that space between where I had just been and where I was about to be, I studied the couples by the lake, one woman naked as if fresh from a swim, and stretched across the white blanket. She sipped a glass of wine and turned toward me, and smiled when she noticed me.

When I scrabbled across the slippery inked landscape to drag myself forward and into my future, a strong hand wrapped itself around my ankle and yanked me in the opposite direction. The lake scene blurred and I slid out of the painting. I spilled onto the cold cement flooring, my dress gathered up around my hips. I licked my lips and swallowed a wave of nausea while my new world, my old world, swirled around me and left me in a vicious state of dizzy.

"Taking a trip?"

I tugged at my hems and cocked my head to see Otto hovering over me. Nicholas stood to the side and held Philippe's arms so far behind him I couldn't figure how that position was physically possible. I didn't know what happened to Philippe's gun while I was in the painting, but it was no longer visible in his waistband.

Otto grabbed my upper arm and lifted me to my feet, then walked a circle around me. Otto clicked his tongue against the roof of his mouth three times and shook his head. "All dressed up and no place to go. Such a pity."

Otto's eyes shifted to the Wentworth and then to me. "I should have known that you would have this ability."

"You," he said flatly to Elizabeth. "I guess you can be bought now that you've been kicked out of your job?"

Elizabeth tried to appear unaffected but fear shone in her wide eyes, and I knew Otto could see it, too.

Otto turned to Philippe. "Did you send them to meet us at the vault?"

Philippe's eyebrows lowered in tandem with his frown and he shook his head slowly. "I don't know what you're talking about."

"Too much of a coincidence when stolen art and FBI show up in the same place."

*FBI...William.*

"Though they didn't get the art, or us. Several did catch a bullet."

*William.* A shifting sadness sloshed between my head and heart. He must have had someone follow us to the warehouse.

"After all I've done for you. This is how you repay me?" He waved toward me.

Otto's eyes fixed on Philippe and I found myself more afraid for Philippe's life than I was for my own.

"You know what you are?" Otto asked.

Philippe's chin jutted out slightly and I felt him steel himself for Otto's answer.

"A regret," Otto said. His eyes moved up and down Philippe's stature with disgust.

Nicholas held Philippe's body firmly, and I waited to hear the crack of Otto's knuckles against Philippe's nose.

Instead he spun around and the back of his hand crashed against my cheek.

"No!" Philippe yelled.

Otto pushed away a lock of hair that had fallen into his face.

"You may not care what happens to you. Though I'm pretty sure you care what happens to her."

I held the side of my face with both hands. My eyes watered with tears.

"I've been fair with you," he walked toward me, his heeled shoes clicking off slow, measured steps against the concrete. "I gave you an opportunity to earn your freedom."

I scoffed.

"Arbeit mach frei. Is that it?" I said, referring to the German phrase displayed at the entryways to Dachau and other internment camps during World War II.

In English the phrase meant Work Makes You Free. It was a cruel suggestion to the tens of millions who entered through the iron gates, that if they just complied, there was a way out.

The truth was the exact opposite.

Otto raised his fist to me.

"I didn't give her a choice!" Philippe said quickly and Otto stopped. "I dropped the hood and the cuffs on her and I brought her here. She didn't choose this."

Otto walked back to Philippe.

His fist cracked against Philippe's jaw.

Philippe spit and blood spattered on the floor.

My heart filled with black dread.

"Now I have to decide if I kill just one of you, or both of you."

I swallowed hard when Otto shifted his glance between Philippe and me. He was going to kill Philippe, then either kill me or lock me away, keeping me alive enough to read art for him.

My life had become more like the last one, where Otto killed Blake, then held me captive until the life drained out of me.

Otto walked toward me and raised his fist to me.

I stepped backward until I caught sight of a movement in the doorway.

"Otto!" She exaggerated the t's when she said his name. "You don't want to do that."

Years dropped from Otto's features when he heard her voice, like she'd spoken to him from a dream. He dropped his fist, then walked slowly toward her.

I stood ready to grab his neck from behind if he tried to hurt her.

But he grazed his fingertips along her cheek. Gently, tenderly.

Carolena returned the touch, her gold and jeweled bracelet dangling against her wrist. Her long black jacket was cut on the angle.. The scarf around her neck was ever-French and carefree. Her entire presentation appeared fresh from fashion week and made her look unaware that people's lives were at stake.

"You came back," he said.

She nodded, her smile warm.

Otto leaned into her touch. He took her hand and kissed it.

"You came back," he said again and this time he swept her into his arms.

## 51

Carolena stared at Philippe's bloodied face, then glanced at me.

I knew the sting and swell on my cheeks must have burned red on my pale face.

She watched us in this godforsaken warehouse, the site of Otto's dreams and nightmares.

Our plans and spirits, broken and bloodied.

I wanted to tell her to run, that she should try to save herself. But I didn't think any of us would live if she did.

"It seems things have gotten beyond your control." Carolena's French accent and royal demeanor continued to ignore the danger of the moment.

"I was just about to remedy that when you walked in." He scowled at Philippe.

"What does this one do for you?" Carolena nodded in my direction.

Otto shrugged. "You left."

Carolena's hand glided over Otto's chest. "There are no replacements for me, my love."

Otto lifted her hand, kissed her knuckles. "You have always been the only one I wanted."

"And are these your boys, all grown up? Philippe, is that you?"

Philippe nodded subtly.

I hoped they could manage the stranger act with success, otherwise she was as dead as the rest of us.

"Oh, Otto, I think he needs help. Did you do this, Nicholas? You boys always played too rough." Carolena reached into her purse, took several tissues, and handed them to Philippe.

Her cover for Otto's cruelty worked. Nicholas released Philippe's arms and backed away from him.

I saw two guns in Nicholas' waistband.

She leaned into Otto's chest, and it was obvious that he was powerless to resist her. "Send them all away so we can have some privacy," she said. "I want to celebrate."

Otto inhaled uncomfortably. "I'm afraid I can't do that."

"Why not? I've come a long way to be with you," she said.

"They know too much." Otto shrugged like a boy.

"Oh." Carolena took in the players around the room. Then she made the move she must have planned since she received my phone message. "Then why don't we leave? Let's go back to the one place where we were really happy with one another. Remember?"

"I remember," Otto said softly.

"I've dreamed of it for so many years," she said. "Si vous plais. Let them go, they can say what they will. No one will ever find us."

Otto studied her. He seemed to search for signs that this might be too good to be true.

I silently begged Carolena not to go anywhere with him —the sacrifice was too extreme.

"I don't guess there's much left for me here, anyway." Otto cut his eyes toward the empty building that used to house his firm. "Except for maybe these." He walked to a storage closet and pulled out three extra-large portfolio cases. "Due to some FBI interference earlier today, I missed an important meeting with the Pulizzi family. They were going to purchase these."

I assumed there was Gardner art inside the cases.

"Then let's do it. Let's run away and live the life we always planned to." Carolena's eyes sparkled and charmed. Otto was utterly powerless to her.

When his expression softened into an uncharacteristic grin, Carolena broadened her *Vogue*-worthy smile. Then she kissed him, and unpacked a traveling outfit.

THEY EMERGED from the bricked room and appeared almost as stunning as they did on their wedding day.

It hurt to think it, but Otto and Carolena were a dashing couple. And Blake's features were evident in each of them.

Carolena wore a beige coat with long, bell-shaped, pleated sleeves and a high-rising burgundy collar over an ornate bronze and navy blue dress.

She was dressed to kill, and I hoped that she would. I hoped that she could.

"Vous êtes magnifique." He raised her left hand to show off her outfit.

"Merci, mon amour. I found it in Paris." She twirled.

"Paris," he echoed, and held her left finger closer to his

face. He angled the sugarloaf cabochon ruby ring and the platinum band twinkled with diamonds. "You wore it."

She smiled. "Let's go. You lead the way."

Carolena walked toward the Wentworth, but Otto guided her back toward the bricked room. "We'll use this one in here," he said. "I kept the path marked off."

"Absolument!" she said enthusiastically, but I felt her disappointment.

Philippe had told her about the one in the safe. She knew the one against the wall wasn't it.

Otto turned toward us. Like he'd just realized we were still there. He opened his mouth, then shut it again. "Are you sure? I don't like to leave loose ends."

"If we leave together then I must do this without anyone's blood on my conscience," she said sternly. "Otherwise it will ruin everything for me. And besides, we are leaving. No one will ever find us."

"I'll make sure of that," Otto said, then he turned to Nicholas. "Let them go. I'll tell you what to do with the Wentworths."

Nicholas pointed to the oversized portfolios that Otto carried. "If we don't deliver that art to the Pulizzis, they're going to search for you. If they can't find you, they might look for me me."

Otto eyed the black cases, then raised his eyes to Nicholas.

"Make a call and tell them how the FBI found us. They can verify the agent's death with a phone call. They'll know the art is too hot right now. Then leave town."

Nicholas nodded and seemed not to realize that that plan didn't leave him any long-term freedom.

"Take them," Otto said to Nicholas, and motioned to

Philippe, Elizabeth and me. "Make sure they leave the property."

PHILIPPE, Elizabeth, and I made it to the van.

Nicholas stood in the doorway and watched us drive away. He held his gun at his side and I knew we'd never see those Wentworths again.

"Take us to Blake's penthouse." My heart ached. I had lost my only chance to get to Blake.

I looked at Elizabeth who hadn't said a word for some time. Her eyes were wide and unbelieving. Her mouth was slightly open.

I spotted my phone in the central console, grabbed it, and called Grace. She, Isabella, and Lexie listened while I told them the story.

"You can't blame yourself," Grace said. "You did everything you could."

"She's right, honey," Isabella said, her voice thick from silent tears. "There are other Wentworths out there and we'll find them."

"Starting with Nicholas," Lexie said. "I've already texted Fowler, and he's going to have some men track him down."

I thanked them for their support. But when they begged me to come home, I turned them down. "I have to stay close to the townhome to watch for messages about Blake."

I called William's cell phone, and it went to voicemail.

## 52

Philippe dropped Elizabeth and me by the townhouse, I checked the book for messages about Blake. No new notes had been delivered, but I sent my grandfather a lengthy and hurried letter that described all that had happened. Including the part about how Carolena and Otto might be headed his way..

Philippe said he would try to track Nicholas and find out what happened to the Wentworths.

I took Elizabeth with me to Blake's penthouse. I didn't think either of us should be alone. Blake had added me to the security system and all the equipment now recognized my thumbprint, retina and security code.

When we got inside Elizabeth turned to me and asked simply, "How?"

I made us some tea, and told her as much as I thought she could handle.

When she had as much information as she could think about, I went to my bedroom.

I took off my unused time-traveling clothes and laid

them neatly on the chair. Then I curled onto the bed and quietly sobbed.

PHILIPPE RETURNED HOME with no news to share. So, the three of us drank red wine, ate frozen pizza, and sat around a warm fire that popped and crackled in the living room. I'd found sweats in Blake's closet, and Philippe and I each wore a pair.

"I've lost him twice now," I said and I stared into the fire. "Once when Otto took him away from me, and then again today." It hurt when I breathed.

"I could have brought him and my father and grandfather home. I know I could have."

"Stop blaming yourself," Elizabeth said. "Otto has a way of...besting everyone."

"What we need to do now is to figure out where Nicholas has gone with the Wentworths," Philippe said. The orangish glow from the fire flickered on his pale skin.

It was late but I texted Lexie for an update from whomever Fowler.

"We need to kidnap and torture Nicholas until he tells us where the Wentworths are," I said.

"I'm impressed," Philippe said.

"And a little afraid." Elizabeth said.

WHEN MORNING CAME I headed to the kitchen for espresso, paper, and a pen. I was deadly serious about kidnapping Nicholas, and I made a list of things we needed.

The swinging door pushed open and Philippe and Elizabeth walked in.

"I got a text," he said.

The sound of locks turned and security key pad beeps interrupted him.

I turned and faced the door. There was only one person who could come through Blake's security system, at this hour or any other.

Anya, Blake's sister, emerged from the private hallway. Her black-as-blue hair was shoulder-length now, still just a mite longer in the front. Her blue eyes danced between the three of us.

"She's gone, isn't she?" Anya asked, and removed a stray piece of hair from her lip gloss "I picked up Carolena when she landed at the airport. But I haven't heard from her since. Did she leave with Otto?"

"Anya, I—I don't even know where to begin," I said.

Anya closed her eyes for a moment, like she realized the worst had happened.

Elizabeth handed me an espresso.

Anya exhaled. Then she nodded and turned to Philippe. "Would you help me?"

They walked to the elevator where a tall, narrow box leaned against the back wall.

"Carolena called me after she received your phone message," Anya said to me. "She told me that she was going to come out of hiding to find Blake."

Anya cut the tape that sealed one edge of the box.

"How did she know where to find us?" I asked.

"I never lost touch with her," Philippe said.

Anya had unveiled the canvas.

"Philippe!"

Philippe took a quick step forward and stooped in front of the art.

"Is it...?" I tucked my hair behind my ears.

"It looks like his signature. There's only one way to find out." He directed me toward the painting.

I placed the third finger of my right hand delicately on the painting and waited for the ink to run up my hand as it had the last time.

But it didn't.

Philippe tilted the painting and examined it from a different angle.

"This is from Carolena?" he asked Anya.

"She had it shipped directly to me," Anya said. "I don't know who sent it to her."

"I found it and gave it to her," Philippe said.

"Where did you get it?"

He nodded to Elizabeth who gave a small wave.

"Otto didn't have an opportunity to get ahold of it, did he?" I asked.

"You used your other hand last time. Try your other hand," Elizabeth said.

I placed two fingertips from my left hand to the canvas, and waited. The colors didn't rise. I shook my head at Philippe.

He walked toward the window. "I thought it was the real thing.

"It was in the Met!" Elizabeth said.

I repositioned my hand and tried to see who really painted this forgery.

"It can't be a forgery," Anya said.

There was no information coming off of the painting. It was like I toughed a dime store poster. "It's not a Wentworth."

I TOOK A HOT SHOWER, drank a hefty dose of caffeine and I felt slightly more human, but no less desperate. I sat on the edge of the bed and stared out the window.

"Are you okay?" I heard Anya say from the doorway.

I didn't answer. I couldn't stop thinking of Blake.

She sat next to me on the bed and hugged me. "Come on, you're going to eat." She led me from the room, leaving me no choice.

"Your son is beautiful," I said.

"Thank you." She squeezed my hand. "Family is everything."

The four of us sat in Blake's rooftop solarium, subtle crunching noises disturbing the sad stillness. I glazed a piece of toast with bright red strawberry jam, my movements rote. I dreaded the moment when I would actually have to put the bread into my mouth.

I spread the tang of red color across the toasted bread, filled the diagonals first in clockwise order, then worked my way to the flat edges. Then, because I wasn't yet ready to put it into my mouth, I slowly added another layer until it was apparent I was creating an art project as opposed to breakfast. I pressed the knife against the jam, and the spongey paste was rubbery against the bread.

I stared at it.

Then I shoved my chair across the floor with a high-pitched screech, and ran from the room.

"Addie!" Elizabeth yelled after me. I rushed through the kitchen and into the main salon where the painting was alone. Waiting. I wiped crumbs and tiny bits of stickiness from my hands. Then I put on the gloves I'd tossed aside earlier and touched the painting.

It was a thin layer, artfully placed and barely noticeable. I pushed it and met its resilience. There was no intelligence placed in the seal, nothing to read.

"It's covered!" I said. "She put a sealant around it, in case it fell into the wrong hands. Brilliant."

"What's a sealant?" Elizabeth asked.

"Can you break through it?" Philippe leaned forward.

I shook my head. "I don't know how to undo them. I just know they exist."

My fingers glided over the slick surface of the cushioned seal. "She's so good. It's flawless. Not very thick, but strong, like armor, and there's no way in as long as it's in place. And I guess, no way out for anyone as well."

I crossed the painting left to right, top to bottom and I searched for any clue she might have left behind. Halfway down the painting I felt tired. "Trying to read through a sealant is like trying to focus in the fog," I said.

"I'll get you some coffee," Elizabeth said, and disappeared into the kitchen.

"Just take your time," Philippe said. "We have time."

"Blake doesn't have any time," I said.

Elizabeth returned with a shot of espresso and my strawberry-sealed toast. I drank the hot coffee in two gulps, took two bites of toast, then I returned to what I very much hoped was a Wentworth.

Slowly, I searched for something genuine to come into focus. I skimmed lightly over the croquet scene. To the right of the red croquet mallet was something unusual. A minuscule divot.

I backed up and went over it again. And again. In the middle was a tiny spot that broke through to the canvas. I pressed against it.

Like magic, the pigments crawled up my finger, covered my nail, and kept climbing.

"Philippe!" I yelled.

He and Elizabeth stood over me and watched.

"You've got it!" she said.

When the scenery from the painting filled the edges of my view of Blake's apartment, I withdrew my hand.

"We've got our way in," I said.

## 53

S harply re-dressed in our 1920s finest, Philippe and I stood once again in front of a Wentworth and prepared to make our sojourn into my once and future past. Philippe checked to make sure we still had our money, and that we'd eaten a solid breakfast of eggs, bacon, and toast.

"The trip takes more out of you than you'd think," he'd insisted.

I spoke to Grace, Isabella, and Lexie to let them know the latest. I also gave them Anya's and Elizabeth's phone numbers.

"Well done, precious girl," Grace said. "Be careful. The world inside of a Wentworth is not your own."

I tried not to think about that, but I knew she was right. Still, I had Philippe, who would get us to the right spot and the right time. Memories of the confusing paths within the Monet haunted me, as well as Grace's stories about how her cousin had gotten forever lost.

"Be careful," Elizabeth said. She stood next to me and primped my hair and dress.

"Oh!" Anya dug through her purse and pulled out an envelope. "Maman wanted you to have this."

MY DEAR ADDIE,

If you're reading this, then I've gone back with Otto.

Do not worry for me. I've known for some time that he wanted to return to the past. Though I hoped and prayed he would not, I've deliberated as to what I would do if he did. The ramifications on the present could be disastrous.

When I heard he sent Blake, I knew what I had to do. Blake won't know how to get back on his own. And though he would not want me to do this, I'm leaving this Wentworth with you so that you can help him.

Get Philippe to help you travel, if he has not already recruited you. You'll find him to be a most loyal ally.

We will probably end up on this day in 1920. I understand that's where your father and grandfather are. Based upon the painting that I think Otto still has, it is my best guess that this is where he took Blake.

It will be up to you and Philippe to find Blake and bring him back.

If you get lost, come back to what you know how to do. Come back to your gifts.

I realize this may not seem helpful now, but hopefully it will once you're on your way.

With all my love,

Carolena

PHILIPPE AND ELIZABETH read the letter as well.

"Do you know what this means?" Elizabeth asked.

I shrugged.

Philippe stepped back. "Carolena has a way of posing riddles instead of just giving answers. She always told me that wisdom becomes our own when we reach for it, not when it's handed to us."

"This really isn't the time for riddles," I said.

"Maybe all that you need to know is too lengthy to explain," Philippe said.

## 54

"Once we're in, hang on to whatever you can," Philippe said. "My hand, my belt...just don't let go."

Philippe sat on the edge of the couch near Anya and pointed to the Wentworth. Elizabeth leaned forward from a nearby chair. A sun-kissed cityscape brightened behind her.

"We'll enter the painting through the front here." Philippe pointed at the Wentworth. "And we'll travel through this scene until we reach the next painting, where we should be able to locate the red cord. This is the same red cord that Otto has always used to guide him from the present to the past and back again.

We'll travel that painting from front to back until it ends. At that point there is fifty to one hundred feet or so of pure blackness. That's where we literally leave this time and enter 1920. We have to be careful at any point within the painting. But we have to be particularly careful at this juncture."

"Aside from the obvious...why, exactly?" Elizabeth asked.

"Because if we misstep in the blackened area, we could

end up missing our intended time entirely." Philippe's tone was stern and serious.

"By a week or so?" I asked. I fiddled with my long-chained bag, which I'd stuffed with everything and anything I thought I might need.

"Try a decade or more. This process is very specific, and any disruption to our travel could throw us off our destination in ways we couldn't recover from. Even if we're a minute off, Addie, we'll miss Blake and your family entirely."

"Blake *is* my family," I said softly. Then I realized that Blake was Philippe's family, too. He just didn't know it.

I HUGGED Elizabeth and repeated the instructions about my townhome, its security, and the F. Scott Fitzgerald book. She promised she'd follow everything as directed. Then I hugged Anya.

"Bring them home safely," she said. There was a softness to the way she looked at me now that hadn't been there before.

"I will," I promised, and hoped I was telling the truth.

"Ready?" Philippe asked.

"Yes," I said and touched the small opening in the painting.

I expected the passage to be roughly the same as the last Wentworth I entered, but the entry point was different this time, and the middle of the croquet game was no place to sit still.

A red wooden mallet cracked my rib. "Ow!" I yelled.

There was genuine shock and surprise on the face of the man who hovered above me. He was tall and thin, and his full mustache and beard-tipped chin were slightly more red than the mostly brown hair that peeked out from his gray cap.

"I dare say," he said with a British accent. "I was aiming for the ball... Where did you come from?"

Everyone in the croquet gathering backed away from me, except for the man with the red mallet who poked me again, like he tried to see if I were real. The subtle brush strokes on his face moved and shifted when he did, the light played the angles of his face. He was an odd representation of real.

Everything in front of me was ripe with meaning and history and I sensed it all.

The red jacket he wore with the gold buttons on his sleeve was his longtime favorite. The female in the blue sundress who stood behind him was his girlfriend and longed to marry him. Even though she knew he wasn't ready yet. Every element had been created with a story and if I stared at any one thing for too long I felt myself move in that direction.

"Sorry. Entirely my fault," I said, and winced against the sharp pain in my side. I crawled upright and away from him. "I wasn't watching where I was going."

"An American, no less!" he huffed, and turned to the rest of the players.

No sooner was I completely upright than Philippe landed at the back of my legs and knocked me onto the ground. My face planted into the soft grass and I saw bits of white beneath it. Canvas, I guessed.

Philippe surveyed the small, sneering crowd and his mouth fell open.

"Sorry." Philippe tipped his hat and took a firm hold on my arm, lifted me to my feet, and led me away.

"Indeed," the croquet player said with a huff.

Philippe nodded toward the woods, and hand in hand we walked across the meadow, the sun's heat cloying with Wentworth's desperation over the loss of his wife and children. The air was meadow sweet and laced with the fragrance of wildflowers. It was an abrupt change from the icy New York winter we'd just left. I removed my winter coat, straightened my twisted dress, smoothed my hair, and tried to center myself. But the wind blew the trees in the distance and I felt the story that Wentworth created there, too.

Philippe quickly grabbed my wrist. "We have to hang on to one another," he whispered. "And don't focus on anything that you don't want to go to."

"Right," I said, and sidled closer to him.

"Is it always this realistic?" I asked, still stunned from my encounter with the croquet player.

"I've never been in this way before. In the other painting we've never had to interact with anyone." Worry painted Philippe's face and I chose to ignore it. We were in this. We had to get through it.

At the edge of the first line of trees, woodsy noises of frogs and crickets started on cue, and soft breezes of crying and sadness blew through my heart.

"Where should the cord be?" I asked, and fought the urge to curl up and sob.

"The edge of those woods begins the next painting," Philippe said. "The cord should be just beyond them, along a dirt path."

We crossed over to the next painting, and there was a shift, like we'd just walked into a different reality.

"It worked," I said, and squeezed Philippe's hand.

"It worked," Philippe said with a sigh.

Once at the dirt path, I placed my left hand into the different footprints that were visible in the soil. The remnants of Otto's energy still rang clear, Carolena's higher-heeled imprints sidled next to his. She was guarded and charming, and played her part to perfection.

I ran my hand through the dirt until I found Blake's prints. Sometimes next to Otto's imprints, and sometimes ahead of his. He was fearful but strong, he worried about me.

I studied their footprints mingled in the dirt, and noticed how, ironically, they gathered here as a family once again.

"Come on." Philippe guided me to the edge of the path. "This is no place to hang out."

I wiped the dirt from my hands onto my dress, immediately regretting doing so, then followed along.

"It's not here," he said. "If the cord were still in the painting it would be tied here, anchored to these trees."

"What do you mean it's not here?"

"I mean, it's gone. Otto's not coming back so he took it away."

"Or he wants to make sure that no one else gets through," I said.

"Either way our guide is gone, and we can't do this." Philippe paced back and forth and cracked his knuckles.

My heart pounded against my chest in three rapid beats. I felt the surrounding hopelessness that carried on the pine scent. I steeled my insides against it, but wondered if it was affecting Philippe more than he let on.

"I have to find Blake," I said. "There isn't another way."

Philippe stared down the pathway. "I don't know that I remember how to get there on my own. I've always had the cord."

I watched him wilt in the onslaught of emotions from

the painting. Then I blurted it out before I lost my nerve to say it. "I'll go alone."

He cast an eye toward the meadow, and I knew he was tempted to go back.

"Philippe."

He looked at me.

I shook my head. "Don't."

He frowned.

"You can't let other people run your life."

"I'm not—"

"You are!" I grabbed his wrist.

He tried to pull away but I held on.

"Strengthen yourself against Wentworth's despair or he's going to own you."

Wentworth's despair was too close to the pain Philippe carried deep inside. I pressed my thumb against his scar. "Know which emotions are yours and which are his."

I'd learned this from Grace a long time ago. "You don't have to carry what's not yours."

Philippe studied me.

Then he pressed his lips together and nodded once, like he understood what I'd said.

He took my hand again and we walked further down the path.

I used each step as an opportunity to strengthen my intent to find Blake, which helped tune out some of Wentworth's depression. When the path broke into three different directions, my concentration waned. We stared at all three options.

"None of this is familiar. The path never divided into three different directions like this before." Philippe pushed his hand across his forehead.

Time passed.

How much time I wasn't sure.

But it was long enough that we both had to sit down.

Eventually I stood again and paced. Frustration built inside of me with every step.

"We need to figure this out!"

A small fire broke out in the brush near Philippe's feet and he quickly stamped it out.

"Your anger," he said. "It's affecting the painting."

Another small fire lit next to Philippe and he jumped to the side, then put that one out, too.

I watched the thin stream of smoke rise from the burnt patch.

"I think Wentworth must have been angry when he painted this section." I swallowed hard. I tried to stem the rage that built up inside. "It's not mine," I whispered.

I glanced at Carolena's footprints. She had been able to do this without a cord. She had found her way to 1920 on many more than one occasion. I could do this, too.

I reached into my purse and unfolded her note:

IT WILL BE UP to you and Philippe to find Blake and bring him home.

*If you get lost, come back to what you know how to do. Come back to your gifts.*

"COME BACK TO MY GIFTS," I said.

"Try it." Philippe said.

I bit the inside of my cheek. "*Everything* in this painting has a story, has history. If I tune in to anything here I'm going to lead us off into some random direction that has nothing to do with getting to Blake."

Philippe sighed. His shoulders tensed. "Whenever we took family trips through this painting, Carolena used to whisper hints and directions to me along the way. It was like she wanted me to learn how to do this. One of the things I remember is her telling me is that you have to have a focus. Know what you want, then tune in to find your way."

I digested Carolena's guidance. "Okay," I closed my eyes. "Have a focus and come back to what I know how to do."

Frogs from the nearby pond croaked.

"Come back to what I know how to do..." I smacked my hand against my forehead. "My gosh, I'm an idiot. Reading art is what I know how to do!"

"I don't know what you mean."

"Okay, have a focus, right? I've always done that when I read art. Now I want to know which path Blake, Otto, and Carolena took. Which path leads us in the direction where they went."

This was a canvas after all, and I could read any canvas I wanted to.

I placed my hands over the dirt paths and read the art I was in.

The path that veered to the left all but reared up to touch my fingers.

"This way," I said. "I hope I'm right about this."

"Me, too," he said.

"Show me the route Blake took to exit the painting," I reaffirmed aloud. I could feel the energetic trail that Blake left behind, faint but present. We continued down that path and cut through the woods, across dense, mossy flooring, and under pine branches. I homed in on it and moved as fast as possible.

*No more time to waste.*

The energetic trail continued, but the dirt path led

straight into a murky pond that reeked of apathy. On the far side, the path continued again.

"There was never a pond here before." Philippe rubbed his face.

"We have to try to go around it."

With Philippe in tow, I dragged us to the right of the pond. Every step felt harder than the last. The farther we walked the wider the pond became.

Philippe refused to walk further. "This isn't going to work."

We moved to the left side of the pond. The same thing happened.

Touching the brown water, I felt Otto's vibe coursing through it like a current. "It's like he has the dang thing programmed!"

There was no response from Philippe. I twisted around in time to see him lunging toward me.

"Watch out!" He yanked me away from the pond, just before an alligator crawled onto the muddy bank. He stared at the both of us, then slowly sank back into the pond, only his eyes above water.

"Can we...die in this painting?" I struggled to catch my breath.

"Yes," he answered, and held on to me. "We have to be more careful."

I stared at the pond and the floating eyeballs. Wentworth's apathy wound itself through my heart. The feeling that Blake and I were destined to be apart, that no matter how we tried we would never win this war, crushed me from the inside. The physical pain of emotional loss dripped through my insides.

"There has to be a way to undo what he's done to this painting."

*Think, Addie.*

"She said come back to what you know how to do. Okay, I read art, I read objects, I'm an empath, sometimes I see past lives... How does any of that help me here?"

I turned to Philippe for an answer but he wasn't there. "Philippe! No!"

Philippe curled up at the base of a nearby tree. "I just need to lie down. I'm so tired."

I tugged hard at his arm. "It's Wentworth's apathy you're feeling—it's not yours. Come on, we've got to get out of here."

"I can't, Addie. This is just too hard," he said. "Nothing is going to work out anyway, and it's easier if we just stop trying."

"This isn't real, Philippe. You're affected by it but it's not real." I studied the pond and the green animal who floated in it. "It's...not real. It's like a forgery—that's it!"

"No."

"Philippe, come on!"

Philippe stumbled to his feet like a drunk. "I've never felt this bad in my life," he moaned.

"Look at me," I said and grabbed the sides of his face. "This is Otto's work, like his forgeries." I edged carefully to the mud at the bank and scooped some into my palm. "I think if he can manipulate it so can we. This isn't real."

The alligator swished his tail in front of us and water splashed across the pond and onto our clothes.

We both considered the damp spots of contrary evidence on his suit and my dress.

"You're sure about this?"

"Pretty sure," I said with a wince of doubt.

Philippe lifted his eyebrows.

"It's not like I've done this before," I said. "It's not like we have other options, either. So, come on. Help me."

I took the mud and formed a step at the bottom of the bank, then added to it until it thickened and hardened. Philippe reluctantly joined me in the effort, and built a muddy ledge on top of mine and held it there until it was firm.

Wentworth's depression made for heavy resistance while we pushed ahead with our arched bridge over the water. His despair was a call to every fear I'd ever known, that feeling that everything important would eventually collapse. His dark sadness and my fears danced with one another in perfect step, and like all fear-based emotions, they worked hard to convince me that I was truly powerless.

The alligator swam beneath us, one pass beneath our mucky, caked bridge, and then another. Like Peter Pan's Tick Tock, he waited for a tasty human treat.

"Argh!" Philippe yelled when we finally arrived at the other side. He swatted at wasps that flew at us and stung our arms and faces.

I shrieked and ducked but the wasps swarmed. They stung my skin.

Philippe grabbed my arm and we sprinted toward a black abyss.

## 55

All that lay ahead of us was a pure blackness.

A subtle burnt scent filled the air.

The pain from the wasp stings pierced my arms like a thousand needles. "What is this?" I asked, out of breath.

"*This* I remember," Philippe said. "This is the back of Wentworth's canvas, in his time. So, we walked through the front side of the painting that exists in our time, we'll exit the front image of the canvas that lives in *his* time. This black zone is where we leave our time, and enter another."

"Just keep your focus—this is not the place where we want to get lost," he said.

We stepped forward, my mind focused again on Blake's trail. Though this section had appeared black to me, once in it, it was filled with the voices, the music, and the different environments that had surrounded the painting over the years.

Too much interest on my part into any one scenario that drifted in front of me, and I knew we'd be anchored to the wrong place in time. Famous faces drifted in front of me—

celebrities, presidents, and other artists perused the painting, stroked their chins, and commented while they stood in front of it.

*Stay focused.*

I ignored them like they were meaningless gnats and directed my focus back to our path.

*Blake. Where he exited the painting.*

The backside of the woods we'd just left came into view and everything laid out ahead of us in reverse. The woods, the dirt path. Thankfully, there was no pond or wasp nest this time, and we sprinted ahead.

The front of the painting was strangely familiar in reverse, and Philippe and I glanced at one another when we heard the muffled sounds of men's voices.

Cautiously, we moved ahead and clung to the edges of the painting until we could see the croquet game on the far side of the meadow, on the other side of the estate.

"We can exit from any painting, right?"

"Should be able to," Philippe said.

The voices became clearer as we edged to the front end of the painting, and one in particular, sounded familiar to me.

"I love the realistic nature of the elements," the voice said. "I can't get over how real the scenes feel—as if I could step right into the painting and begin life."

"Everything in the painting is a character to me," another voice said. "I imagine a history for each one."

"Extraordinary," the first voice said.

"I know that voice," I whispered, my heart fluttering at the sound of it. From the lower left hand corner, I peered outward into what appeared to be an artist's atelier. Two men stood in front of my canvas-based reality and shook hands.

"Thank you, Monsieur Wentworth. These are extraordinary pieces."

His sandy-blond hair and blue eyes were just as I had always seen them, though this was the first time I had witnessed them outside of a dream or a reading.

It was Jack. The man Blake used to be when he lived in the 1920s, the man he was when we shared our last life together.

Still joined palm to palm, Philippe stiffened his arm and stopped me from moving ahead.

"Can they see us?" I whispered.

"I don't know," he said. "I'd prefer they didn't."

## 56

W hen the dizziness and nausea finally faded, we bundled ourselves against the weather and walked down the sidewalk with all the other pedestrians.

No one hurried in 1920, not the way they did in the life we'd just left. Here, people looked you directly in the eye, interested to know more about you. Gentlemen tipped their hats. There were no headphones or cell phones or other weapons of mass distraction.

"Do you think he'll be there?" Philippe asked. He ran his fingers through his hair and tried to smooth a few of the turbulent waves.

"I don't know. That's where their last photo was taken. They were searching the Met for another Wentworth."

We weren't far from the museum, but the walk felt an eternity. When the park benches came into view, it was plain to see how empty they were. I slowed my approach, and prayed with every step that Otto hadn't had access enough to Blake to hurt him or kill him or throw him into the painting to be lost in time.

I felt a little bit of comfort in the fact that if he had, Carolena would have found the strength of ten men to snap Otto's neck in half.

Philippe and I sat. And waited. We hoped we might find them exiting the museum. I felt oddly at home in 1920 and yet completely out of place.

"Should we try the hospitals instead?" I asked.

"Which ones? There are several in the city."

I drew in a deep inhale, the cold air burned my lungs.. The pedestrian traffic had slowed significantly and there were very few prospects to consider. The adrenaline that pumped through my system on our journey here was now replaced by an empty ache.

He patted my hand. "We can try the hospitals tomorrow. Let's get to The Plaza and get a hot meal and a warm bath. We might find them there."

I rested my head on Philippe's shoulder and stared down the empty street. "There really aren't any guarantees in life, are there?"

He squeezed my hand. "Not a one. Come on, let's get to the hotel. You're freezing and we really should have eaten something by now."

We hopped on the subway that was littered only with elegant clientele. Philippe marveled at the ceiling fans, leather seating, and drop-sash windows, while I searched for any energetic traces of Blake or my father or grandfather. We exited the train and entered The Plaza Hotel on Fifth Ave at 59th Street.

"Let's hope they've already invented the Martini," I said.

"The random pieces of information you have in your head." Philippe grinned. "How about we try for a sandwich first."

We were guided to the restaurant, away from the

raucous cheering and music of the ballroom. I searched every face for one I might recognize. Far hungrier than I realized, I quickly ate a meal of roasted chicken, mashed potatoes, and several thick slices of hot, buttered bread.

"It makes you hungry, doesn't it?" Philippe said.

"What...the travel?" I whispered the word travel as if someone might know what we were talking about.

Philippe nodded. "There's something about it that just wipes you out."

"I think I'm going to fall over," I said, suddenly tired and dizzy.

"I'll check us in. Separate rooms," he said and winked at me.

I waited next to a potted palm in the wide lobby while Philippe spoke to the broadly mustached employee at the front desk. The hotel clerk glared at me like I was someone who had wandered in from the street. I decided to move.

A sign rested on a gold easel to the side of the room: The New Plaza Hotel—Light Comfortable Airy—Room with Bath and Shower—$3

I brought my purse closer to my body now that I realized just how far Philippe's and my cash would last us at these prices.

Hot jazz floated out of the ballroom and ambled through the wide hallway where I slumped, pigeon-toed on a golden upholstered bench. I felt I'd run away from home. I caught sight of myself in one of the tall hallway mirrors.

My dress was covered with mud, my neck and arms were splattered with wasp stings, and my hair had completely fallen out of the style Elizabeth had so kindly pinned together. My lips and nose were swollen where Otto punched me. A bluish green tint colored the areas. I turned away from the image. No wonder the clerk didn't want to give us a room. I resembled a homeless person.

I guessed I was.

Music and couples swayed out of the dancehall, singing and holding glasses of champagne, their laughter floated above the din. They were the happiest drunks I'd ever seen. I tiptoed down the hall and peeked into the ballroom to see if my family was inside. They weren't.

You could feel it in the air though, something was about to happen. The general vibe boasted an excitement of better things to come and it was a tune everyone wanted to sing. I walked toward the foyer and struggled to remember my history lessons. What was it about 1920 that set the stage for one of the most exciting and stylish decades of the century? The end of World War I, perhaps.

Philippe handed me a large brass key. It was connected by a chain to a fob with The Plaza Hotel insignia on it and weighed at least a pound. "I told him you were my sister. I don't think he believed me."

"Sir, sir!" the clerk called, and ran to where we stood. "You must sign the registry." The clerk paused, studied me from top to bottom, then turned with his nose in the air as if he wished he hadn't seen me.

While I waited for Philippe to finish the registration, I stared out the gracious windows that framed Fifth Avenue. The street was moderately busy, not at all what it was like at home at this hour.

Time had fallen away in the place where I stood. Across the street were several tall buildings that didn't appear much different than they had when I last saw them in my own time. Excepting the skyscraper background, of course.

The brilliant white building with double-story arched windows was home to a bank in my time. A copper-colored building with rectangle windows and an arched doorway occupied the opposite corner and seemed familiar, but I couldn't remember what businesses lived there in current day. I started to look at the next landmark, but my eyes got hung up on the large white sign that was suspended in the largest window:

Montgomery and Associates
Fine Art Appraisals and Dealers

MY BREATH TOOK off in a rapid pant and I headed toward the front door of the hotel, my eyes held tight to the sign.

"Where are you going?" Philippe called after me as I sprinted through the lobby.

"The sign!" I crashed into someone and ended up on all fours.

"Di Mi!" a woman squealed.

I moved several frizzy strands of hair from my eyes and saw an elegant blond woman in a long, white sequined dress who stabled herself against her suited date.

"Is this your tomato?" he asked.

I saw Philippe running in my direction.

"Yes, she's mine," Philippe said and helped me up. "Sorry about that."

"Argh!" The woman gasped and picked bits of dried mud from her outfit.

"I'm sorry, so sorry," I said to the couple. "There's a sign," I said to Philippe, as if he knew what that meant, and I fled from the hotel with him quick on my heels.

"Addie! No!" Philippe yelled from the sidewalk.

The yellow double-decker bus's squeaky brakes filled the night. I narrowly missed contact with the its front bumper. The driver's panicked expression was far too clear.

I clung to the twenty-five-foot traffic tower that stood in the middle of the four lanes of Fifth Avenue. The bus driver yelled a mild "Watch it!" He drove away.

I looked back at Philippe, who held both sides of his head.

"I'm okay," I mouthed to him with a nod and a wave. "I'm okay," I assured myself in a whisper.

"What in the heck are you doing?" Philippe fussed when he caught up with me.

I took a long, deep breath. "There's a sign," I pointed to the white placard that hung in front and to the right of us.

"Oh my gosh." Philippe's brown eyes widened and his jaw dropped. "All right. Let's not have a repeat of *An Affair to Remember*, though. Accidents only work out well in the movies." Philippe took a firm grip on my hand and escorted me to the other side of the street.

Once in front of Montgomery & Associates, I peered through the larger than life corner window but found only the blackened insides of a gallery. I ran to the front door and banged on the center glass. No one appeared. I yanked on the frigid brass door handle and felt a twinge in my shoulder. The door was locked up tight.

"Is everything okay?" A deep, clear male voice asked.

"She's fine," Philippe tore me away from the front door and tucked me under his arm. "She just left something in there earlier today. We were hoping to retrieve it." He gathered me closer.

The policeman cleared his throat. He wore a double-breasted uniform jacket, blue with gold buttons, his billy club rested firm in his hand. He surveyed my dress and face and his somber eyes narrowed.

"Sorry." I swallowed hard and leaned close to Philippe.

"Why don't the two of you move along for tonight?" The policeman waved his club at our muddy attire. "You can visit them tomorrow to get whatever you left behind." He extended his left hand as if to show us the way to go.

"Yes, officer." Philippe tipped his hat and held me around the waist with a death grip. "You have to be more careful," he scolded me in a low whisper.

"Okay," I said.

Philippe turned us right at the corner and we strolled slowly past the other side of the gallery. I cut my eyes to the gallery for any movements through the glass, but dared not turn my head for fear that the policeman still watched us from Fifth Avenue.

A few steps later, Philippe spun in front of me with a gentle dance, took both of my hands in his, and kissed me on the lips.

"What was that for?"

"Just making sure the policeman was gone and this was the only way I could think to do it without him noticing. Sorry, love." He caressed my face.

"Is he gone?" I asked.

"He just passed that building." Philippe gestured across the street. "Still, you've got to be more careful. In this world you have to be a subtle observer—you can't rock any boats. Every ripple here could send a tidal wave back home."

I stopped and scanned the building that was as secure as Fort Knox, then blew a hefty exhale with puffy cheeks. "I'm sorry. I thought he'd be inside."

"We'll find him." Philippe hugged me close. "We just

don't want Otto to find us in the process, so don't draw any attention to yourself."

"Right. Of course," I clasped my hands together against the cold and tried to prepare myself. It might be several days before I saw Blake or my father or grandfather. Blake was probably at one of the hospitals.

"Let's get back to the hotel and get cleaned up. I'll ask where we can get clothes for the morning—"

A squeaky door opened behind us and I turned to see an older man with graying blond hair, a plaid jacket and short brimmed newsboy cap. I realized he was leaving through the service door that led to the gallery, and I took off in what felt like slow motion.

The man's eyes widened as if he thought I might try to take him out. He inhaled against the open door and I passed him. At least I thought I might until his hands grabbed me around the waist. I dragged him several feet down the hall before he stopped me.

"Oh, no ya don't, miss, they're closed now. Ya have to come back tomorrow." His Irish accent was strong. So was he for a man his age. I worked to get his hands off of me.

"I just have to—John Montgomery!" I yelled and I tore from the man's grasp again. "Campbell!" I made it several more steps before he caught me again.

"Miss, I told ya—" He struggled for a firm hold on my arm.

"John!"

"Sorry," Philippe appeared in the darkened hallway. He seemed unsure of what to apologize for next. "Sorry." He let his arms flap by his side.

"Does she belong to you?" The man wrestled my flailing arm.

"Yes." Philippe walked toward me. "Sorry, she knows the

owners and thought they might be in at this hour." He glared at me and took possession of me from the man in the thick, plaid jacket.

"I'm under strict orders to keep all people out after hours when they're here." The man nodded toward the gallery. "You can't be too careful with folks nowadays."

"When who's here?" Philippe asked, his head cocked sideways.

The man stopped abruptly, his eyes bouncing once between Philippe and me.

"Run!" Philippe shoved me toward the open gallery and he tackled the man against the wall and held him there.

I ran through the hidden areas of the blackened office space. "John!" I called for my grandfather.

The sounds of struggle carried through the area, and I figured as long as they continued I had time. I scrambled through the two small rooms in the rear corner, opened doors and flicked on lights, but only empty offices revealed themselves. I turned the last corner and found myself where I started, with Philippe and the man in plaid having taken to fisticuffs.

"Dang it!" There was nowhere left to search. My only hope was to leave the way I came and escape to the hotel. Maybe Philippe could get away as soon as he knew I was free. Hopefully, the police would not be called.

*No, this can't be right.*

There had to be an area for storage, or maybe a vault. I turned and searched along the wall of the small, pitch-black alcove for another doorway. There was nothing.

Then I found the outline of a door and, finally, the small round doorknob. I took one step into the dark and fell. Head first, down into an abyss of narrow walls and hard, wooden stair edges. The opposite wall at the end of the flight stopped me.

I opened my eyes. I stared across a hallway and into a small kitchen.

The great love of more than just one of my lives sat on a wooden stool, cleanly shaven and leaning over a light wood table. A map was laid before him.

He frowned at me with his head cocked in the classic RCA dog pose. He tried to figure who this strange muddy woman was who'd dropped from above. I moved my long, straggling hair from across my face.

Blake jumped up. The wooden stool clattered on the cement floor. He lifted me slowly from my crunched, end-of-the-trail position and held me fast. The natural cologne of his skin reached my heart and the tears of two lifetimes fell down my cheeks.

I hadn't lost him.

We did beat Otto.

Through it all we were still together.

He pushed me at arm's length and grasped my shoulders, like he needed to prove that I was really there. He tucked a lock of my unruly hair behind my ear, examined me from tip to toe, and shook his head.

"You're really here," he said.

"You're okay? What about your arm? Weren't you in the hospital?" I asked.

His mouth rushed to mine.

It felt like our first kiss.

Our last kiss.

The only one that ever mattered.

## 57

The four of us stood near the service door of Montgomery & Associates, my hand fastened tight to Blake's. One lone globe sconce on the wall of the hallway to light the night.

"It's my fault, Alfred. I ought to have let you know that we were expecting guests. I apologize." Blake said.

"Well, see that ya remember next time." The man in plaid jutted his chin out, his eyes darkened to a shade of meanness. "I have strict orders." He pressed a handkerchief to his bloodied nose. He eyed Philippe, who came out of the altercation with a bruised cheek and what would probably turn into a black eye.

"I understand." Blake was firm, and Philippe ushered Alfred out.

Blake took my face in his hands, his fingertips grazed the sore places that Otto left behind and I flinched. "What happened?"

"Doesn't matter now. How is your arm?" I asked.

"Healing. No fever. Painkillers suck in 1920." He cocked a sideways grin. "I can't believe you're here."

"Neither can I," a male voice said.

Though I hadn't heard that voice in many years, its unique timbre awakened the memories of my heart and little girl tears welled up in my eyes. I peered over Blake's shoulder, my mouth ajar.

"Daddy," I whispered when I saw his face. I walked toward him at a turtle's pace. I hugged him tight, my hand brushed across the gold chain I'd always known him to wear.

He stood back, shell-shocked to see me. Twenty-five long years.

"Addie?" he questioned.

"It's me." I swiped the tears from my cheeks.

His voice was exactly the same as I'd remembered it. I wished for Alexa, Isabella, and Grace to hear it, too.

His chestnut-colored hair was a much shorter style and streaked with gray at the temples. I reached up to touch it and he grabbed my hand, kissed it, and held it to his heart.

"My princess." He laughed. His eyes filled with tears.

"Who's here?" The tall, gray-haired man stamped the snowy wet off of his shoes. He was debonair and aloof, and barely noticed his surroundings. But the woman who clung to his arm was smitten. She giggled and swiveled her hips, all the while through long, fluttery lashes.

His eyes finally caught me and his world stopped. "Addie-belle."

"Who is she?" the brightly blond woman accused.

"Addie-belle!" My grandfather's laughter roared, his voice boomed, and he scooped me off my feet in a giant bear of a hug.

"Blake said he was afraid you'd do such a thing." He kissed my right cheek five times before he set me down. He spread my arms. "Look at you. Obviously you take after our side of the family." He glanced back at my father. "Because you're just gorgeous and...muddy."

"Oh. Well." I crossed my arms over my time-traveled dress. "It was something of a bumpy ride on the way over." I glanced at Philippe, who stood off to the side.

"Grandpa, Daddy, this is Philippe. He played a big part in getting us here."

"Well, it was more of a team effort, I think," Philippe said. His eye was starting to swell.

My grandfather walked over and shook Philippe's hand.

"You're Otto's boy?" he asked.

"Yes sir," Philippe said.

"Take after your mother, I see," my grandfather said, and he examined Philippe's face. "In more ways than one I would suspect."

"Yes," Philippe said, and seemed to take that as a compliment.

My father gave him a vigorous handshake. "Thank you, son, for helping to get her here safely."

"If it weren't for her, we wouldn't be here." Philippe's dapper smile was now crooked, the result of a swelling cheek. My grandfather's pat to Philippe's back was a zealous and muted wallop against his thick jacket.

My grandfather strolled over to me, an admiring gleam in his eye. "Little Addie-belle-a-rina always did have all the talent in the family. Not that any of the women in our clan would give her credit for it, though."

The blond woman cleared her throat and my grandfather raised his finger to me. "Just a quick minute." His signature Montgomery blues fully lit from within, his face animated and lively.

"This is my granddaughter," he said to the woman. She mouthed an "Oh" in return. "Why don't you scoot your pretty self back to the hotel and I'll be there shortly. I need a few minutes with her."

She nodded, giggled, and pranced. He patted her on the bottom and shooed her out the door.

My grandfather walked in to the room and stood between Blake and my father. I clasped my hands at my chest.

I was finally in the same room with the three great loves of my life.

## 58

"There's not a red cord in place anymore, but I think I could get all of us back. Though Otto booby-trapped the path, we managed to get around it," I said.

I pushed a lock of my still-messy hair behind my ear, dabbed a baking soda mixture on my wasp stings, and launched into great detail about our harrowing journey. "So, Wentworth's atelier is now on a little side street, not far from the Met."

"Then we should leave first thing in the morning, so we don't lose access to the painting," my father said. "I think you should have some rest first, sweetheart."

"Agreed," my grandfather said. "Do you have a place to stay?"

"I checked us into The Plaza across the street. That's how Addie saw your sign," Philippe said. He adjusted the makeshift bag of ice on his eye.

"I knew it had to be yours," I said.

My father reached out and squeezed my hand. "I'm so

grateful you saw it, Addie. We own the townhome now if you'd rather stay there tonight."

"You own the townhome already?" I asked.

"We had to buy it," my grandfather said. "Getting in and out of there when it was a bed and breakfast was too hard, and we had to have access to the book to communicate with Grace and Isabella.

"And Ellen," I said with a nod to the stack of ribbon-clad letters that he'd placed next to him on the table.

"You know about Ellen?"

"And Nathan."

My grandfather swallowed visibly. "I suppose that was inevitable with the two of you working together."

"Who's Nathan?" Blake asked.

"I'll tell you later," I said. "That reminds me," I said to my father and grandfather. "I had a dream a few months back. A vision. The two of you were in it, it seemed so real. Like you were trying to send me a message. Were you?"

My grandfather and father exchanged a glance, then looked back at me. "Grace wrote to us that you were working with Otto. We wanted to see if we could warn you about him and what we thought he was up to," my father said. "We stood just outside the front door of the townhouse and focused together on getting that message to you."

"It worked," I said. "I don't know how, but it worked."

The broken icicles my father had gathered shifted against each other in Philippe's pseudo-ice pack, which was really my father's white handkerchief, insulated with some plastic wrap.

"Y'all aware that Carolena and Otto are here?" I asked.

Three of the four men nodded.

Blake grimaced.

"Without her, we wouldn't be alive." I squeezed Blake's hand.

"Carolena has been very good to me throughout my life," Philippe said. "She's watched out for me and protected me from Otto wherever she could. Though I've tried, I don't think I could ever fully repay her for the love and kindness she's given to me." Philippe lowered the batch of ice from his face. The combination of his physical brawn and emotional sensitivity was a beautiful mix, and I understood Carolena's need to protect him.

"I'll do whatever you need to help find her and return her to the present." Philippe placed his hand on Blake's shoulder.

Blake's expression warmed and he hugged Philippe.

"Thanks, man," Blake said with two hearty back slaps.

"You have our support as well, whatever you need." My father's old smile had returned, the one that wasn't evident in the photographs they'd sent through the books. "Grace wrote and told us you're family now. So, if it wasn't already, that makes it official."

We all laughed in symphony at my father's statement. Grace did set the rules.

"Absolutely," my grandfather said. "Anything for you and Carolena."

"Thank you. Your support means a lot, but you've waited a long time to get home. I don't want to get in the way of that." Blake turned to me. "I have to talk with Addie about next steps. My home is where she is."

I sighed without any sense of conflict. "It sounds to me as though these two men have already made their decisions. For me, my home is wherever you are," I said. "I understand if we need to stay and find Carolena. She's your mother."

Blake held my face in his hands and kissed me. "Thank you."

"We'll have to make arrangements for one of us to keep an eye on the art. Wentworth moves it every now and then. We don't want to lose track of it."

"Campbell and I have several men working for us. We can post them outside of his atelier in shifts to make sure we don't lose it," my grandfather said.

"What about Otto?" I asked. "We can't leave him in the past. He could completely destroy the future."

Blake, my father, and grandfather studied one another. Transporting a man as dangerous as Otto from past to present was even more difficult than it sounded.

"We'll have to devise a plan," my father said. He always was the planner, easily his mother's son. He reached across the table. His hands were cool as they always were in winter weather, but soft to the touch as though they'd been well cared for.

I nodded. "Yes, we'll need some time to sort it out."

My father squeezed my hands. A strength and solidity that had been missing for over twenty years, returned to me. I clasped his hand in return. My eyes clouded with tears.

"This is wonderful, thank you," Blake said. "Thank you for understanding."

I ran a hand across his shorter hair. "This is family. It's what we do. Tristan."

Blake's breath caught on his inhale and his eyes widened.

My grandfather's brilliant laughter rumbled against every wall of the small room like an explosion. "Never keep a secret from our Addie, my friend. She'll find you out."

Blake smiled with pride. "So I'm learning," he said with

another kiss. "Why don't we sleep on it? We'll discuss our decisions in the morning over an early breakfast."

"Good idea, son," my father said.

My heart swelled with joy at the sound of my father calling Blake "son."

"Why don't you stay with us at the town home, Philippe, and let Blake and Addie have The Plaza?" my grandfather said.

"We have separate rooms," Philippe said.

Blake raised our joined hands to his lips and kissed one of my fingers.

We all pushed away from the small table and our wooden stools screeched against the cement floor. We agreed to meet at eight the next morning.

We stepped outside into the frigid, quiet dark of the night. Traffic had died down significantly. We could hear the distant sounds of the party that carried on inside the ballroom of The Plaza.

I felt a little lost without my cellphone, I wouldn't be able to text anyone to let them know I was running late, or early, for that matter. I couldn't call them to find out where they were if they didn't show up on time, and I couldn't email them late tonight and ask questions about our plans.

It was all rather freeing.

"Wait for me, Campbell. I need to check in with Mary before we leave. I also want to see if she can loan Addie some clothes. She's a real fashion plate and I think you two are about the same size," my grandfather said, and glanced at my dress.

The idea of me being the same size as my grandfather's newest lover creeped me out.

My father stood next to a shiny black Ford Model T with the door open and one foot inside. "Well, I'll just walk with you. No sense in standing out here in the cold." He gave the door a solid slam then raised his collar against the wind. "Plus, it would give me a few more minutes with my princess." He wrapped his arm around me and squeezed me three times, his version of the triple pat.

The five of us crossed Fifth Avenue, safely this time. My father and I held our arms snugly around each other while Blake and I held hands. My grandfather led the way in animated regale of his first days in the past, and Philippe kept pace each step of the way.

We entered the lobby. My grandfather flagged a young photographer who was on his way out. "I say, young man, take our picture, would you?" My grandfather leaned forward with paper money in his outstretched hand.

The boy pocketed the money and smiled happily. We arranged ourselves together for the photo. The flash was blinding and it took several seconds before I could see anything again.

"Send it to this address, please. Thank you, sport." My grandfather handed the boy a business card. "We'll send that to Grace and your mother when we get it. What room are you in?" my grandfather asked.

"I—uh, don't know," I said and fumbled into my pocket for the key.

"She's in 502," Philippe said. "The other room is right next door."

"I'll have Mary drop off an outfit for you and I'll see you for breakfast." My grandfather kissed my cheek, shook Blake's hand and disappeared into an elevator.

"Get good rest, my love." My father hugged me long and tight. "Tomorrow's going to be a big day."

He shook Blake's hand, then hugged him as well.

B  lake shut our hotel room door behind us, swept me into his arms, and twirled me across the room. We reached the window that overlooked Central Park. He pressed his lips to mine in a long, slow kiss, the kind that brought forever into a moment.

"I thought I'd lost you." Moonbeams illuminated his face and accentuated the beautiful crystal blue of his eyes.

"You didn't." I stroked the stubble-free angles of his jaw and marveled at the clean-cut boyish handsomeness of his face.

"We could have been parted forever, lost in different directions of time." He drew me close.

"We're together. We made it. We win this time, remember?" I said. "Carolena was right. Wisdom earned is wisdom kept."

Blake took a red rose from the nearby vase and handed it to me. Its scent was delicate and intoxicating, a song to my senses.

"It seems we've traded emotional places on this issue," he said.

I laughed quietly and unbuttoned his vest and crisp white shirt, needing his skin beneath my fingers. "I guess I've conquered a few fears since we last saw one another."

He turned me around slowly, moved my hair aside, and unzipped my dress.

I stepped behind the triple-arched vanity screen made of bronze and quartz and lapis lazuli. My dress was heavy with blotches of mud, and it thudded to the floor. Blake handed me a robe and I slipped it on.

"There was this moment in Wentworth's painting when I really didn't know if Philippe and I would make it. Otto's obstacles in the path were incredibly realistic, Wentworth's emotions were crippling, and every fear of loss I've ever had came out to play.

"But I faced them. Then hope showed up, and strength wasn't too far behind it.

"That's when I realized all I had was whatever I could fight for. And I was going to fight for my family. I wasn't going to let Otto take you away from me again." I stepped around the folding screen.

Blake's grin widened, all traces of his fears vanished. "Family is an important thing."

"Family is everything." I slid my hands into his, our fingers twined together at my side. Beneath the glow of the 1920s moon that we had lived under once before, he kissed me. On this occasion, time didn't stand still. It ceased to exist. We had conquered it.

Blake sat me at the vanity and tried to dismantle the rest of my failing hairdo.

With the knowledge that he, my father, and grandfather were safe, my shoulders relaxed and my mind calmed. No matter where we landed in time, it was home as long as Blake and I were together.

The snow-dusted park glistened below us like a page from a storybook. "The simplicity here is so peaceful. There's very little to resist. Not at all like it is where we come from."

He lifted the mudded dress from the floor and laid it on an armless chair next to me. The chair was covered in slate blue fabric with gold vines and floral blooms running vertically. Normally I would have thought it a beautiful antique, but I realized it was quite a current fashion. The silk was cool to my touch.

"What's it like here?" I raised my eyes and found Blake staring at me in the mirror, his own eyes soft. His gaze was full of something deeper, less fearful. He tipped my chin and touched his lips to mine, slow and full of love, mixed with passion.

"Nice," he said when he leaned back.

"Nice?"

"1920s New York. It's nice." He laughed.

I smiled.

"There's something...special about this decade. People are excited to be alive and they're looking forward to a bright future. Most are concerned with what really matters in life, not their social media pages—a refreshing change."

"It's like being in a dream." I marveled at the park below us, which felt tranquil and crime-free.

He plucked the remaining pins from my hair, dropped them on the dresser, and thick, mudded curls fell onto my upper back.

"Tell me what it was like to see them," he said.

"A lifelong dream come true." I sighed. "In many ways, everything I thought it would be. Minus the mud and the wasp stings, I guess."

He chuckled and tried to run a flat-bristled brush through the length of my hair.

The brush scratched pitifully against the surface of the tangles. "I'm glad you found them. It was a long-overdue reunion."

I nodded. "What do you think Carolena's plan is?"

Blake shrugged. "I don't always know with her. She has more secrets than...than —"

"Than Grace?"

"Than Grace." He laughed and brushed another length of my hair and found a hidden hair pin. He dropped it on the vanity with the others and it made a thin, tinny sound. "John thinks they might go to that house they built. I don't know what Carolena has up her sleeve."

I thought about how we'd step out of the hotel in the morning into a bustling 1920 to begin what was next. Very few the wiser that we weren't from this time.

"I think you're just going to have to wash this out in the tub," he said. "I'm sure there's shampoo in there."

He ran a warm sudsy bath.

I climbed in. Eerily, the tub reminded me of the one I'd crawled into after Jack had been killed.

Blake waited in the bedroom.

"How is your arm?" I asked.

"Better," he said. "I'm lucky to be alive."

"Thank God you are," I said. "At least we did that right this time."

"We've done a lot of things right this time."

"You're right," I said, and thought of all we'd overcome.

I lathered my hair and the scent of coconut filled the room. I wondered how my hair would look after a run with 1920s shampoo. The watery mud ran down my skin and I realized that it wasn't mud at all.

"This is paint. Wentworth's paint." I rubbed a chunk of it between my fingers and thumb, studied it closely as it melted. "Makes sense, I guess."

A quiet knock sounded from the hotel room door. Blake answered it.

I rinsed and combed through my tropical-scented hair and dried it to damp with a fresh towel.

Wrapped in my robe again, I emerged to find Blake pouring red wine into flat-bottomed wine glasses.

"Someone deliver that?" I asked.

"Your grandfather has been importing French wine over the last few years. He doesn't plan on suffering through prohibition."

"Bless him," I said.

"He also brought you those, they're from his lady friend." He nodded toward a black velvet coat with gold beaded art deco design along the hem. A navy blue velvet dress with silvery details was laid on the chair next to it. Metallic shoes sat on the floor, ready to wear. An enamel mesh handbag with a tiny clock in the metalwork hung on the chair back.

"She really is a fashion plate," I said of my grandfather's friend.

Blake handed the glasses of wine to me, and notes of ripe berries, chocolate, and a hint of licorice swirled through the air.

"I don't think I've ever had wine from the early part of the 1900s before," I said, and inhaled the flavors.

"It's pretty amazing." Blake said.

"Ooooh, you're ahead of me on this time-warped wine tasting thing."

"Hard not to be. Your grandfather has a warehouse full of the stuff."

"Love that man," I said, and stepped closer.

We posed our glasses to face one another. I exhaled deep and slow, grateful that we were together again.

"To...finding Carolena?" I suggested.

"We'll find Carolena," he said, his intent firm and clear.

"To the end of Otto." I raised my glass and enjoyed the feeling of having trumped him.

"Oh, this will be the end of Otto," Blake said.

I had no doubt.

He leaned in and I realized just what that something deeper was that I'd seen earlier. Trust.

"To our love. It has survived the curse of death and passed the tests of time. May it always," he said.

"May it always," I said. Our glasses clinked together.

Blake pressed his lips against mine with a love that sealed the circle of our past and present, and shone a bright light on our future.

Continue the adventure with LOST IN TIME (THE FINE ART OF DECEPTION, BOOK 3)

# AUTHOR'S NOTE

What a joy it has been to write Blake and Addie's story. And what a story it is—spanning several lifetimes and three books! The entire trilogy has been released and you can read their full story back to back with SOMEWHERE IN TIME AND LOST IN TIME. (Both are free through Amazon's Kindle Unlimited) I do hope you enjoy reading these books as much as I enjoyed writing them!

After I finished LOST IN TIME I fully planned to continue writing in that world. Until the idea for THE HAUNTING OF ALCOTT MANOR landed on me. Sometimes stories choose their author and that was definitely the case with this one!

When you've finished THE FINE ART OF DECEPTION SERIES, you might want to try THE HAUNTING OF ALCOTT MANOR Series. It's a contemporary gothic romance that's full of mysteries, twists and surprises!

I love to hear from my readers and you're welcome to get in touch with me at AuthorAlyssaRichards@proton mail.com or via my website. While you're there, sign up for my mailing list so I can let you know when I have a new title.

I hope you enjoy your journey through time with Blake and Addie!

Alyssa Richards

# THE FINE ART OF DECEPTION SERIES, BOOK 3

## LOST IN TIME

## Chapter One

Blake held on to the side of the windshield of John's Model T and braced himself, both for the next hard-hit bump and for the night that lay ahead.

Dust from the vacant dirt road kicked up and found its way into his nose and mouth. Tiny granules of grit crunched between his teeth and he spit out the open window.

He didn't have to turn his head to the left to see John's occasional stare bearing down on him—he could feel the hardness of it on the side of his face. John didn't want them to make this trip.

"Everyone in this meeting is armed. None of these guys know you so they'll assume that you're either a copper trying to take their operation down or a rival who wants to take their business away from them." John Montgomery, Addie's grandfather, white-knuckled his hands at ten and two on the thin black wheel. His car hit almost every hole on the rarely traveled road and jostled them like children on a cheap carnival scrambler.

John smoothed one side of his perfect white hair. "They're always thinking about how to kill you. Remember that and don't turn your back on anyone. Even when you're inspecting the pieces. Got it?"

"Got it." Blake stared straight ahead. He'd spent the last hour of the drive trying to ignore the fear and the worry that had grown intertwining roots in his heart. Fear that no matter what he did, he might not find his mother. Worry that he couldn't do enough to protect Addie.

He swallowed hard against his throat, which had become as narrow and dry as the road. This was the last sign of nervousness he could allow himself for the next few hours.

The car slowed when they entered the grass-edged drive of the warehouse-type building. A round man in a brown pinstriped suit stood at the doorway and held his tommy gun at his side. Finger on the trigger.

Several men were ahead of the. They stepped from their cars, and searched the darkened lot. They looked around once again, then they went inside.

Blake seen that look before. It was a paranoid-guilty expression that settled scores too quickly.

There weren't any windows on the oversized, silver-tinned shack, but he knew what was going on inside. Even though this was only 1922, the black market for antiquities was already an ancient and dangerous tradition. And where there was art theft, Otto was bound to be nearby.

"Floyd," John said to the guard in the pinstriped suit.

"John." He nudged the end of his tommy gun into Blake's chest. "Who's 'dis?"

"Nephew of mine. I brought him into the business a couple of years ago." John moved the tip of the gun away from Blake's chest. "If you blow a hole in him my sister will never speak to me again."

"I wasn't expectin' no one else with you." Floyd returned his aim to Blake.

Blake's heart pounded hard in his chest.

"Floyd." John faced both palms outward in surrender. In slow-motion carefulness, he reached into his jacket pocket and retrieved a fat cigar, and handed it to the man with the gun. "I take responsibility for him—he's my blood."

Floyd accepted the cigar and nodded to the entrance. "It will be if anything goes wrong in there."

The windowless tin warehouse was empty except for the four men who stood around a few opened crates, three of the men held tommy guns.

The one man who didn't hold a gun extended a hand to John. His brown eyes, flat with unfeeling meanness, locked hard enough on Blake to leave a mark. "John. Who's this?"

The man's long dark hair was slicked obsessively neat across the top, excepting two pieces of hair that fell onto the shaved sides of his head. He attempted style and attitude with a tipped-up collar on his knee-length trench coat. He missed the mark with rumpled, high-waisted pants that were held up with a belt as well as suspenders. Blake recognized him immediately, even though he had only seen him in a photo a few years ago.

"My sister's son. I brought him into the gallery a while back. He has a thing for art. He's good."

Blake held still, his hands out and on his hips where everyone could see he didn't hold a gun.

He'd been shot by this man before.

Not in his current life, but in his past life when he was Jack. The fear that it could happen again remained like a memory in his soul. That trace sent a shot of adrenaline into his heart that felt remarkably like a bullet.

The man was Gary Walker. Otto's past-life incarnation.

If it wouldn't have ended his own life again, Blake would have killed Gary on the spot.

Click here to continue the adventure with LOST IN TIME!

## ALSO BY ALYSSA RICHARDS

**THE FINE ART OF DECEPTION SERIES**

THE FINE ART OF DECEPTION, UNDOING TIME

SOMEWHERE IN TIME

LOST IN TIME

THE FINE ART OF DECEPTION, BOXED SET

**THE ALCOTT MANOR SERIES**

THE HAUNTING AT ALCOTT MANOR

A MURDER AT ALCOTT MANOR

A STRANGER AT ALCOTT MANOR

**THE CHASING SECRETS SERIES**

CHASING SECRETS

FORCED PERSPECTIVE

**Be the first to know about Alyssa Richards' next novel, sign up here:** www.AlyssaRichards.com

and follow her on Amazon or BookBub to receive a new release alert!

# ABOUT THE AUTHOR

ALYSSA RICHARDS is the USA TODAY BESTSELLING AUTHOR of romantic suspense and mystery thriller novels. She loves living in the South with her husband and two children. She also loves good espresso, her rescue dogs, magnolias and gardenias, and, of course, reading a great book. She grew up running barefoot in the Blue Ridge Mountains of North Carolina, where her favorite weekly adventure was a trip to the library with her mom.

Sign up for Alyssa's newsletter at www.alyssarichards.com to receive special offers, and news about her latest releases.

*For More information*
www.AlyssaRichards.com
Contact Alyssa at:
authoralyssarichards@protonmail.com

# ACKNOWLEDGMENTS

My heartfelt gratitude ...

...to my husband for his continued support and encouragement & to my boys for being such brilliant blessings in my life, the three of you make life worth living.

...to Libby Murphy for being the most amazing editor.

...to Hughes for his kindness to read and critique.

...to Lucinda for reading, for her feedback and for her generous friendship.

www.ingramcontent.com/pod-product-compliance
Lightning Source LLC
Chambersburg PA
CBHW072014110726
47910CB00005B/1751